The Fifth Level

BY THE SAME AUTHOR

September Song

Out of the Shadows

The Burned Woman

Another Path, Another Dragon

Natural Prey

Dark Streaks and Empty Places

From a High Place

The Fifth Level

/♦/

EDWARD MATHIS

CHARLES SCRIBNER'S SONS
New York

MAXWELL MACMILLAN CANADA
Toronto

MAXWELL MACMILLAN INTERNATIONAL
New York Oxford Singapore Sydney

Charles Scribner's Sons
Macmillan Publishing Company
866 Third Avenue, New York, NY 10022

Maxwell Macmillan Canada, Inc.
1200 Eglinton Avenue East, Suite 200
Don Mills, Ontario M3C 3N1

Macmillan Publishing Company is part of the Maxwell Communication Group of Companies.

This is a work of fiction. Names, characters, places, and incidents either are the product of the author's imagination or are used fictitiously. Any resemblance to events or persons, living or dead, is entirely coincidental.

Library of Congress Cataloging-in-Publication Data
Mathis, Edward.
The fifth level / Edward Mathis.
p. cm.
ISBN 0-684-19386-8
I. Title.
PS3563.A8364F5 1992
813'.54—dc20 91-28468

10 9 8 7 6 5 4 3 2 1

Printed in the United States of America

To my grandchildren:
Brian, Casey, and Kelly Davis

The Fifth Level

/1/

My father died a lonely, broken man. A righteous, God-fearing teetotaler until the time of my mother's death five years before his own, he had become a source of bewilderment and deep concern not only for me, his only offspring, but for all his friends and neighbors living in and around the small southeast Texas community of Butler Wells.

My mother died during the month of October, only a few weeks into my senior year in high school; by Christmas my father had discovered the panacea of the bottle and by the time I graduated high school his life revolved around it. Four years later he froze to death in a Texas norther. A small, self-effacing man, he died as quietly as he had lived.

At the time, I was halfway around the world, an unwilling guest in a misbegotten Asian war that only a few people wanted and nobody understood. By the time the Red Cross finally caught up with me he had been buried almost two months.

He died alone, penniless, fifteen feet from the door of a two-room hunting shack he and I had built on four hundred acres of land he had placed in irrevocable trust for me when I was born. The rest of the ranch was gone, uprooted and swept away in a gurgling, never-ending torrent of booze, leached away by the unabashed larceny of drunken cronies more cunning and accomplished than he, by barroom maidens who whispered of sweet love and ecstasy, who delivered cold couplings with no more meaning than the itch that spawned them.

But he did not die entirely in vain. He left me a legacy: the frightening awareness of possible genetic susceptibility, the deadly certainty that booze could kill.

And battle-weary warrior that I was, I cried above his grave and swore a mighty blood oath that I would never succumb to the sly seduction of demon rum, blithely ignoring the fact of innocence already lost, of drunken sorties into the sewers of Saigon, of R and R oblivion in Japan.

But tears dry up and sorrow fades and graveside resolve withers and dies when balanced against the irresistible imperative of coated tongue and burning throat; clear resolution shimmers and dissolves before the sorry rationalization that one more drink don't make a drunk. But maybe, not being a man who always knows right from wrong, maybe it's not all that sorry after all. Maybe it's just sad. And painful. It's damned sure painful; I can jump up and clap my hands and testify to that.

But sad or not, sorry or not, I had done it one more time, breached the narrow rift between the nursers and the sippers, the dilettantes and those of us who understand that life is sometimes too complex to bear, too absurd to face without fortification, be it drugs or alcohol or simple insanity.

And I was paying my dues, a fermenting head and a crusty mouth that tasted like the walls of a well-used garbage compactor, dark painful bruises on my knees from kneeling too long with my face in the toilet, humble and sick and despairing in my knowledge of the cussed foolishness of man.

And, as if that wasn't enough to cope with on that bright sunshiny day in autumn, I was being bombarded with strange vibrations from Susie, and slowly, tenderly, I moved my eyes away from the glare of the bay windows that flanked the kitchen table. I fixed my head as rigid as a bird dog on point and warily watched her elegant profile at the kitchen stove.

She was smiling a little—and humming, casting dark-eyed glances at me from eyes almost hidden behind a luxuriant cascade of shining black hair. It was a pleasing sound, an enchanting sight I would have delighted in on any other occasion. But not today. Today was the morning after booze-and-poker night and anything other than cold haughty disdain was to be viewed with suspicion and alarm.

Sweet sounds and a forgiving smile? I shuddered at the sinister implications of that, at the chilling connotation of heinous retribution inherent in such uncharacteristic behavior.

I watched her dump eggs into the frying pan, cupped my aching head gently in my hands. I closed my eyes and stoically awaited her pleasure and my fate, which had, in some inexplicable fashion, become irretrievably intertwined in some long-ago karma.

"What I want to know is," she said a moment later, dropping a plate of bacon and eggs on the table with a horrendous clatter that sent a dibble of pain lancing through my head, "when are we going to get married again?"

"Please don't shout," I whispered, cutting into the eggs slowly and carefully, holding my head perfectly still, dreading to take the first glutinous bite, but knowing from experience that that way lay the only path to salvation after a reckless, self-destructive night of poker and tequila.

"I'm not shouting, darling," she said pertly, dragging a chair back from the table with a shattering screech. She dropped a place mat on the table and sat down with a piece of toast and a cup of coffee. She chewed thoughtfully, her dark eyes gazing at me solicitously. "But I might," she said, after a while. "If you don't answer my question."

"Please, Susie, can't we talk about that some other time?" It hurt like hell even to chew.

"No. I want to talk about it now." She set her coffee cup on the table with a bang.

I winced, jerking my head sideways, then dropped the knife and fork and grabbed my head with both hands to keep it from exploding.

"Jesus," I whined. "You could have a little consideration."

"Like you did last night," she said coldly. "Out all night getting drunk as a loon, doing heaven knows what with whom, and *I* should have consideration."

"You know where I was," I mumbled.

"What? I can't hear you."

"Dammit, I said you know where I was."

"I know where you said you were, but that could be light-years from where you really were." She took a sip of coffee, then said primly, "Besides, that's no reason for you to curse at the breakfast table."

I took another bite of egg, wallowed it around my mouth a few times, then swallowed it without chewing. I gave her a weak smile. "You could call Homer."

"Hah! That bastard would lie to anything you asked him to." Her eyes were flashing and her voice was still frigid, but there was a hint of a smile at the edges of her mouth and I knew I had about finished paying my dues.

She snipped off another bite of toast with even white teeth. "Besides, we're getting off the subject, Danny boy." Her voice was back to sweet again, her eyes warm and liquid over the rim of her cup.

"If I'm such a rum-dum," I growled, "why would you want to marry me again anyhow?"

She cocked her head reflectively, her teeth worrying her full lower lip. "Weeell, I've given that some thought. I guess because I have a few years invested in you, because you damn well need someone to straighten you out again, and . . ." She paused and wrinkled her nose. "And I guess mostly because I happen to still love you." She was holding the coffee cup suspended between the slim fingers of both hands, her elbows propped on the table, and she peeked at me around it, her lips crooked in a smile that seemed somehow vulnerable. "Is them reasons good enough?" she said, doing a pretty fair imitation of my gravelly voice.

"Them's purty good reasons," I conceded. I turned my head carefully and looked at the clock over the sink, wondering where in hell I was going from here.

She eyed me steadily for a moment and I cringed inwardly. Then, to my relief, she laughed and got up and came around the table and kissed me. "Okay, buster," she said, her clear lovely eyes inches from my bleary ones, "you're on parole for now. We'll talk about this tonight. Really talk. Okay?"

She brushed my cheek with her lips again, touched me lightly on the neck, then turned and marched sturdily out of the room, slender, yet full-bodied, very nearly voluptuous in the charcoal pants and red blouse. I looked after her, feeling a pang of guilt, wondering morosely for the thousandth time what in the shades of hell was wrong with me. I pushed away from the table.

I caught up with her in the entry hall reaching for the door. Ignoring the fireball dancing around in my head, I gathered her in my arms and kissed her. We drew apart and she leaned back in the circle of my arms, her face rosy.

"Wow, what was that for?"

"Do I have to have a reason?"

She smiled and straightened the collar of my shirt. "You usually do."

"Maybe it's because you're such a nice little girl."

She poked me in the stomach. "Dammit, don't talk down to me."

"Hey, come on. I'm not talking down to you. Who's talking down to you? If you can't tell the difference between talking down and condescension you ain't got much chance with me, little girl."

Her smile was becoming strained, rimmed with white. "You know you make me feel awfully small."

"Hey, why not? I'll bet you won't go a hundred and twenty soaking wet."

"You always make me feel like I'm begging you to marry me again."

"Aw, come on. That's pretty strong, isn't it? Begging? Maybe beseeching . . ."

She stiffened in my arms. "All right, be a wiseass. You are just punishing me for divorcing you."

"You're wrong. It's not that." My mouth was suddenly dry, my throat parched, the words coming out like the rasp of a file on metal.

"Then what, Danny? You still love me. I'm not mistaken about that. Are we back to the differences in our ages again?"

I started to shake my head, thought better of it. "No. I just need a little more time."

"Oh, God." It was half laugh, half sob. "Time? Tell me, Danny, what are we waiting for now?"

I stared at her dumbly, finally looked away.

She writhed in my arms, wrenched herself free. She whirled and grabbed the doorknob, ripped the door open and leaped headlong into the arms of a startled young man standing there with his right arm outstretched in a pose reminiscent of the days of Hitler.

* * *

He was big and gangling and flustered and not as young as I had thought at first glance. He turned from watching Susie march down the walk, his broad face the color of new copper. He gave me a confused, apologetic smile.

"I'm sure sorry, Mr. Roman. I hope I didn't scare your daughter too much. I rang your bell and I was just getting ready to knock." His face looked vaguely familiar, but I couldn't put a name with it.

"She's not my daughter," I said dryly, "and I'm certain she'll get over it." His skin took on an even deeper hue and he took a step forward and held out his hand.

"I guess you don't know me, but I'm one of your neighbors. I live four houses down." He gave a small apologetic laugh. "The one with the Arizona front yard. Cactus and rock."

"Sure," I said, taking his big limp hand. "Leroy Ulster's place. Didn't know he'd sold out." His hand engulfed mine, but I had the feeling that if I bore down he would just duck his head and smile that apologetic smile.

He gave me a funny look. "He died. Two years ago. I bought the place from his widow right after that."

"Oh," I said. "Well, I don't keep up much with the neighbors."

"Yeah, well, right." He looked confused again. He shuffled his feet and stuck his hands in his pockets.

I stepped out on the porch. I'm a great believer in neighborhood harmony, and if pressed would do a lot of things to promote it, but entertaining a neighbor at seven o'clock in the morning is not one of them.

I found and lit a cigarette while he shuffled some more, studiously avoiding my eyes. Up close he looked bigger; at least four inches higher than my six feet, arms thick and muscular, pectorals high and well defined under the white tank top he was wearing. And I revised my original estimate of his age upward, to somewhere around thirty-eight or thirty-nine. I decided it was the big cow-brown eyes and the thick tangle of auburn hair that curled around his ears and dangled down over his forehead that promulgated the illusion of youth.

The silence was becoming awkward, but he didn't seem to notice. After a couple more puffs on my cigarette I had to say something.

"Well, what do you think of this nice weather we've been having?"

"Yeah, well, it sure is," he said; and followed that with, "Somebody has been trying to kill me, Mr. Roman." He looked at me then, with that small apologetic smile.

I stared back at him, not real sure he had said what I had heard. "Let's run through that again. I said something about the weather . . . and you said?"

His chuckle was too high for a man his size—almost a giggle. "I know it sounds kinda stupid when I just say it out like that, but I'm pretty sure somebody is trying to do it."

"By that you mean trying to kill you?"

He shoved his hands back into his pockets and nodded—with that silly damn grin still on his face.

I'm hallucinating, I thought desperately. This is just a figment of my imagination; my body trying to tell me something: cut out the shit, lay off the booze, get some sleep. I took a deep breath, then flipped my hand and cursed as the cigarette burned down to my fingers. Okay. I was awake. This yo-yo was real. So it had to be Homer Sellers or Tom Jeffers getting even for last night's poker game. I looked around, halfway expecting to see their convulsed faces peeking around a tree.

"Mr. Roman, are you okay?" He was peering at me with alarm, the grin finally gone off his face.

I decided to go along with the joke and grinned at him. But that caused my head to pound even more and I made a noise that probably sounded like a fart to him and turned toward the front door.

"It was nice talking to you, neighbor," I said. "Stop by again sometime."

"Hey," he said, his voice halting, apologetic. "I—uh, I—aren't you a detective?"

I turned wearily. "Only sometimes, friend. Only when I feel like it. Only when someone is lost and somebody wants to find them bad enough to pay good money to do it."

I was confusing him again. "Well," he said, his broad face wrinkled with worry. Then it brightened. "Mr.—uh, Captain Sellers sent me."

I smiled thinly. "I'll just bet he did."

"He said that you might be able to help me. He said there wasn't anything the police could do."

I snorted. "There very rarely is. Look, you go back and tell Homer—aw, shit, I'll tell the asshole myself." I stopped with my hand on the knob. "Who are you, anyhow? You're not young enough to be one of his rookies."

His face was a blueprint of bewilderment. "I'm Warren Stillwell, Mr. Roman. I'm your neighbor. I live four houses down. You know, the one—"

"Yeah, cactus and rocks." I shook my head in disgust—which was a mistake; I looked at him one more time—which was another. He was standing slump-shouldered, hands deep in his pants pockets, his big cow eyes filled with a quiet desperation and the kind of pathetic hopelessness you see in the eyes of puppies dropped on back country roads. He was either a consummate actor or he was on the level and I was the world's biggest idiot, and for the first time I was beginning to have doubts.

We looked at each other for a while, but that wasn't proving anything one way or the other, so I lit another cigarette, coughed up a lungful of bitter smoke, gingerly fingered the back of my head, and finally sighed.

"Okay, neighbor, I'll listen to your story, for all the damn good it will do. I don't hire out as a bodyguard, or a gofer, or much of anything else except finding lost people. You might keep that in mind."

I opened the door and stepped back for him to enter, and I didn't say it, but it occurred to me that right then he looked about as lost as anyone could get.

/2/

There was still some of Susie's coffee hot on the stove, but Warren Stillwell declined, and since I can't stomach the foul brew, I mixed myself a Bloody Mary at the leather-and-chrome monstrosity in my den that the builder had proudly billed as a "genuine wet bar." I drank half of it at the bar and consoled myself with the notion that it was strictly medicinal. And besides, I had a visitor; it's the solitary stuff that really gets you.

Stillwell sat watching me, patiently waiting. I glanced at him expecting at least a trace of censure at this ungodly early morning indulgence. But his face was curiously empty, benignly immobile, a tiny tilt at the corners of his wide mouth all that remained of that fatuous, ingratiating smile that I had grown so fond of.

"So somebody's trying to rub you out, hey, bucko?" I said in my best Bogart imitation. But it went right over his tousled head. He nodded solemnly.

"It sure looks that way, Mr. Roman."

He was sitting in my favorite chair, so I dropped into an imitation leather recliner-rocker facing him from the other side of the fireplace.

"All right, Mr. Stillwell, why don't you tell me about it?" I said quietly.

"All right," he said. "It was about two months ago that the first thing happened. It started down in Dallas. I was at this nightclub. It's a real nice place, floor show and everything. And when I came out these two men—"

"Whoa," I said. "Were you alone?"

"Yes. Well, when I came out these two men seemed to come from nowhere. I was at my car—"

"How much did you have to drink?"

He nodded. "I had quite a bit, I guess. I was pretty drunk, but not drunk enough not to remember what happened . . ." He stopped and frowned. "Well, most of it, anyway."

"Go on."

"Well, these two men came up beside me at my car. They had guns, both of them. They made me get in my car and lay down on the back seat . . . well, first they put the handcuffs on me—"

"Handcuffs? Were they police?"

"I don't know. They didn't say anything except to tell me what to do. I kept trying to say something, ask them what was going on. But every time I did, the one who wasn't driving would hit me on the head with something hard. After we started driving they never said a word—except when I tried to talk and once the man hit me and the other one, the driver, said something like 'Watch out for the bruises, stupid, this is supposed to be an accident.' "

"Did they ever call you by name?"

He shook his shaggy head. "No. They never really said much of anything. Just what I've told you." His eyes searched my face for a clue, but found none, and he went on in a hushed, curiously didactic voice.

"They took me to Grapevine Lake. I didn't know that until later, but that's where it was. They stopped the car on a boat ramp somewhere on the north side. It was way after midnight by then. They got me out of the car and handed me a bathing suit and told me to put it on. They took off the handcuffs and the driver stood behind me with a gun against my head while I undressed. I was down to my skivvies and . . . I guess I was crying . . . a little. I remember I tried to talk to them again . . . ask them why they were doing it . . . but the driver shoved the gun in my ear and said one more word and to hell with the accident, that he'd blow my damn head off." He stopped and stared into the dead fireplace, his face suddenly pale and haunted, his eyes slightly out of kilter. He sucked his lips into his mouth and wet them, then went on in a hollow toneless voice. "This is where it gets . . . hazy. I remember having the man's wrist in my hand . . . hearing him scream. I was fighting, somehow . . . doing things, I—I don't know what exactly . . . but then they were both there on the ground . . . one of them moaning . . . like a small scream. I remember there was blood coming out . . . out of his mouth, and he was trying to crawl away from me."

"Do you think you might have shot him?"

"No. I can't remember any gunshot. I think I would remember something like that. No, whatever I did . . . whatever it was . . . I did it with my hands." He looked down, turned his big hands over in his lap, staring at them with wonder, as if they were something alien that had suddenly sprouted at the end of his arms.

"That's what's so funny," he said slowly. "I'm not a violent man. I guess you could even call me a pacifist. I haven't had a fight since I was in grade school."

"How about military service?"

He nodded. "I was in the army."

"Vietnam?"

"Yes, but I never fired a shot in anger. I was in Supply."

"How about hand-to-hand combat training? You must have had that in basic."

"No. My mother died. They gave me a seventy-two-hour leave. I guess my company had that while I was gone."

I lit a cigarette and watched him for a moment, still searching his hands for answers, his broad face a mixture of wonder and disbelief.

"All right, Warren, what happened then?"

He sat back in the chair and assumed a position like a man being strapped in an electric chair: his body upright, knees together, feet firmly on the floor, his arms resting lightly on the chair arms, fingers curled slightly over the ends.

"I drove home."

"You didn't go to the police?"

"No. Not until the next day. Don't ask me why. I was scared, I guess. Sick. I just got back into my clothes and got away from there. Anne was out of town overnight and I fell into bed with my clothes on."

"Anne your wife?"

"No, my sister. I'm not married."

"Then you went to the Grapevine police the next day?"

"No. I have a friend . . . well, an acquaintance really, on the Midway City force. I called him. Lieutenant Royce. We're in the same bowling league. I—he went with me to Grapevine. We went out to the lake with some other officers." He took a deep breath.

"And?"

"Nothing," he said dully. "It's a gravel ramp and I took them to the exact spot. But there was nothing. Not even drops of blood on the gravel. There should have been blood; one of them was bleeding badly from the mouth."

"Maybe you took them to the wrong ramp."

"No chance. I've been there before. I discovered that on the way out. It was the right ramp." He laughed hollowly, apologetically. "Crazy, huh?"

"No blood on you? Or your underwear?"

"All I had on was shorts. I didn't notice any when I showered the next morning and by the time I got around to remembering the shorts, Anne had already run them through the washer. She didn't mention anything and I didn't ask. She doesn't know anything about this."

"What did the police say?"

He rolled his heavy shoulders in a despairing shrug. "Nothing really. I don't think they really believed me. Especially after I told them where it happened, that I had been drinking pretty heavily."

"How about your friend Royce?"

"I don't know. He seemed to, but I'm not sure." He frowned. "There was one other thing. They were waiting for someone at the lake. I'd forgotten about that. One said something I didn't make out and the other one said they'd just have to wait until he got there. He said it twice, 'We'll just have to wait until he gets here, that's all there is to it.' "

"You said that was the first thing that happened?"

He nodded and slid forward on the edge of his chair. "Yes. About two weeks later, I was working late—I work at United Labs in Dallas—and it was raining. I didn't have a raincoat and I was running to my car holding a piece of cardboard over my head. This big car—it just came out of nowhere, no lights, so I didn't see it until it was right on me. It was accelerating, making no attempt to stop, and if I hadn't slipped and fell and rolled, it would have nailed me good. I think maybe the rain saved me. The rear end seemed to be fishtailing, losing traction. I could hear the tires screaming. That's what caused me to look up and lose my footing."

"You don't think it could have been an accident? It can be tricky in the rain."

He shook his head vehemently. "No. There were two men in the car and they were looking right at me. I saw that much before I fell."

"Did you report it?"

"Who to?" he said bitterly. "There were no witnesses as far as I know. What could the police do? Even if they believed me," he added morosely.

He was watching me intently. I lit a cigarette, keeping my face expressionless. I studied the patterns of drifting smoke for a few moments before I returned his look.

"Okay," I said. "We have two incidents. Just for the sake of argument, what if the first time was a case of mistaken identity? And the second thing in the parking lot *could* have been an accident. Will you concede . . ." But he was shaking his head doggedly, a fist-sized ball of auburn hair falling forward on his forehead.

"No," he said emphatically. "Because we don't have two attempts; we have three."

"Three?" I echoed.

"That's right. Three weeks ago. In my own garage. A little weasel of a man was attempting to wire something to my car. I caught him flat-footed. If I wasn't so big and clumsy I would have had him. He barely got away the way it was."

"Wire something? A bomb?"

"Exactly. A bundle of dynamite sticks. I'd stake my life on it. They were lying on the car fender when I opened the door and switched on the light. No farther than from here to you. I saw them at the same time I saw him. He had the hood up and was evidently just beginning, because he grabbed the dynamite and ran like a rabbit."

"He got away clean then?" I was feeling a tingle of something that could have been excitement. For the first time I was beginning to believe the big shaggy man might have something besides a bad case of paranoia.

He nodded grimly. "I have a big boat in my garage. There's not much room between it and the car on the right side. I have to sidle through sideways. If it hadn't been for that I think I could have caught him. But he got a head start and he was just too fast."

"What time was this?"

"Around one o'clock in the morning. I had already been to bed. But I had forgotten that I had a battery charging in my boat. I got up to turn it off. I was barefoot and I didn't turn on any lights until I opened the garage door."

"You'd never seen the man before?"

"No. I don't think I'd ever forget that weasel face."

"You reported this to the Midway police?"

"Yes. I went back into the house and called them right then. They sent out a patrol car. He made out a report, but . . ." He stopped and lifted his shoulders in another shrug.

"But what?"

He coughed into his fist. "Well, they kept trying to call it an attempted robbery, insisted I look around to see if anything was missing—like that."

"They didn't buy your story about the dynamite?"

"Oh, he wrote it down, but they didn't talk about it a whole lot."

I smiled a little. "Small-town cops. That sort of thing happens in the big cities. Gangster-type stuff."

He nodded glumly and I thought of something. "You said Homer Sellers sent you to me. I played poker with Homer most of last night. Funny he didn't mention it."

He twisted uneasily in the chair and his face took on some of its former copper hue. "Well, he didn't exactly send me," he said, smiling sheepishly. "He came into Lieutenant Royce's office when I was there and he happened to mention that you lived here and that you were a former policeman and a friend of his. I took it as a sort of a suggestion that I come see you. Maybe I read something into it that wasn't there, but he sure gave you a good recommendation." That note of humble apology was back in his voice. It was beginning to set my teeth on edge.

"I'll have to thank him," I said dryly. That Bloody Mary had helped so much with my hangover, I decided another one might very well cure me. I went to the bar.

"You sure you won't have something?"

"No, thank you," he said gravely, but I thought I detected a faint note of hesitation. There was no censure in his voice, but for some reason I felt compelled to offer an explanation.

"I don't normally drink so early, but you may have noticed I'm a little hung over this morning." I resumed my seat and sucked up some of the red penicillin.

"I'm curious about something," I said. "Why did you wait so long to come see me?"

"I don't know," he said simply. "Every day I'd think about it and I'd just keep putting it off. I did walk down here a couple of times, but your car was gone." He smiled faintly. "Maybe I was afraid you would think I was paranoid too."

"Why should I think that?"

He spread his hands wide, then brought them back together and steepled his fingers. "Well, I can't really prove any of this, can I?"

"No, but I can't think of any reasons offhand why you'd lie either."

"Then you believe me?" he asked quietly.

It was my turn to shrug. "I don't have any reason not to." I set the drink on the brick fireplace ledge beside me and lit a cigarette. "Okay. If we accept that someone is trying to do away with you, then there's one logically obvious question that has to be answered."

"What?"

"Why?"

"I don't know why," he said quickly; maybe too quickly.

"There's got to be a reason," I said irritably. "Plain damn common sense tells us that. Three planned attempts at murder. Someone has to want you dead pretty badly."

"I've thought about that," he said soberly.

"That's good," I said, unable to keep the sarcasm out of my voice. "And you can't think of anyone, right?"

He squirmed and answered in a low voice. "No, I can't."

"Come on, Warren. Nobody reaches damn near middle age without making a few enemies." I thought about some of mine and finished the rest of the Bloody Mary.

He shook his head silently.

"How about where you work—what was it? United Labs?"

"Nobody. I work by myself mostly."

"What kind of work?"

"It's kind of hard to explain. Computers mostly."

"No enemies? Somebody who might want your job, maybe?"

"No."

"Before United Labs?"

"I went to school."

"Before that?"

"Army."

"How about ex-girlfriends, ex-wives . . . ?"

"I was married for a while. It didn't work out. She's remarried and very happy."

"Ex-girlfriends?"

"A few. Casual, nothing serious or important."

"I'll decide what's important, dammit. How about ex-boyfriends?"

He lifted his head and gave me the ghost of a smile. "I'm afraid not."

"Come on, Warren, dammit. Nobody exists in a vacuum. How about relatives? Any rich old aunts about ready to kick off and leave you a bundle?"

"No, my mother is dead. My only living relative is my sister. My father died years ago when I was little. I don't even remember him."

"What about your sister? What does she do?"

"She's a secretary in an office in downtown Dallas. A small oil company."

"There's no such thing as a small oil company. Not anymore. She younger than you?"

"Yes. By three years. She's thirty-six."

"Married?"

"Widow. Her husband was killed in a car wreck."

I sighed and thought about it for a moment. "You're sure about where you work? No professional jealousy, that kind of thing?"

"Yes, I'm sure. My work is research, primarily allied with the medical field. All of us are pretty much autonomous. Sometimes our projects overlap to a degree, but then it's simply a matter of cooperation and sharing pertinent data."

"Yeah, sounds great." I got up and walked around the room, then came back and sat down. "Okay. There's damn well got to be something. We'll just have to backtrack. All right, how long have you worked at United?"

"Eight years."

"Okay, before that you said school. How long?"

He shifted in his seat and rubbed his chin thoughtfully. "Well, I got out of the Army in 1973. I started that fall."

I did some quick figuring. "Jesus Christ. You went to school for seven years?"

He smiled faintly. "Something like that."

"You said medical research. You a doctor?"

"Not hardly."

"What then?"

"Mathematician."

"Seven years for that? What do you have, a master's?"

He smiled apologetically.

"Doctoral level?"

He nodded. "It's hard to believe, isn't it?"

I grinned. "A little. Okay, you got out of the army in 'seventy-three. When did you go in?"

"I went in at eighteen, 1967."

"That gives you six years in the army. How long were you in 'Nam?"

"Eighteen months more or less."

"Okay, now think about it. Anything happen while you were in the army? You make any enemies for any reason at all?"

He made such an obvious show of thinking about it, wrinkling his brow, screwing up his face, that I almost laughed.

"No," he said, after a while. "I can't think of anything."

"All right," I said wearily. "How about when you were in school?" He was already shaking his head ruefully before I finished the question, and I exploded.

"Dammit! Nobody's that perfect! How about sex? Did you whang your dong all those years or did you stick it in some professor's wife? Come on, Warren, what?"

"I was married during most of those years."

"Oh," I sneered. "Your wife put you through school and you dumped her. Right?" But he refused to rise to the bait.

"No," he said placidly. "It wasn't like that at all."

"Jesus Christ!"

"She's married to a brain surgeon in Boston. She left me for him."

"Maybe it's him. Maybe he's trying to get back at you for divorcing her."

He chuckled a little, then it seemed to strike him funny and he let out a bellowing guffaw.

"This is not a damn bit funny, you know," I said coldly, but he was enjoying himself so much, his merriment so contagious, that I soon joined in.

I waited until he quieted down. "Well, we've established one thing."

"What's that?" he asked, poking at his eyes with fingers as big as sausages.

"You're about as non-damn-violent as anyone I've ever met."

He nodded solemnly. "I told you that."

We'd accomplished one other thing also, I thought. We'd gotten rid of my hangover and relieved the boredom of an otherwise dull morning. And to think I'd about swallowed the whole thing like a hungry bass after a purple worm. If they hadn't thrown in that bit about the doctorate in mathematics. Jesus Christ! Talk about shopworn clichés: kidnapping, miraculous escapes from deadly killers, attempted murder by hit-and-run, and, for pete's sake, a bomb yet! You'd think a captain of Homicide could come up with something a little more original than that. I wondered if Lee Swain was in on it too. That bit about the mathematics sounded like his type of input into the scenario. The only thing that bothered me was how they had set it up so fast; less than five hours ago I had been counting their money, fielding snide remarks about bottom dealing, marked cards, and not too subtle references to my ancestry. But maybe it had been set up earlier, the impromptu card game last night just a coincidence. Both Homer Sellers and Tom Jeffers were hard-core practical jokers, painstaking and ruthless. Like the time Lee Swain had dashed off to Chicago as the result of a telegram confirming his hotel reservations for an architect's convention and congratulating him on being chosen architect of the year. He had returned the next day red-faced with blood in his eye, thirsting for revenge. Sellers and Jeffers giggled about that one for months. Homer had had one of his cop friends in Chicago send the wire.

"Well, what do you think, Mr. Roman?" Stillwell was asking humbly, his brown eyes anxious and apologetic at the same time. He was pretty good. I'd have to give him that.

I frowned in my best judicatory manner, fingered a pimple on my chin, and even picked my nose thoughtfully for a while. Then I coughed up some tobacco phlegm and lit a cigarette.

"Okay, Warren. Why don't you run on along now and give me time to assimilate all this. I'm not sure yet what I can do to help you—if anything."

He got up immediately and bobbed his head. "That'll be fine, Mr. Roman. I'd sure appreciate it," he said earnestly, the helpless, guileless look on his face so realistic I faltered for a second.

I patted his thick shoulder and steered him toward the door. "Just sit tight, Warren, I'll be in touch with you one way or the other." Then I added grimly, "You be careful now, you hear?"

"Yes sir, I will." He bobbed and shuffled to the edge of the porch, then turned hesitantly. "You think you might take my case, Mr. Roman?" he asked hopefully.

I smiled at him. "I'll have to think on it, Warren. There seems to be more than meets the eye here, and whatever happens I surely hope you don't live to regret coming to see me this morning."

There was a flicker of something in his eyes before confusion swamped his face again and he nodded uncertainly. "Well, all right, Mr. Roman, I'll wait to hear from you."

"You do that, Warren," I said softly, but he was already trundling across my yard toward the street.

/3/

Homer Sellers's official title was Captain of Homicide, but he was also in charge of burglary, armed robbery, and just about all of the other assorted offenses of mayhem and general skulduggery the citizens of Midway City, Texas, insisted on occasionally perpetrating against each other. There was one other captain on the Midway City force; he handled traffic, traffic-related crimes, auto theft, and arson.

Homer Sellers was a huge genial bear of a man. Affable, garrulous, he was fully as tall as Warren Stillwell, but with considerably more padding on his enormous frame. He had deceptively gentle blue eyes, slightly myopic behind thick glasses that continually slid forward on his big nose, and a loud booming laugh that he used often, particularly during a poker game. After a lot of fruitless study, a lot more lost money, I had suddenly discovered one fine night that the pitch and timbre of that laugh changed slightly when he was bluffing. From that moment on, he was mine.

He was sitting hunched over his battered desk, leafing slowly through a porno magazine. There was a stack of them on the corner of the desk and he looked up in irritation when I barged in without knocking. The look changed to sour disgust when he saw who it was.

"Come here to gloat, I suppose," he rumbled. Without waiting for me to answer, he pointed with his head toward the magazines on his desk. "Look at this crap. This is what our kids are reading today."

"Who're you kidding? These for your collection, or what?" I picked up one of the magazines and flipped through it. Nothing there I hadn't seen—or done. I tossed it back on the stack. "Where'd you get them?"

"Arnico and Collins raided that bookstore over on Tower."

"I thought this stuff was legal. Thought you couldn't touch them."

"Law says they have to be a thousand feet from any public building." He grinned suddenly, showing me an even row of big white teeth. "The corner of their store is nine hundred and ninety-five feet from the city garage. That's a public building."

I laughed. "I'll bet that tickled their funny bone."

"Pissed them off some," he admitted. He put the magazine with the others and leaned back in his squeaking swivel chair. He produced a cigar from his breast pocket and wet the end of it, his blue eyes watching me expressionlessly. He got it drawing good, then blew a puff of smoke in my direction.

"Well, Slick, you here to crow about last night, or what? If I had my sooners, I'd just as soon not seen you for a few days."

"Oh, hell, Homer, it wasn't all that bad. I was just on a roll. We all have nights like that once in a while."

"Uh-huh. Wonder when my time's coming? Seems like here lately every time I run a damn bluff, you ram it up my ass all the way to the third knuckle."

I grinned. "Don't blame me. I offered to give you guys lessons . . ."

He slapped his desk, his booming laugh rattling the windows. Sounds genuine as hell, I thought, perfect pitch. "You done that, son, but you didn't tell us it was going to be so expensive."

I laughed with him for a few moments, then I zoomed in on his eyes and got to it.

"Actually, Homer, I was wondering what you could tell me about Warren Stillwell."

He puffed slowly on the cigar, his wide brow wrinkling. "Stillwell? Don't think . . . yeah, yeah, I remember. That's that neighbor of yours, ain't it? In here about a month ago. Something about somebody trying to kill him. Yeah. What about him?" He held my gaze, his eyes as clear and innocent as young love.

"Just wondered what your people might have come up with."

"He come to see you?"

"Yeah."

He shrugged. "I don't know, Dan. Never heard any more about it after I saw him in Royce's office that day. John wanted me to listen to his story, get my feeling. Seemed a little flaky to me at the time. No corroboration, no witnesses. I don't know, maybe John carried it a little further. I understood they were friends. John never did come back for my input, but as I recall, I wasn't too impressed with his story. Still . . ." He laid a big-knuckled finger on one of the buttons on his phone deck. "Want me to check?"

"Might not hurt," I said, my eyes never leaving his as he pushed on the button and spoke into the box. "Mitzi. See if Royce is in, would you? And bring in the file on a Warren Stillwell—if we have one."

He leaned back and picked a fleck of cigar tobacco off his lip, rolled it around in his fingers, and dropped it in the ashtray.

"You taking him on, Dan? When did you start doing lifeguard work?"

"Just being neighborly, Homer." A small pocket of

unease was beginning to form in the nether regions of my stomach. Homer just wasn't devious enough to carry it this far—I didn't think.

He grunted and leaned forward and propped his elbows on the desk. "Ever been sorry you left the force, Dan?"

The door opened before I could answer. Mitzi trotted in, dropped a file folder in front of Homer, and without a word, trotted right back out.

Homer looked at me and grinned.

"Still goes in a run, I see."

He shook his head. "Can you beat it? She's been here for years and I've never seen her walking." He turned the folder around and opened it, then looked up as the door opened again.

It was a man this time: tall, wiry, as dapper as a three-button suit can make you. John Royce had a prominent nose, an easy, friendly grin, cold eyes, and very little hair. What there was, was coal black.

He stopped beside my chair and held out his hand. "Hello, Lieutenant. You probably don't remember me. I was just starting out here when you left." He dropped my hand and raked his fingers across his scalp. "Besides, that was a whole head of hair ago."

"I think I've seen you around," I said, just to be polite.

"What about this buddy of yours, John? Warren Stillwell. What happened on that beef of his a few weeks ago?"

"Not exactly a friend, Captain. We bowl in the same league." He slid the pile of magazines over to make room to sit on Homer's desk. "Wasn't much of anywhere to go with it. He couldn't come up with anybody who might want a piece of his hide, and there was nothing to prove or disprove his story." He stopped and gave one manicured nail a critical examination. "And he is something of a lush, Homer. There's that to consider."

"What do you make of that thing up at Grapevine Lake?" I asked.

He shrugged eloquently. "Same thing. Nothing for or against. Just his word." He sighed. "I don't know. The only thing I was able to corroborate was his being at the Steerhorn Bar in Dallas that night. They know him there. Only thing is, he was pretty well looped when he left, according to the night bartender."

"He admitted that," I said. I could feel the small balloon of discomfort begin to expand as I realized that the whole thing hadn't been a put-on by Homer, that right or wrong, the poor sad bastard had been telling it like it was—or at least his version of how it was.

"You say he's a lush?" Homer asked. "How bad?"

Royce shrugged again. "He's been pulled in three times here for public drunkenness. One DWI arrest, and would have had another except he used my name and the officer called me and I asked them to take him on home. I've seen him falling-down drunk at the bowling alley several times. If he does most of his drinking in Dallas, he might have a sheet over there . . ." He paused and looked from me to Homer. "My opinion, the guy's all screwed up."

"You mean mentally?"

He thought about it for a moment, his lips pursed in a soundless whistle. "I don't know. The guy's just so . . . so . . ." He stopped, unable to find the right word.

"Passive," I said.

"Yeah. Passive. And he's too damn friendly. Anybody pat him on the head and he wiggles like a big damn Saint Bernard. Any minute you expect him to start licking your hand."

Homer closed the folder and held it out to me. "Nothing else in here. You want to see it?"

I shook my head. "No. I guess I got what I came for."

She swung the door open in the middle of my second stab at the bell. It was easy to see that they were brother and sister because they had the same big brown eyes. The only difference was, on her they looked warm and bold and alluring instead of weak and defenseless. They had the same auburn hair also, but there the resemblance ended. She was trim and firm in the pale pink dress. Pink probably wasn't her very best color, but that meant she had worn it because she liked it and not because it went well with her pale ivory skin and the smattering of freckles across her nose and upper cheeks. Her mouth was rimmed with a muted red ring of lipstick, the interior portion of her lips a pale pink, as if she had just finished eating and hadn't had time to make repairs.

"Yes?" The ring of lipstick and her raised eyebrows gave her a rakish appearance.

"You shouldn't open your door like that," I said. "I might be a bad person: a robber, a rapist, or a salesman."

She laughed. "I looked first. I could tell right off you were a good guy." Her eyes twinkled mischievously. "Anyhow, I know you."

"You do?"

"Four houses up the street. The old English brick with all the conifers."

"I'll take your word about that last part. I thought they were Italian cypress."

She laughed again, and I decided I liked it: rich and full and no trace of a giggle.

"I've seen you out working in your yard lots of times . . ." She paused, then added, "In your shorts."

"Well, there goes any chance for a lasting relationship."

"Oh, I don't know. I like knobby-kneed men." She smiled to take the sting out of it and stepped back. "Won't you come in, Mr. . . ."

"Dan," I said.

"Won't you come in, Mr. Dan?" If she was putting me on, she handled it well.

"Just Dan," I said. "Roman is my last name."

"Oh," she said, flustered. "How stupid."

I grinned. "Well, I've never thought much about it, but I see what you mean. It is a pretty stupid name."

She was really flustered now. "Oh, no! I never meant . . . oh, lordy, you must think I'm . . . I didn't mean . . ." Her face was rosy. I could see pink all the way to the top of her breasts.

"I'm sorry," I said. "That was a gutter ball. I know what you meant. Sometimes I get carried away."

She smiled. "Don't we all." The color was rapidly receding; she might rattle easily, but she recovered just as fast. "Let's start over. Won't you come in, Mr. Roman?"

"Dan," I said, and she laughed that lusty laugh again.

"All right. Dan. My name is Anne Lawrence." She held out a slender, short-fingered hand. I discovered that limp grips didn't run in the family; hers was surprisingly firm, her palm warm and dry.

"We've been living here over a year," she said as I followed her down a short entrance hall into an expansive family room, tastefully furnished in brown and beige. "And except for my next-door neighbors and Mrs. Libby, across the street from you, you're the only other person on the block I've met."

"That about says it for me too, and I've lived here over twelve years. It's not a very friendly block."

"Oh, I don't know. Everyone's busy. Most of the women work, I understand. And I'm gone most of the time. Even when I'm home, there's always so much to do, I don't have much time for visiting—could I get you some coffee, Dan?"

"No, thanks. I really stopped by to have a chat with your brother."

"Oh, have you two met? He didn't tell me." There was a minute difference in her voice, an almost unnoticeable change of pitch. "Please sit down, Dan."

I took the chair she indicated and she sat down across from me on the edge of a chocolate-and-beige couch, her hands clasped demurely in her lap, her eyes filled with a lively interest.

"It was just this morning."

"Oh, during his morning run? He usually goes the other direction. He likes the challenge of the hill in the park."

I nodded. "I don't think he jogged this morning. He came to see me." I sat back in the chair, and since there was a smoking stand beside me with lipstick-ringed butts, I lit up. "Maybe it's just as well Warren isn't here, Mrs. Lawrence. Your brother has a problem and it might be well if you and I discussed it."

"You mean his drinking," she said, her voice small and weary. Her friendly smile had vanished and the freckles seemed to be more prominent against her pale skin. "Mrs. Libby told me you were a detective. Is Warren in trouble with the law, Mr. Roman?" Her voice was cool and I noticed she had dropped the Dan.

I smiled and shook my head. "No, he's not. I'm not a police officer. When I work at it, I'm a private investigator. Warren's problem is more . . . well, he seems to believe someone is . . . threatening him."

She looked stunned. "Threatening him?" she echoed incredulously. "Why, for heaven's sake?"

"He doesn't know why. That's a big part of the problem. Actually, Mrs. Lawrence, Warren believes someone is trying to kill him."

One small hand flew to her mouth and she sat frozen for a second, her eyes wide with disbelief.

"Kill him? My God, Dan, why?"

"He doesn't know why," I repeated patiently. "All he knows—or believes—is that someone has made three attempts on his life." I hesitated. "Anne, has Warren ever had . . . well, delusions?"

She stiffened, color rushing back into her face; and this time it was anger instead of embarrassment. "There's nothing wrong with Warren's mind," she said coldly. "If that's what you're trying to imply."

"I'm not implying anything. Look, Anne, your brother came to me this morning for help. He was very clear about what he thinks has happened to him. It was his behavior that made me wonder if he might not be imagining things, or at best, be weaving a series of coincidental incidents into a pattern to fit into his . . . well, paranoia." I held up my hand as her head jerked angrily. "I'm not a doctor. Warren came to me with a story that can't be substantiated in any way by the law in two cities. Which doesn't necessarily mean anything except that if his stories were true at least one of the episodes should have been provable. There was supposedly a lot of blood at the scene, but the police found no traces the very next day."

"Blood?"

"Yes. He was kidnapped by two men outside a bar in Dallas. They had guns and they took him to Lake Grapevine to kill him—" I broke off as she gasped, both hands covering her mouth, her face ashen. "I'm sorry," I said gently. "I know this is upsetting, but it has to be faced. I'm pretty well convinced he believes what he says, although he seemed mystified himself about how he subdued the two men and escaped. He remembers one of the men was badly injured, but he doesn't remember how. From what I've seen and heard about him, it seems completely out of character for him to do the kind of things that would be required to make that happen. He looks strong enough, but it would take more than strength if the two men were professionals—which is what he seems to think." She was sitting rigidly upright, staring stonily at her hands in her lap. "All I'm saying is I think maybe he needs a doctor more than he needs a detective."

"He's a kind, sweet, gentle man," she said tonelessly. "No, I agree with you. He couldn't possibly hurt anyone." She took a long deep shuddering breath, then looked at me with a wan smile. "Warren's been to a doctor. For almost two years. I think he stopped a few months ago. He won't discuss it and I stopped pressing him about it." She shook her head, then met my eyes steadily. "He wasn't going because there's anything wrong with his head. He was going because of the dreams."

"Dreams?"

"Nightmares. Terrible nightmares. He's had them for years, I guess. I didn't know about it until my husband died and I came to live with him. Many nights I had to wake him . . . yelling, screaming in his sleep. And he would be so upset later. Usually he would stay up the rest of the night . . . as if he was afraid to go back to sleep."

"What were the dreams about?"

"He would never say. He usually told me he couldn't remember; other times he would laugh the next day and say it was probably his libido repaying him for a starvation diet."

"Any problems with his sex life?"

She threw me a quick, slightly annoyed look. "Not that I know about," she said stiffly. "He goes out with girls, if that's what you're getting at."

"I'm not just being nosy, Anne. But you're right, his sex life is none of my business." Which was a big damn lie, I thought. I was curious.

"Well," she said slowly, somewhat mollified, "he did come to you for help, I guess."

"That brings up another thing," I said. "Even if what he says is true, I don't think I can help him. I'm not a bodyguard. The only cases I normally take are rounding up strays."

She looked at me curiously. "What's that?"

I shrugged. "Runaways. Husbands, wives, children, whatever."

"That sounds like good honest labor," she said, a caustic edge to her voice.

"It beats pimping," I said, putting a little edge in my own voice. I caught all the snide remarks about my line of work I could handle from Homer and Susie. I didn't need any more, particularly from somebody working for an oil company.

"Then why are you here?" It was an honest question, even reasonable, but for some reason it sent a thrill of anger surging through me.

I got to my feet. "You're right. What *am* I doing here?" I smiled at her, the skin on my face feeling tight and unnatural.

She was watching me with wide questing eyes. She blinked. "I'm sorry," she said, as if I had just accused her of not measuring up to my expectations. "I wasn't trying to be offensive."

"I know," I said. "I came to talk to your brother, remember. He has me perplexed and I don't like to be perplexed. I even hate riddles. I thought that talking to him again might somehow . . ." I let it trail off into a meaningless wave of my hand.

"Please," she said. "Warren needs . . . we need help, I think."

"I get three hundred dollars a day plus expenses," I said, still feeling a residue of the unreasonable anger.

"That's all right," she said.

"But it won't matter," I said bluntly, "if he can't convince me this is not a dipso dream of some kind."

"All right," she repeated humbly, completely subdued, as artless as a child. Maybe she was more her brother's sister than I had thought.

"Tell him to come see me—not call, come. And not at seven in the morning. Okay?"

She nodded silently and I moved to the doorway.

"Good-bye," I said, and she looked up and murmured something. I went out the door and left her sitting there, looking as helpless and vulnerable as a kitten on a freeway.

I walked home through the blaze of the late-afternoon Texas sun, feeling low down and shitty, and when I went into my house and found Susie lying curled up on the sofa in the den, her feet lashed together, her hands tied behind her naked body, her eyes, filled with horror, staring at me over the dirty sock stuffed in her mouth, when I found her like that and found out the who and the why, for one blinding moment I hated Warren Stillwell with a helpless rage that shook me like a willow in a high wind.

I held her shaking body and soothed her as best I could, her arms fiercely clutching my neck, and her cheek, wet and cold and slippery, mashed against mine.

"Oh, God, Danny!" she wailed. "I was so . . . so . . . scared."

"Hush, hush, baby," I crooned, rocking her like the baby I never had. "It's all right, it's okay, I'm here, Danny's here, nobody's going to hurt you again." I cradled her and rocked her until the wrenching sobs began to dwindle, die, and finally I lifted her tear-mottled face and kissed her cheeks.

"Who was it, baby?" I asked softly. "Who did this to you?"

She whimpered and sniffled and tried to hide her face in my shoulder, but I wouldn't let her.

"Who was it, Susie honey? You have to tell me."

She shook her head and hiccuped, her lips trembling. "I don't know, Danny. Two . . . two men . . . they were in . . . in the house when I came . . . home. I don't know . . ."

"Who, Susie? Dammit, tell me who!"

"I don't know who . . ." Her voice sailed off into a wail and another paroxysm of sobbing. I waited patiently, her grief touching a defenseless spot somewhere deep inside me, tightening my throat. I tucked the blanket around her more securely.

"All right, baby," I said after a while. "You didn't know them. What . . . what did they . . . want?" I forced the words out, my voice sounding like I was talking under water.

Her arms tightened convulsively. "They didn't . . . do it . . . to me, Danny," she said. "They told me to tell you . . . they said for you to stay away from Warren Stillwell . . . they made me repeat it over and over. Warren Stillwell. Who is he, Danny?"

"Dammit!" I breathed, my skin crawling with heat, my muscles pulling taut, shock dropping to the pit of my stomach like a hot splash of lead.

"They said tell you next time . . . the next time—" She broke off as my arms contracted, shutting off the words.

"No!" I said savagely. "No! There won't be a next time! I promise you, baby. Not again!"

"Danny! Danny, please!" She was squirming, breaking out of my arms, twisting to face me, holding my face between her ice-cold palms. "Please, honey! They didn't really hurt me! Please, honey." Her arms encircled my head, pulled me against the sweet silkiness of her breasts; it was my turn to be held and rocked and soothed. The soft crooning voice washing away the crazy mixture of helpless rage and hopeless fear, until it was nothing but a faint murky taste, like the bitter residue of yesterday's booze.

But proximity has other rewards, and as is often the case after great emotional trauma and stress, the human body sends out a demand for reaffirmation; and this time was no exception. I felt soft lips and warm breath at my ear, and moments later at my mouth. The kiss was long and deep and initiated its own form of emotional stress. She wriggled out of the blanket and stretched across me, warm and smooth and supple, her eyes sparkling eagerly with young lust and old knowledge as ageless as woman herself. Her gentle crooning had at some time become a husky whimper that fired my blood and brought us together in a tender-loving-savage embrace that soon, too soon, carried us to the crest—and breath-holding time.

4

After we finished, we feasted royally on peanut butter, crackers, and Cokes, and later made love again, slowly and languorously this time, taking all the turns and making all the stops that we had missed the first time, shopping leisurely at all the quaint lovely little nooks along the way.

I left Susie in my bed literally purring with contentment, her dark eyes drooping, her legs drawing upward into her going-to-sleep curl. I staggered into the kitchen, fought the tab off a can of beer, and collapsed in front of the TV to watch the news, my body demolished, my brain still in high gear.

There were a few interesting bits interspersed amongst the usual robbing and raping and killing going on. One was an interview with a Vietnam vet who had spent a goodly portion of the entire war in the clutches of the enemy, a sad-looking man who wondered why there had been no parades for him, no visits to the White House, no ticker-tape madness. Watching his tired young-old face I got the impression that he didn't really give a damn, but what the hell, how many times do you get a chance to go on national TV? He had the look of a guy who had been there and back, an air of cynical tolerance, or maybe indifference, a man soured on life; a man who might make your cars, fix your washer, your TV. A man who might gouge you a little and rationalize it away as playing the game, doing unto others while they were doing unto you. The good old American way, getting yours while there was still some left to get. A small immorality in a world filled with immorality. A world where politicians scream austerity and vote themselves raises; where they proudly display their pampered wives in ten-thousand-dollar designer dresses while sanctimoniously espousing the tightening of belts among the poor, the ruthless weeding out of the laggards, the freeloaders, the apportioning of their largess on the basis of slide rule predetermined need; where even the president quotes thinly veiled parables about ungrateful children who cannot seem to learn the virtues of prudence and thrift, and therefore must be bridled like unruly colts, taught the harsh realities of life by a stern but kindly father who will, for their own good, of course, curtail their allowance.

I finished my beer, watching Johnny Carson for a while, then dragged myself off to bed when the fat lady started singing.

Susie woke me the next morning with a breakfast tray. She was glowing, effervescent, bubbling over like foam on a glass of good lager beer. She bustled around, arranging the tray, bolstering my back with pillows, touching and poking and prodding until everything was just so. Then she sat on the edge of the bed watching fondly while I ate, sharing a piece of my bacon, regaling me with juicy bits of gossip about her coworkers in the newsroom of the local independent television station. She had gone back to work, and her goal in life was to become an anchorperson again.

Watching her, I was struck again by the air of expectancy about her; as if the very next sixty seconds were going to be the best minute of her life.

After breakfast I dressed while she disposed of the dishes. Then I took her by the hand and led her into her bedroom. I opened her closet, found two suitcases, and threw them on her bed. She watched me with slowly widening eyes, her lips beginning to flatten and thin. She opened her mouth angrily, then took another look at my face and slowly let it close.

"Pack them, Susie," I said quietly.

"Why, Danny? Why do I have to leave?" Her voice was a shaky whisper.

"You know why, Susie." I sat down on the edge of the bed and pulled her between my knees. Her face was beginning to contort and there was a sheen of moisture in her eyes.

"Please, Danny? What did I do wrong? Was it last night . . . ?"

"No! Hell, no! It was yesterday, baby. It was the men, those two men . . ."

"Oh, God, Danny, you scared me!" She was laughing and crying at the same time. She sucked in a deep shuddering breath. "I thought you . . . you wanted me to go away. I thought . . ."

I shook her gently. "Never mind what you thought. It isn't true. Those men scare me, Susie. They were professionals. They didn't just break into this house. They came in through locked doors—good locks. They had to know what they were doing and I have to believe they meant what they said to you. That's why you're going to your grandmother's."

"I can't do that, Danny! That's in Waco. What about my job? What—"

"To hell with the job! I'll give your boss a call, but if they won't hold your job . . . well, that's just tough. You're going, and you're going this morning!" I was almost shouting, and I could see the beginning of indignation and defiance.

We glared at each other for a long moment before she tried to twist away from me. But I snared her around the waist and pulled her resisting body in close. "Susie," I said, making an effort to soften my tone. "Don't fight me on this. I lost one woman I loved because I let her sway me, because I let her talk me into doing things the way she wanted instead of the way reason told me they should have been done. Well, I'm not going to lose another one." I cupped her cheek in my hand, then stood up and pulled her against me. "Look, it may be for only a day or two. Just until this mess gets straightened out." I could feel her body relaxing, clinging, and her touch started a keen vibration that tightened my already thrumming nerves.

She lifted her head and looked at me almost shyly,

her face filled with a solemn softness that brought a lurch to my heart, a painful sensation as real as the phantom pain of a lost limb.

"Look," I said softly. "There's no way you can know how I felt yesterday. That first second when I saw you there on the couch—not knowing what had happened, if you were hurt, if you had been raped, or even if you were dead. My heart stopped, Susie. The whole damn world stopped. I don't want ever to go through that again, hell, I don't know if I *can* go through it again."

Her lips quirked with the beginning of a tremulous smile, her eyes warm and damp and luminous. "I think this would be a very good time to visit Ma-Ma, don't you, Danny?" she said innocently, and laughed.

While Susie packed, I called Homer Sellers, pausing frequently in my story to wait for his fervent cursing to subside.

"Dammit, Dan, why didn't you report this yesterday?"

"What the hell for?" I shouted back. "So those apes of yours could come lunging around like blind coyotes in a henhouse? She was upset enough the way it was. Those men could have been halfway to Texarkana by the time I found her."

"How's Susie doing?" And I knew the concern in his voice was genuine.

"She's fine, Homer. All they really hurt was her pride, I guess. It's what they said that scares the hell out of me."

"What're you gonna do?"

"First thing is get her out of here. She's going to her grandmother's in Waco until I can find out what's going on."

"You gonna take her?"

"No. She wants to take her car. I'm going to follow her a ways to make sure nobody gets cute."

"Don't have to," he rumbled, "if you don't want to. I got a man going to Austin to pick up a prisoner. He can follow her all the way, right to her grandma's door. Make sure no son of a bitch is following her, too."

"Thanks, Homer, I'd appreciate it."

"Well," he said slowly, "like the whore said when she rubbed on the axle grease, I guess this will make things a little more slippery."

"Yeah. Looks like Warren is not as befuddled as he appears."

"You talked to him today?"

"No. He and his sister both work. I plan on calling him at the job."

"You gonna get mixed up in this thing then?"

"I already am, Homer. Whether I want to be or not. At least until . . ." I let it fade away.

"At least until they get him." His voice was bland, casual.

"That's a shitty thing to say."

"Truth, ain't it?"

"Well, you're the damn police, why don't you protect him?"

"If the damn citizens reported things when they was supposed to instead of—"

"Homer, shove it. Just shove it."

"Okay, son. Did Susie give you a description on them two bastards?"

"Yeah. I'll bring it by."

"Why don't you bring her in, see if we can work up a sketch?"

"No! No damn way, Homer. She's getting out of this town, now. If you want sketches call the Waco police. She can work with them. But she leaves here within an hour. If your man isn't ready to go, just say so."

"No need to get all pissed, litte buddy. My man will be there in a few minutes."

"Okay, Homer, and thanks."

"You come make that report, hear?"

"Sure, Homer," I said, and hung up.

There were two men instead of one in the police car that showed up a few minutes later. The older one I knew, Bill Askew; the other one, a tall randy-looking young man in a natty brown suit, had the studiously bored indifference of a new plainclothesman. He took one look at Susie and went into his mating dance, leaping forward with alacrity to carry her bags while Bill and I grinned at each other behind his back.

"Don't worry about her, Dan," Bill said, looking to where Susie and the young cop had the map spread on the hood of the car, plotting the route to Interstate 35. "We'll drop her off at the door and I got some buddies in Waco who'll spread the word to check her out regular."

"Thanks, Bill. Shouldn't be any problems in Waco, but I appreciate it just the same."

Susie broke the young cop's heart by giving me a long kiss and a hug, and then another kiss before climbing into her Dodge and driving off misty-eyed down the street. The unmarked police car followed and I caught a glimpse of the young cop's red face and Bill's grinning one.

I watched until they were out of sight. I went back into the house and looked up Warren Stillwell's telephone number and dialed it. I let it ring ten times just for the hell of it, then hung up and got a Coors out of the refrigerator. I flopped down in front of the TV and watched a game show while I drank my beer.

I gave it a lot of thought, but I couldn't come up with a thing I could do until I talked with Warren Stillwell again, doubted seriously whether there would be anything even then.

Despite the mindless babble coming from the set, the house seemed cold and empty all of a sudden without Susie, and I did the only thing I could think to do to keep from brooding about her; I went to sleep.

"Hello. This is Warren Stillwell."

"Dan Roman, Warren."

"Oh, hello, Mr. Roman. I'm sorry you had to wait but we don't have phones in the lab." Even on the phone his voice had a hesitant, ingratiating quality.

"That's all right, Warren. I think you and I need to have a talk."

The line hummed emptily for a moment. "Anne told me you came by the house yesterday."

"Yes. I came to see you, but she said you were working late."

"Yes. We're pretty busy. I have to work again tonight too."

"I don't think so, Warren. Not tonight. And I want you to come straight home from work. What time do you normally quit?"

He was silent for so long I began to wonder if I had lost him.

"Warren?"

"Does this mean you believe me, Mr. Roman?"

"I suppose you could say that."

"Did Anne change your mind, Mr. Roman? I wish you hadn't told her."

"Don't you think she has a right to know if your life is in danger?"

"Maybe so, but she was awfully upset."

"I can imagine," I said dryly. "What time do you quit?"

"Five o'clock."

"What time do you get home?"

"Around five-thirty."

"Okay. I'll be waiting at your house at five-thirty. Will your sister be home?"

"I think so."

"Okay. You'll remember to come straight home?"

"Yes sir, Mr. Roman." There was a note of amusement in his voice, and I hung up the phone suddenly aware that I had been talking to him as if he were a child. Well, why not, I thought. You judge a man by the way he acts.

I rummaged in the refrigerator and found a couple of pieces of bologna with brown curling edges and made a sandwich. I opened a can of beer to go with it, stuck an apple in my pocket, and went out into the front yard.

It was October and hot. But I can take only so much refrigerated air and for a few minutes the heat felt good; long enough for me to drag a metal lawn chair into the pool of shade under a big oak. The bologna tasted funny and the beer more bitter than I remembered, but I was hungry after my nap and the hot dry air made the brew go down easy.

I propped my feet against the rough bark of the oak and watched the kids stream down the hill from the school into the park at the end of my street a city block away.

Not too long ago it had been woods, part of a thousand-acre ranch with real cows and horses and cowboys, only the cowboys didn't ride the horses anymore; they drove around in pickups and Jeeps and it got harder and harder to tell them from anybody else. But it didn't matter a lot because pretty soon the city fathers decided that we needed a city park and they passed a few ordinances, waited a while, passed a few more, and before you could say cat spit they were bringing in the bulldozers, backhoes, chain saws, and concrete trucks, and almost overnight we had us a five-hundred-acre expanse of verdant wasteland with precision-spaced trees, bicycle trails, and lighted tennis courts. It was used mainly as a shortcut by the kids who lived in the postage stamp houses that now occupied the other five hundred acres of the ranch. But it wasn't all a complete waste; it gave the town drunks a place to sleep in the summertime, and an occasional jogger could be seen staggering red-faced and gasping along its winding trails.

The ragged line of kids straggled across the park and disappeared and there was one lone figure left. An old man by the look of him, mounted on a three-wheeler bike and wearing a white crash helmet, pumping slowly and steadily along a trail that entered the park at the end of my street. He paused cautiously at the cross street, then pushed off and came toward me, bare legs flashing in a slow methodical cadence. He was wearing white walking shorts, a white polo shirt, and was within a hundred feet before I realized the crash helmet was hair, white and frothy as cotton candy.

He rode militarily erect, his eyes straight ahead, seemingly oblivious to everything around him. Ten feet from the edge of my driveway his head moved and he seemed to see me for the first time. I lifted my hand and he nodded, then turned the bike into my driveway as if that was where he had been headed all along. He coasted to a stop a few feet away.

"Good afternoon, sir." His voice was strong and resonant, somehow unsuited to the thin wiry frame. His face, long and angular and pleasant, was almost the same color as his hair, and there was a crisp expectant look about him, as if nobody had ever taken the time to explain that life was a very complex affair and that no one was ever really meant to be happy.

"How do you do," I said. I dropped the empty beer can at the base of the tree and got up and shook his hand. "My name is Dan Roman. You must be one of my neighbors. I don't think you'd be riding too far on a day like this."

His laugh was almost musical. "Lionel Whitecomb, sir. Very perceptive deduction. I am a neighbor, and I can see where you get your reputation as a detective."

It was my turn to laugh. "Hardly a Sherlock Holmes deduction, Mr. Whitecomb. It must be eighty at least." I took a closer look at him. "Have we met before, Mr. Whitecomb?"

He shook his head, the halo of hair glinting like spun silver in the sunlight. "No sir, we have not." He paused, lively blue eyes gleaming. "And that, sir, is my loss."

"Very nice of you to say so. Would you like to come in out of the sun? I can get another chair from the porch, or we could go inside and cool off."

"I will sit a bit, if you don't mind, but here in the shade will do fine." There was an upward curl at the corners of his mouth, a slight parting of the lips over convex teeth that gave his features the perpetual appearance of the beginning of a whimsical smile. He climbed stiffly and carefully off the bike and I went to the porch and brought back another chair. "We all get far too much refrigerated air, I'm afraid," he said. He lowered himself cautiously into the chair and I noticed that his knees were crisscrossed with a network of slick, uneven scars.

He caught my glance and smiled. "They look much worse than they actually are. They mesh well enough to ride the bicycle. It's when they're in a locked position that I must be careful."

"Football?"

His eyes twinkled. "Oh, my, no. Onset of old age, I'm afraid. Deterioration of the cartilage. One of nature's little painful reminders that we're all vulnerable."

I lighted a cigarette and offered him the pack. He shook his head with a doleful sigh. "Had to give them up. Along with most of the other small pleasures of life." He crossed his legs with the aid of his hands and squirmed into a more comfortable position. His blue eyes regarded me shrewdly.

"I'm sure by now, Mr. Roman, you have deduced that my happening along this afternoon was not merely an accident."

I smiled a little and nodded sagely. "I was wondering," I confessed. It was just a small lie. I saw no reason to shatter his illusions. I had had no inkling that his visit was not a spur-of-the-moment thing, an old man's whimsy.

He nodded his head in satisfaction. "I was sure of it," he said. "You seem to be a very astute young man." He looked toward the park, his lips pursed, his brow wrinkled. After a moment, he cleared his throat. "This is very embarrassing for me, Mr. Roman. I dislike having to air family problems this way, but I suppose there comes a time in each man's life when he must seek aid beyond his own capabilities to fend for himself." He turned toward me with a small apologetic smile. Abruptly he turned back to face the park. "I have a daughter, a grown woman. A grown woman with a good husband and two small children. A very pretty lady who was always a sweet obedient child, an honor student in school . . . and up until two months ago, a loving mother and wife." He stopped and breathed deeply, his left hand idly massaging the thin muscle of his thigh. "But that's all changed. Two months ago she ran off with another man, leaving two wonderful children and a husband who's almost in a state of shock." He turned his head and looked at me intently, expectantly, as if to see horror in my face, or, failing that, at least a modicum of censure. His expression demanded answers and I trembled on the verge of telling him to go home, to get back on his tricycle and pedal back the way he had come, that I had no solutions, no answers to the anomalies of human behavior that had begun with a ripe red fruit in a lush green garden. But instead I nodded wisely.

"I see."

"A kid," he said bitterly. "A lazy, shiftless, long-haired punk who doesn't even have sense enough to know that prayer beads and dirty feet went out with the sixties." His kindly eyes were suddenly chips of blue-green ice. "I want to hire you to find them, Mr. Roman. I can bring my daughter to her senses. She had always been a reasonable, well-behaved child, and if I can just talk to her I'm sure I can make her see how illogical, how irresponsible, her behavior is."

I shook my head. "Logic and reason have nothing to do with it, sir," I said, my voice harsher than I had intended. "Believe me, I've seen it often enough to know. I don't know your daughter, of course, and I don't pretend to be an analyst, but I've chased and caught enough runaway wives to know that no amount of talking, or cajoling, or threatening will bring them home. It's love we're dealing with here, Mr. Whitecomb. Or the illusion of it, which is the same thing, and usually comes down to a plain old-fashioned case of hot pants. There's only one way to deal with it effectively, and it takes guts and patience and a hell of a lot of caring. You have to let it go, let it run its course. Sooner or later she's going to realize that all she's been chasing is her youth. One day she's going to wake up and discover that her husband and all that housework weren't nearly as bad as she thought, and that suddenly her kids are the most precious thing in life to her. And she's going to panic, afraid that she's lost them forever—and that's when she'll come home, Mr. Whitecomb—and not before."

He was staring at me fixedly, a look of such despondency on his pale face that I palliated my stern lecture with a smile. "Maybe it will happen soon, Mr. Whitecomb. Two months is a long time. By the same token, they may be out of the state by now, New York or San Francisco . . ."

He shook his head sadly. "No. They're still here. A friend of Jack's saw them a few days ago . . ." He paused, his face darkening. "On a motorcycle in Dallas."

I flipped the cigarette butt out into the street and reached for another. "I'm sorry. Ordinarily, if you were still determined to find her after my little speech, I could probably help you. But right now I'm working on another case and I have no way of knowing how long it will take. Believe me, sir, I think you would be wasting your money."

"That doesn't matter," he said stiffly. "I am a retired army officer. I have the necessary money. As much as it takes."

"I'm sure you do, sir. I only meant—"

He lifted his hand. "I know what you mean, Mr. Roman," he said gently. "And I understand, of course. You must honor your prior commitments. A gentleman can do no less. Perhaps later . . ." He let it drift vaguely away and rose awkwardly to his feet, his knees not the only things that were stiff. He stood as rigidly erect as the oak tree beside us, and I could sense his pride, as fragile as a baby's tears.

He extended his hand. "Thank you for your time, sir, and it was a pleasure meeting you. I ride this way quite often of late. Perhaps we will see each other again."

"I hope so, sir," I said, a small shaft of guilt penetrating the bubble of empathy already fermenting inside, adding scope and dimension.

He was starting to mount the three-wheeler when I stopped him.

"Mr. Whitecomb, look, maybe I could manage to work in a few hours a day. Who knows, I may get lucky. It happens that way sometimes. If they're still in this area they shouldn't be too hard to locate."

He gave me a level, penetrating stare. "Are you certain it wouldn't interfere with your present commitment?"

"I won't allow it to. I'll spend what spare time I can afford on finding your daughter. Most of the preliminary work I can handle by telephone. I'm sure we can work something out if you find the arrangement satisfactory."

"That will be most satisfactory." He hesitated. "About your fee, sir . . ."

"Oh, I think seventy-five dollars a day would be more than enough."

His lips thinned and his head came up sharply. "I will not accept charity, Mr. Roman. I am sure your usual fee is substantially more than that."

"That's so," I admitted, "but that's for a full eight-hour day. I can't expect you to pay for something you're not getting." I smiled reassuringly, forcing myself to return his gaze steadily.

"Very well," he said, after a long moment. There was a battered briefcase in the bicycle's basket and he opened it and removed a large manila envelope and a checkbook. "There are pictures of my daughter in here and I have written down everything we know about the young man, including his motorcycle tag number Jack's friend was good enough to obtain for us. If I could just borrow a pen, Mr. Roman, I will give you a retainer."

I accepted the manila envelope. "You've been watching too much TV, Mr. Whitecomb: real-life private investigators don't get paid until they deliver." I busied myself with the envelope to avoid his eyes. There was a five-by-seven photograph of a rather plain woman who appeared to be in her early thirties. She had her father's small mouth without the mitigating influence of the upward curl to relieve its severity; her nose was a smidgen too long and had a slight hook; her eyes were big and blue and sad, almost hidden by straight lank hair that was obviously artificially blond.

I dropped the picture back into the envelope. "One thing, Mr. Whitecomb. Do you know if they had any money?"

"No, they didn't," he said slowly, reluctantly replacing the checkbook in the briefcase. "Sherry drew three hundred from their account, and the bum never had a dime to his name."

I nodded. "Well, that won't last them very long. One of them will have to be working by now. Did your daughter work before or after she was married?"

"She worked as a waitress for about a year after they were married, until the first boy came. The punk was some kind of mechanic. Motorcyles, I believe." He snapped the catches on the briefcase. "When he worked, that is."

"You don't happen to have a picture of him?"

"No. I'm sorry."

"Don't be." I grinned. "If you make things too easy, I won't have anything to do to earn my money."

"I doubt that," he said dryly.

I held up the envelope. "Do I have your telephone number in here?"

He waited until he was positioned on the bicycle before answering. "If you don't mind, Mr. Roman, I'd rather not give you my number. To be perfectly honest, my son-in-law, Jack, would be terribly upset if he knew I was doing . . . this. He swears he will not have her back, and I would just as soon not have him know that I'm . . . well, meddling in their affairs. I know he will come around once Sherry is back home, but until then, if he should get wind of my actions, I'm afraid he would take the children and return to his hometown. I hope you understand. I am staying with him, helping with the children, and since he works at home it would be difficult not to arouse his suspicions if I were to start receiving telephone calls. However, if I could call you?"

"Certainly, Mr. Whitecomb, I understand. For the next few days, at least, I expect to be home most of the time. My number is in the book."

He nodded. "Thank you, Mr. Roman." He turned the three-wheeler and pushed himself out of the driveway, his legs moving jerkily at first, then, seeming to gain lubricity, strength, began to pick up a smooth rhythm. I lit another cigarette and watched until his brittle white figure disappeared in the park.

/5/

I was standing beside my station wagon smoking when Anne Lawrence's small red Ford came zipping down the street and pulled into her driveway. She sat looking at me for a moment. Then she got out.

"Hello, Mr. Roman."

"Mrs. Lawrence." I walked across the grass and intercepted her halfway up the walk.

Her eyes searched my face. "Is there something wrong?"

"Yes," I said, taking her elbow and moving toward the front door. "There is something wrong, but if you don't mind I'll wait until your brother comes before we discuss it. Save telling it twice."

She selected a key and inserted it into the door. "I think Warren said something about working late tonight. But please come on in." There was a vertical worry line in the center of her forehead and most of the lipstick was gone from her lips again. Either a very sloppy young lady or a very secure one, I thought.

"He won't be. I talked to him today."

"You did?" She glanced at me from the corner of her eye, then turned to face me squarely. "Has something else happened today, Mr. Roman? I want to know."

"Dan," I said.

"All right, Dan. Tell me."

"No. I promise you. Nothing has happened today—that I know about, anyway."

Her face plainly said that she didn't believe me, but she let it go. "Could I get you something to drink, Dan? Coffee? Coke?" She laughed at the expression on my face. "I'm sorry we don't have something with more punch."

"I don't like punch either," I said, wondering what it was about her that brought out the frivolity in me. Maybe it was her ready, appreciative laugh.

I moved toward the chair I had used the day before, then stopped and turned as the front door burst open and Warren Stillwell came lumbering in, his face red and anxious. He was breathing hard, as if he had been jogging. He stopped in the doorway and smiled apologetically.

"I'm a little late," he said, his shaggy head swinging from me to Anne and back again.

"At least you found the right house," I said, and felt as much as saw the quick hard look Anne gave me.

"I'm sorry," Warren said. "We were right in the middle of—"

"You don't have to explain, War," Anne said sharply.

I ignored her. "This work you do. Is it possible anyone else might be interested in it?"

He looked perplexed. "Oh, sure. A lot of people. They call us all the time to see how we're getting along. Doctors, pharmaceutical companies, hospital administrators, all kinds of people."

"I don't mean that exactly," I said patiently. "I mean other research outfits who might be working on the same thing. Who might be afraid you were getting the jump on them."

He looked at Anne, then back at me. "I don't know what you mean. A lot of people are working on cancer research . . ."

"That's what it is? Cancer research?"

"Yes. I thought you knew that."

"I thought you were a mathematician."

He gave me a puzzled, pitying look. "Everything is based on mathematics, Mr. Roman. I thought everybody knew that." His tone was querulous, filled with reproach.

Anne laughed. "Not everyone loves mathematics like you do, War."

I ignored her again. "Then there is absolutely no reason for anyone to be concerned about your work because it might affect them adversely, either monetarily or personally?"

"No," he said, a tiny needle of petulance in his voice. "I already told you that."

"All right, big man," I said, letting a savage edge creep into my own voice, "tell me this—tell me why two men came into my house yesterday. Ripped the clothing off my . . . girl . . . threatened her with rape, and worse, if I didn't stay away from you."

"Oh, no!" Anne's hand flew to cover her open mouth. "Oh, my God, Dan, did they hurt her?"

"Not physically," I said, watching Warren Stillwell, watching the color leaving his face as if all the blood were being sucked to an empty heart.

"Jesus, I'm sorry, Mr. Roman. I can't believe anybody'd do that."

"It happened. And that's why I'm here. I sent Susie to a safe place until I can find out what this is all about. The only way I know to do that is through you." I stopped and let both of them get a good look at my face. "I've decided to take your case, Warren, but God help you if I find out you're not leveling with me."

"I'm not lying, Mr. Roman. Not one little bit of it. It happened just the way I said." He was bobbing his head emphatically, as if to lend credibility to his declaration.

"All right, Warren, I believe you. But there is one

thing both of you have to agree to. You have to do exactly like I tell you. Is that agreed?" Warren's head was already moving up and down. I turned to Anne. "You have any objections?"

"No sir," she said demurely, a small enigmatic smile working at her lips.

"All right. The first thing I want you to do is go pack enough clothes for at least three days."

"Pack?" Anne sat up straight, the smile sliding off her face. "Where are we going?"

There was truculence in her voice and I could see rebellion brewing in her eyes.

I grinned. "You're going down the street. To my place. If I'm going to have to baby-sit Baby Huey here, it will have to be on my own turf, where I can have at least some control of the situation."

"Why not here?" Anne asked as a token to women's lib, but the fight had gone out of her.

"I just told you," I said shortly. "My place is better situated for defense, if it comes to that."

"Sounds like you expect a siege," she said abstractedly, her mind obviously somewhere else. Undoubtedly cataloging the things she would have to take. Without waiting for an answer, she got up and left the room.

"Okay with you, Warren?"

"Yes," he said, but there was something in his face, in the way he met my eyes uneasily.

"Something bothering you, Warren?"

"Yes, Mr. Roman, there is. I don't enjoy being talked down to."

"I wasn't aware that I was doing that."

"I think you are," he said quietly.

"Okay, Warren, was it the Baby Huey thing?"

"Yes. Partly. And I understand why. I realize that my physical characteristics make me look like a big buffoon, and that sometimes I even talk like one. I'm not certain why. But I just wanted you to know that I knew."

"I'm sorry, Warren. It won't happen again."

He smiled suddenly. "Yes it will, Mr. Roman. Sometimes I deserve it."

I smiled back at him. "Okay, if it does, then you know there's no malicious intent."

He got up and headed for the door. "As long as we both know," he said genially. "I'll go pack."

"This will be your bedroom," I told Warren. "You may have to move some of Susie's things to another closet. There's some space in the front bedroom closet. This room only has one window and it's small and pretty high. It's the safest room in the house."

I went on down the hallway and Anne followed behind. "I've turned the front bedroom into a sort of reading room, so I suppose you and I will have to share this one."

I grinned down at her and she arched an eyebrow. "If you're trying to scare me," she said, "you have."

"It's a great big bed," I said. "You'll never even know I'm there."

"You bet I won't." Her eyes were flashing and the rosy glow was mounting in her cheeks.

I laughed. "Okay, kidding's over. We'll both be using it but at different times. You'll be sleeping nights, and I'll be sleeping days."

She glanced at me, startled. "You're going to stay up all night?"

"Yes. I'll do my sleeping while you and Warren are at work."

She looked around the bedroom, then back at me, the blush fading, her face worried. "You really think all this is necessary?"

I nodded. "It's necessary. Look at it this way. They've tried three times. By now they know that I'm working for you, they probably know you're here. You can bet we're being watched. So they know the only way they can get to Warren now is to come in and get him or try to snipe him on the way to or from work. But I'm going to make that as difficult as possible. I take both of you to work and I pick you up. I cover you here at night while you sleep."

"But this could go on forever."

"It could. But I don't think so. They know now they're out in the open. Maybe they're under some kind of pressure. Time limitation. Something. But one thing they do know is they're not after a helpless man now. He has help. So, unless time is of no importance to them, I think they'll come after him. If that doesn't happen in a reasonable time, I'd suggest you just pick up and leave. Go to another part of the country—"

"I can't do that." Warren was standing in the doorway. "I've put too much time into this project. I have to see it through."

"You can't see it through if you're dead."

He folded his arms and stared at me stubbornly. "It doesn't matter."

"Then why in hell am I helping you?" I blazed.

His lips tightened and his eyes, shiny and blank, touched mine briefly, then flicked away. "For three hundred a day, I guess," he said.

I didn't put everything I had into it, but then I don't think it would have mattered much. His jaw felt like a seasoned oak plank and the pain lanced up my arm and skyrocketed in my brain. He grunted and shook his head and trundled off down the hall. And I could swear I heard him chuckle.

"Oh, Jesus," I moaned. "I broke the damned thing."

"Here, let me see."

She took my burning hand in her cool ones and led me into the bathroom and ran cold water over it. "That wasn't nice," she clucked. "You might have hurt him."

I worked the fingers back and forth and it hurt like hell, but nothing grated. "I'll tell you one damned thing."

"What?"

"If I knew how to find these damn bastards I'd send them a wire telling them where that big son of a bitch is. I'd sign a damn peace treaty with them and let them have his damn big ass."

She clucked again. "No you wouldn't." She worked the fingers around and around, alternated between stinging hot water and cold, and I don't know if that's the prescribed treatment, but it wasn't long before it began to feel better.

She patted it dry, examined it one more time, then gave me a bright smile. "There, as good as new. Now don't you think you should go apologize to him?"

"I'll be ducked in sheep shit first."

She cocked her head at me. "You really wouldn't do it, would you?"

"What?"

"Tell them to come get Warren."

I sighed. "No, I guess I really wouldn't do it."

"I don't see why I can't drive my own car," Anne grumbled as I helped her into the camper on the back of Hector Johnson's Ford pickup. Hector was my next-door neighbor, and I had talked him into a temporary vehicle swap. He was a retired accountant and vacillated between vicarious titillation over what his overactive imagination considered to be the more exciting aspects of my life and being repelled by the violence in it. Hector watched far too much TV.

"You could," I said, "but do you think they would hesitate for a minute to use you to get to Warren?"

"Oh, all right," she said sullenly. "Get in, Warren."

He climbed awkwardly through the narrow door and sat down on the bunk across from Anne. I closed the door and pushed the buttons on the garage door activator. I climbed into the truck and slid open the window between the cab and the camper.

"They're going to know you're in there, but keep the drapes closed anyhow. They can't tell exactly where you are. If I yell, hit the floor and stay there."

"Oh, God," Anne mumbled, "classic paranoia."

I smiled and drove out into the morning sunshine.

Except for the choking, paralyzing traffic on Stemmons Freeway, the ride was uneventful. I dropped Warren off first; a large brick building a mile beyond the Trinity River bridge and two blocks off the freeway. Anne worked at an office building closer to downtown. We drove the two miles in strained silence. She leaped out of the camper almost before I came to a complete stop. She slammed the door and marched up the walk without looking back. I watched her go inside, then shrugged, yawned, and drove off the lot into the westbound traffic.

Home again, I backed the pickup into the garage, the top of the shell camper barely clearing the raised door. I showered and shaved and checked the doors, promising myself for the thousandth time to install dead bolts. There was a subtle smell of perfume in the bedroom, and I crawled into bed vaguely wondering if Anne Lawrence had freckles on the rest of her body.

Hector Johnson's dog, Rowdy, woke me at two-thirty. I looked out the window. My station wagon was gone from Hector's driveway and Rowdy was sitting at the chain-link gate, gazing down the driveway and expressing his boredom in an occasional guttural bark. I opened the window and yelled at him. He flattened his ears, gave me a sheepish dog-grin, and trotted out of sight around the house.

I went back to bed, but it was too late. I was more than half awake and I finally said to hell with it and shuffled wearily into the den. I lit a cigarette and sat in my leather chair and tried to decide if I wanted breakfast or lunch. I opted for lunch and dropped a couple of wieners in a pan of water on the stove.

Lionel Whitecomb's manila envelope was lying on the dining table and while I waited for my food to heat, I looked at its contents. Besides the photograph I had already seen there was a single sheet of typing paper half filled with neat precise printing. There was a lot of information about Sherry Bascomb, most of it useless; the only really important items were her Social Security number and her vital statistics. There was a detailed description of her lover, but no name. But that didn't matter too much if the motorcycle was registered to him. I looked at the photograph again, at the quiet, pleasant face, the sad eyes, and wondered what depths of desperation, and quiet frustration, had sparked her rebellion. Was it reaching the nominal midway point in life, the sudden realization that life didn't necessarily get progressively better as one got older? That what she had was all there was? That a couple of screaming kids and a tired irritable husband failed miserably to compensate for faded childhood dreams of fame and fortune and undying love. The real world. Most people accept it, or at least tolerate it, but there are some, a few, for whom it represents a living nightmare, an intolerable condition from which they must escape. Some do it by quietly folding in on themselves, withdrawing, creating their own worlds, safe and secure from the madness. Others, by abandoning what they know and fear and hate, leaping headlong into the unknown, sustaining themselves with the sorry rationalization that whatever lies ahead must be better than what they are leaving behind.

I wondered if Sherry Bascomb was one of the latter.

I fixed my hot dogs and sat down in front of the phone. Homer Sellers's phone was busy and I was on my second hot dog before I was able to reach him.

"Sellers."

"Hi, Homer, how's my best buddy?"

"What do you want, Dan? I'm busy."

"What've you got? Some more of those porno magazines to investigate?"

He made an exasperated sound. "You calling about this week's game, or what?"

"Okay, sorehead. How would you like to make a bet?"

"What kind of bet?"

"Well, you know that hand drill press that's been gathering dust out in my garage for years—the one you were hinting you'd like to have?"

"Yeah, what about it? You gonna give it to me?"

"Not exactly. I was thinking more in terms of a bet; the press against twenty dollars."

"For what?"

"That you can't get me a name and address from a motorcycle tag—wait a minute—and find out if there's been any input into a certain Social Security number recently, and do it in thirty minutes."

"Thirty minutes! Can't be done. I can give you the name on the tag in five, but that other shit takes time. Anyhow, I told you I'm busy."

"That press sure would come in handy mounted on the corner of your worktable."

"That's outright bribery. That's against the law."

"So's gambling. Okay, we'll make it an hour."

"Two hours and you got a deal. This got something to do with that Stillwell thing?"

"No. Some old geezer trying to find his runaway daughter. Another one of my neighbors."

"Damn, they never learn."

I gave him the numbers. "Remember, two hours."

His laugh rumbled like a subterranean well bubbling. "I can do it in one easy. I got a cousin works up there. That is, if he ain't hanging around the coffee machine."

"I appreciate it, Homer."

"Well, seeing's how I would have ended up doing it for nothing anyhow . . ." He hesitated. "In view of what happened with Susie, I could probably get that guy Stillwell into protective custody."

"You mean in a jail cell?"

"Yeah."

"He'd never go for it, Homer."

"It's his ass." He hung up.

I finished the rest of my cold dog and opened another can of beer.

He was chuckling when I picked up the phone forty-five minutes later. "Here you go, little buddy. Got a pencil and paper?"

"Shoot, Homer."

"Drew a blank on the Social Security number. Belongs to a Sherry Lee Bascomb . . ."

"I knew that, Homer. No input on recent earnings?"

"Nope, I'm afraid not."

"Okay. How about the tag number?"

"Theron William Brody, last known address, Apartment 214, Dockweiler Apartments, Irving, Texas."

"All right. Anything on him?"

"Got two outstanding speeding tickets. One in Dallas last July. Another one in Irving on September twenty-fourth."

"Dallas got a warrant out on him?"

"You kidding? They're probably a year behind at least. This the guy the girl cut out with?"

"Not exactly a girl, Homer. She's in her early thirties. Got two kids and a husband."

"Crap. This guy Brody's only twenty-two."

"The vigor of youth, Homer."

"And the stupid jerk wants her back?"

"Her father does."

"Yeah, well, I guess I can understand that."

"Tough cop with a heart of gold."

"When do I get my drill press, little buddy?"

"Just as soon as you come over here and unbolt it from my workbench." I hung up in the middle of his bellow.

/6/

Wednesday morning's trip into Dallas was a replica of Tuesday's. On the way I swung off the freeway at Story Road in Irving and drove to the Dockweiler Apartments. It was a relatively small two-story complex built of beige brick, possibly fifty apartments in all. Apartment 214 was on the second floor in the rear. I rang the bell several times and then tried knocking. No answer. I drove home and went to bed.

Wednesday afternoon I left early and stopped by there again on my way in to Dallas. Still no answer. I walked back down the stairs and around to the manager's office in the front of the building.

A small wiry man with reddish brown hair and an

incredibly lined face got up from a lawn chair behind the counter. He watched me approach with wary unblinking eyes.

"Hi," I said. "I've been trying to catch the Brodys at home, but I'm not having much luck. Apartment 214. I was wondering if you might happen to know if they're working—or what?"

"Don't know 'em," he said. He spoke rapidly, his mouth barely moving, a harsh clipped accent—definitely not a Texan. He had pinpoint pupils in eyes the color of dishwater.

I dropped the picture of Sherry Bascomb on the counter. "This is the lady. Perhaps you might recognize her."

"Don't know her either," he said, his pale eyes never leaving my face. "You a bill collector, salesman, or what?" There was a hint of a sneer in his voice.

"I'd like to be their friend," I said mildly. "I'd like to be your friend too, friend. Why don't you take a closer look at the picture?"

"Told you I didn't know 'em. Now why don't you shove off, friend." He smiled, showing me a set of too-white teeth with pale pink gums—the kind they give you in prison.

"Would it make any difference if I told you I wasn't a bill collector or a salesman? Would that improve your disposition any?"

"Not even if you told me you was the Pope." He just stood there smiling at me, a little ugly man who didn't like big men who weren't so ugly. A little ex-con, stoned just enough to feel ten feet tall and weasel mean. He'd seen and done it all, or had it done to him. That made him special, and his crazy washed-out eyes told me he knew I knew it. A man who truly loved to hate and be hated; I could smell his virulence, and I felt a stir of gut-level response.

I grinned down at him. I picked up the photo and put it in my jacket pocket. "Sorry, little man, not today. But there are bars all over Dallas full of guys who'd be tickled to oblige you."

I went out still smiling, but shaken; shaken by the swift, atavistic surge of fear. Not fear of the little man, but of myself, of the primitive urge to retaliate, the compelling desire to accept the challenge, to rend and tear and mutilate, to destroy.

I climbed into the truck and lit a cigarette with trembling hands. Jesus Christ! If my skin of civilization was so thin, so fragile, that it could not withstand the assault of one small man's unreasoning, baleful rage, then what chance was there for me, for anyone?

I picked Anne up first, waiting impatiently just inside the door of her office building. She marched down the walk and climbed into the cab with me. She gave me a cool look. "I'm not riding back there anymore," she said defiantly. "I ruined my best panty hose this morning on that damn bunk."

I shrugged. "Suit yourself." We drove the two miles to Warren's lab in silence. I'd about had my fill of truculent little people for the moment. He came shuffling out fifteen minutes late, a scowl on his broad face, his voice sullen as he clambered awkwardly into the camper.

"Dammit, I needed to work tonight."

"Then do it, dammit!" I twisted in the seat, glared at him through the open window, my nerves suddenly thrumming with a cold icy rage. "Go on! Get your ass back in there and work all you want. You're not doing me any bloody favor, you know."

"Naw, that's all right," he said sulkily.

I slammed the gear selector into Park and shut off the engine. "No, it's damn well not all right! I think it's time you two understood something. All this hassle and inconvenience is not for my benefit. I'm damn tired of you two acting like spoiled children. I didn't take you to raise, I'm just trying my damnedest to save your lives, and I'm risking my own in the process. If you think three hundred dollars a day is compensation for that, then you're incredibly naive or dumber than I think. This is it. Decision time. You either do as I say without all this childish bullshit or we forget it. Make up your mind. Do we go to your place or do we go to mine?" I lit a cigarette and stared through the windshield, cold and calm, no longer caring one way or the other.

Seconds later I felt Anne's hand on my arm. "We're sorry, Dan. You're right. We have been acting badly. I wouldn't blame you if you kicked us out of your house. We'll do better, I promise. Won't we, War?"

"Yeah, we will, Mr. Roman." It was an earnest, worried rumble.

"Okay." I started the truck, then glanced back through the window. "Warren, you can quit calling me mister, if you don't mind. I'm not that much older than you."

Anne laughed gaily and the big man's head bobbed happily. "You bet, Dan," he said.

The tension eased; Anne chattered all the way home about nothing, her dark eyes warm and liquid; Warren's deep bellow occasionally punctuated one of her more vapid absurdities. I listened good-naturedly, marveling at the astonishing ease with which these two unlikely siblings could reverse their moods.

"How would you two like a really good meal?" Anne bubbled enthusiastically. "What's your favorite, Dan?"

"Well, I'm kinda partial to steak and potatoes. Nothing fancy. A salad and maybe some corn on the cob. Susie and I usually cook the steaks and the corn on the charcoal grill. It makes a pretty good meal."

"Mmmm. Sounds delicious. Good. If you'll stop at the store, I'll run in and pick up—"

"No need for that," I said. "I've got everything we need."

"Terrific! I'm going to make both of you old bachelors wish you had a woman around all the time." Her eyes sparkled, glinted at me slyly. "Oh, but I forgot. You do have a woman, don't you?"

I nodded, keeping my eyes on the street.

"I've seen her driving by in her little car. She's very lovely." There was no hint of malice in her voice; but there was something, a touch of something I couldn't identify.

"Thank you," I said flatly. "Just for the record, I'm sixteen years older than she, we are divorced, but I plan to marry her again." I met her eyes levelly. "That's in case anyone should mention it."

If my bluntness flustered her, she didn't show it. "That's very nice, Dan," she said warmly, her bright smile unfaltering. "Good for you. It's how you feel that counts, not how long you've been around."

I eased out of the flow of traffic onto the off ramp. "I'll buy that," I said. "Up to a point, up to the point of diminishing returns." I braked to a stop at Highway 157, then eased around the corner. "But I'm not sure where that is. I think I'm too old for her. She doesn't think so. So, like most people, I'm letting my heart overrule my head."

"Don't be silly," she said earnestly. "Nobody ever has any guarantees. So what if it ends in ten, fifteen years? Or even twenty? If they're happy years, what have you lost? Nothing. Sometimes a year can be a lifetime. Just like the beer commercial says, you only get one chance at the gusto."

I laughed. "That's pretty close." I looked at her curiously. "You're the first woman I've talked about this with. Somehow, I thought you'd disapprove."

She shook her head, her fingers idly combing through the thick russet strands. "No, I don't disapprove. Life is usually a mess at best. We deserve all the happiness we can grab just for living through it."

I checked the side mirror one more time before I turned in to my street. The street behind was empty. I backed into the driveway while Anne worked the garage door activator.

I backed slowly into the garage, checking the interior through the wide-angle mirror. Anne slid across the seat and got out on my side. The truck rocked and pitched as Warren fought his way out of the narrow rear door. "That's a tight fit," he said cheerily.

"You guys give me thirty minutes in the kitchen, then you can start the fire."

"All right!" Warren said exuberantly, his big hands rubbing together with the sound of sandpaper.

The dinner was delicious; the steaks pink on the inside, charred on the out, something that takes a great deal of expert timing when they're frozen. The corn was tender and sweet, the salad crisp. The baked potato was flaky and smooth and the rolls hot from the oven. Anne and Warren drank iced tea, and I settled for a more plebeian can of Coors. It was the kind of meal that goes a long way toward righting the wrongs of the world—at least for me.

Anne shooed us out of the kitchen and we caught the last five minutes of news on TV. Following that we sat through a game show with a screaming crowd and an electronic dragon. Warren enjoyed it immensely, slapping his thighs and joining with the studio audience in yelling advice to the participants. A drama followed at seven o'clock, an age-old dilemma: a young girl pregnant and afraid to tell her boyfriend.

Warren soon became bored and restless. He got up and wandered around the room, ending up eventually in front of my gun cabinet. He stood there so long, I finally got up and walked over to join him.

"You interested in guns, Warren?"

He moved his shaggy head. "No. I don't know much about them."

I opened the case and withdrew a .308 Remington, my favorite deer rifle. "Here, see how this feels to you."

He accepted the gun reluctantly, then automatically opened the bolt, checked the chamber, snapped it shut, and swung the gun to his shoulder with a swift fluid grace. He sighted through the scope and I saw his finger press lightly on the trigger. Abruptly, he lowered the weapon and handed it to me.

"Feels well balanced," he said, his voice suddenly thick, his face pale. He turned away. "I don't like guns," he said in a dull monotone. "I don't like to kill things."

"I don't like it that much myself," I said dryly. "But it somehow seems foolish to go to all the expense and trouble and not bring something home."

"Then why hunt?" Anne was standing in the kitchen doorway. She shivered. "I don't see how you men can kill those poor helpless little animals."

"Well," I said slowly, not sure how to continue. She was voicing the one legitimate complaint about hunting that was getting harder and harder for me to rationalize away. "Well, when I was a kid in East Texas, there were many times when a cottontail or a squirrel, or maybe a brace of quail, meant the difference between a good meal and a damn poor one. I don't have to justify that."

"Yes, but," she said, swinging into the next predictable step of the nonhunter's incantation, "you don't have to do that anymore. You can buy all the meat you want."

"Yeah, I know," I said, feeling the usual annoyance when faced with someone else's immutable logic. "But, dammit, I happen to *like* rabbit and squirrel and quail and deer. I like it better than beef or pork or chicken when it comes right down to it." There was a small lie in there somewhere, but I was warming to my subject. "Besides, I never kill anything I can't eat."

She came into the room and sat down in a small flurry of skirts. "Oh, well, it's a silly argument." She smiled and wrinkled her nose. "Like arguing about religion."

I wiped the gun with a slightly oiled rag and replaced it in the gun case. "You're right. Religion or politics." But she wasn't listening. She was watching the TV, already absorbed in the young girl's heartrending problems. Warren was glowering at the wall from deep within my favorite chair. I shook my head and went down the hall to the back bathroom for a quick shower and a shave.

Anne was still glued to the television when I returned. Warren was gone. I walked on through the room and opened a can of beer. I sat with Anne and watched the predictable ending unfold until the next commercial.

"Warren go to bed?" I asked.

She yawned. "No. He's sweeping the patio."

I got up and opened the drapes on the sliding door. He was squatting at the edge of the patio intently watching something out in the yard. "He shouldn't be out there, Anne." I scanned the edge of the woods across the field. The sun was dropping slowly behind the trees and there were deep uneven shadows stretching out across the gently sloping hill. I opened the door and walked out onto the concrete. Warren was still squatting at the upper edge of the three-foot sloping bank and I followed his gaze.

A small brown bird was standing in the grass fifteen feet away, unmoving, its wings drooping, dragging the ground. It appeared to be frozen, sick, or dying. Then I noticed the tree limb, round and black, as big around as my wrist, as long as my arm. The bird was standing eighteen inches away, its tiny head lowered, staring fixedly at the limb as if it were a giant black worm.

And then the limb moved, and I knew instantly what was happening. I had seen it once before, as a kid: a dusty road in East Texas, a long varicolored chicken snake, a huddled bird, mesmerized, waiting helplessly for the killing strike. I had disrupted that chilling scenario, and this one was no different.

"Jesus Christ!"

Two long swift strides brought me to Warren; I jerked the broom out of his hand and started down the bank. Too late! The snake had completed its coil and the flat black head flicked forward. There was no sound, a brief flurry of wings, two clawed feet scratching at the grass, and it was over.

I stood over them, the musky taste of sick disgust in my mouth. The snake lay motionless, its eyes watching me with reptilian intensity, the bird's head in its mouth, its thick stubby tail an inch off the grass. I walked around it and its eyes followed me, but still it refused to relinquish its prey.

"What is it?" Anne asked from the patio.

"It's a cottonmouth." I took a quick step and smashed my boot heel against its spade-shaped head. I felt the give of its thin skull bones and the whiplash of its tail against the back of my leg. I twisted my heel. "You got it, bastard, but you're not going to enjoy it."

I stepped back and lit a cigarette for the taste in my mouth. I watched until the writhing died to a slow sinuous wiggle, then I picked the snake up by the tail and carried it and the hapless bird to the back fence. I whirled the snake like a rope and let it fly into the bushes across the small creek. I threw the bird after it.

Warren and Anne were still watching from the patio. I glanced at Warren, his broad expressionless face.

"You could have stopped that," I said quietly. "Why didn't you?"

He stared at me blankly for a moment, then turned and went into the house.

I looked at Anne's ashen face and shrugged. "He was watching it."

She came and stood in front of me, her hand on my arm. "Please don't be too hard on him, Dan. He doesn't always . . . react like . . . other people. Ever since the coma . . ." Her voice trailed away and she nibbled at her lower lip.

"What coma?"

She sighed and looked away. "It's . . . when he was in the army. He was in a coma . . . for two years."

"He didn't tell me about that."

Her hair stirred silkily as she shook her head. "He wouldn't. . . . He doesn't like for people to know. . . . He thinks they will think . . . you know, that there's something wrong with his mind."

"How long has it been?"

"He came out of it in 1973. He said it was almost two years to the day as far as he could determine."

"In 1973?" My mind went back to our first conversation. "That gave him seven years to get a doctor's degree in mathematics?"

She smiled wanly and nodded. "He did it in a little less than seven years. He has total recall in most things. It seems to be selective. Mathematics and physics . . . oh, he has a master's degree in physics too."

"My God, I can't believe it!"

"Well, I've heard that Einstein couldn't talk, or was it walk, until he was five, and failed mathematics in school."

"But why is he so . . . so . . ."

"Childlike? I don't know, Dan. He didn't used to be like that. He was always a bright kid but nothing much above normal. At least his grades in high school didn't show it. He was an exceptional athlete, though. That's really all he was interested in in high school—except girls, of course." She smiled. "He was certainly normal in that respect."

"What brought on the coma?"

"They told him it was an accident. He was due for discharge from the army in a month—that was in 1971. He doesn't remember the accident or anything else until he woke up in an army hospital in California. That was in July 1973."

"What about his family—you? Didn't you find out anything about it?"

She ducked her head, a pained expression in her eyes. "No. Our folks are dead. I lost track of War . . . well, we lost touch when I got married. Bill and War didn't have much in common. . . . To be honest about it, they disliked each other intensely. I lived in New York with my husband and War was at several army bases, then overseas for a long time. We . . . we just lost touch. I didn't see him until September 1973. He had gotten my address from an aunt in New Mexico. He came to see me in New York."

"Then you didn't know anything about the coma while it was happening?"

"No. He didn't tell me until after Bill was killed and I came to stay with him."

"Why would he work for a small place like United Labs? Jesus, he could name his own price with any research outfit in the country."

"He's happy there. They pay him well and they leave him alone. That's what's important to War. Nobody bothers him. He doesn't have to deal with people. He hates having to do that. He's just not good at it."

I lit a cigarette and we sat in silence. The sun was almost completely gone now, the shadows from the woods reaching almost to infinity. I could hear the laugh track from one of the latest T and A shows and an occasional guffaw from Warren. I laughed softly. "It doesn't take much to make him happy, does it?"

"No," she said seriously. "For someone with such a sophisticated mind, he exists on a very elemental level away from his work. He gets bored very easily, restless. But on the other hand, it doesn't take much to divert him—for a time. He loves the game shows. Probably because he knows all the answers. I think it makes him feel superior. He actually gets upset sometimes when someone misses what he thinks is a very easy answer."

"He like cop shows, violence, that kind of thing?"

"No. Definitely not. He just won't watch it. Or anything that has a lot of human conflict between the characters. All he really likes are game shows and the comedy programs." She folded her arms across her breast, her face gradually growing indistinct in the twilight. "It's . . . it's almost as if he had a complete personality reversal after the coma."

"How so?"

She slapped at a mosquito on her arm, then scratched the bite idly. "He was just the opposite before. He used to love all the cop shows when we were kids. . . . *The Untouchables* was one of his favorites. *Dragnet.* He liked that, but not as much as some of the others with more action. He was . . . well, he was something of a tough himself. I guess you could say a bully. He wasn't vicious or anything like that, but he loved to wrestle, fight, anything that was rough-and-tumble. And he was so big, he almost always won."

Her face became softly blurred as she smiled gently. "He was always good to me, though. Always so protective."

"Does he have any scars from the accident?"

"Just some tiny ones on his head. He said a doctor told him they were from punctures to relieve pressure on his brain or something like that. He has one or two on his chest that look like dimples. If he has any anywhere else he hasn't said."

"What hospital was he in when he woke up?"

"I don't know. I don't think War does either. Two days after he came out of it he was transferred to Walter Reed. He called it a small army hospital. It was in . . . I told you that . . . in California."

"He doesn't receive any kind of disability?"

"No. He . . ." She pursed her lips thoughtfully. "There was one thing he thought was funny though."

"What?"

"Well, his body, you know, his muscles and . . . well, his body in general. He said he couldn't see that he was deteriorated in any way. He felt strong, alert, as if he had only been sleeping . . . you know."

"Had he lost weight?"

"No. He was about the same. He couldn't understand that either."

"Well, they feed you through the veins. Some types of coma victims can even eat, hear, understand to a degree. They just can't wake up. And I'm sure they gave him physical therapy while he was out. Exercised his arms, legs, like that."

"Yes, well, I don't know," she said dubiously.

The outside light came on and Warren stuck his head out the sliding door. "Telephone, Mr. Roman . . . uh, Dan. I think it's your . . . Susie."

"Okay, thanks. Get your head back inside, Warren."

His head disappeared and Anne chuckled. "I think you scare him."

"I hope so," I said, moving to the door. "Maybe then he'll listen to me."

I went into the bedroom and picked up the extension. "Hi, Susie."

"Danny! Well hi. When did you get a butler?"

"Afraid not, sugar. That was Mr. Stillwell."

"How's everything going, honey?"

"Pretty slow, Susie. How's your grandmother?"

"Okay. You haven't found out anything yet?" There was disappointment in her tone.

"No. Mr. Stillwell and his sister are staying here with me."

"Is she young?"

"Who?"

"You know who. His sister."

"Naw. She's pretty old. Pushing forty."

"Is she pretty?"

"Ah, ravishing!"

"Danny!"

"Well, not bad in a motherly sort of way. But she's way too old for me."

"You just remember that, buster. Where's she sleeping."

"Well . . . in my bed."

The lines hummed emptily.

"Where are you sleeping?"

"Well . . ."

"Danny?"

"Well, I'm sleeping in my bed too, but—"

"You better be lying to me!"

I laughed. "Before you get in a snit. She's sleeping nights and I'm sleeping days . . . and never the twain shall meet."

"I'm coming home!"

"You just stay where you are, young lady. I've got enough on my hands the way it is. I hope you're not going to be one of those jealous wives who—"

"What did you say?"

"I said I hope you're not the jealous type."

"No, you didn't! You said wife . . . didn't you, Danny?"

"Maybe I did, but that was just a slip of the tongue."

She laughed delightedly. "A Freudian slip, you mean!"

"Might not be such a bad idea at that. Keep these young bucks away from you. I saw that redheaded cop strutting around like a spring gobbler."

"He was very nice.

"I'll bet he was. Very helpful."

Her voice gurgled with laughter. "He kept asking me if there was anything . . . *anything* he could do for me."

"Yeah, I'll bet."

"See. Other men find me attractive."

"That was never the problem, Susie."

"Then what?"

"Let's wait and discuss it later, okay?"

"Okay, Danny. I called Mr. Proctor and he gave me my week's vacation early, but he thinks I'm coming back Monday. Will I be able to?"

"That's too far ahead to tell, honey. Call me this weekend. I'll know more then."

"All right, Danny. I miss you."

"I miss you too."

"I love you."

"Okay. I'll be talk—"

"Okay what? I said I love you."

"You know I do you too."

"Well then, say it."

"I do."

"Is there someone listening?"

"No."

"Well, then say it."

I sighed. "Okay, Susie, I love you."

"See, that wasn't so hard."

"It wasn't easy . . ." I was talking to a dead phone.

/7/

Thursday morning after I drove Anne and Warren to work, I stopped at the Dockweiler Apartments again. There was still no answer to my finger on the bell, but this time the front blinds were open and I could see a picture on a television set in the living room, rolling and flickering.

I knocked on the door. Again, louder. I was reaching to do it again when a chain rattled, the doorknob turned, and a face poked out at me. There was a muttered curse as the bright sunlight hit him and he recoiled and shaded his eyes with a palm and peered up at me; an Indian scout in an old movie. He was naked enough for the part. Except for a pair of skintight Jockey shorts, he was completely nude.

"Mr. Brody, Theron Brody?"

"Who're you?" He was squinting, his eyes having difficulty focusing.

"Who is it, baby?" A feminine voice from somewhere in the apartment.

"You the fuzz?"

"I wonder if I could talk to you, Mr. Brody?"

"Who is it, Billy?" The same female voice, querulous, faintly apprehensive.

"I think it's the fuzz," he shouted. There was a muted flurry of sound and the gushing roar of a toilet flushing.

"I think you might have just wasted some good dope, Billy," I said. "I'm not the police."

"Who the hell are you then?" He was straightening slowly, his face scowling.

"Just a man who wants to talk to you. My name wouldn't mean anything." I was beginning to see why a woman of thirty might have flipped over him. He was tall, muscular, and exceptionally handsome. Hell, any woman would have flipped over him.

"What about?" He was growing increasingly wary, his marbled eyes losing a little of the glaze. A muscle twitched in his cheek and he sniffed. Coming down, I thought.

"Why don't we talk inside?" I suggested. "We wouldn't want to bother the neighbors."

"I don't give a damn about the neighbors! You ain't coming in until you tell me what the hell you want." It was pure bravado, almost convincing, but his eyes betrayed him.

"All right, Billy. I'm looking for a lady. A lady named Sherry Bascomb."

"I don't know no Sherry."

"How about the young lady in the bedroom, Billy?"

"Her name's Betty, dammit. Ain't none of your damned business anyway!"

"Mind if I just take a quick look? Won't take but a second."

"I damn sure do mind! Get the hell out of here, buddy."

He stepped back to slam the door, but I got my shoulder into it before he was set. It moved inward easily and he squawked and leaped backwards. He landed heavily on his heels, then went into a picturesque stance, his feet apart, his hands tensed and moving in tight graceful circles.

"All right, asshole," he said menacingly, a tight-lipped grin on his handsome face. "Now I'm gonna take your head off."

"Really?" I opened my jacket and put my hands on my hips so he could get a good look at the gun. "I thought you were gonna dance for me, Billy."

He straightened abruptly. "Aw, dammit, you are the law."

A face popped around the doorjamb behind him. A young face, round and pretty, framed with blond ringlets. She squealed once and disappeared. The door slammed.

"All right, Billy. So you got a Betty back there in the bedroom now. What I want to know is what happened to Sherry Bascomb."

"Dammit, man, I don't know no Sherry."

"You got a motorcycle?"

"Yeah. What . . . ?"

"License number UG 502?"

"That sounds right. Yeah, that's mine. What . . . ?"

I stepped in close and smiled. I touched him on the neck below his left ear. He leaped back. "Hey! Man!" He grabbed his neck and stared at me.

"Sherry Bascomb, around thirty, has a husband and two sweet kids." I stepped in close again and touched his left nipple with one finger, lightly. I may as well have touched him with a branding iron. He leaped sideways, slammed into the wall, bounced off, and staggered to the middle of the room. "Hey, man, please, come on!"

I followed him. He was watching my finger with bulging eyes, his mouth twisting in hysterical fear.

It's the menace of the unknown. Fists and boots and curses they can understand and live with as an inevitable part of their lives, and spit back into your face. Present them with an anomaly, quiet intimidation instead of shouts and threats, the sinister horror of a smile instead of a threatening grimace, and their drug-weakened, vulnerable minds cannot cope with it, cannot abide this reminder of their monster-infested nightmares.

I wondered what particular significance my pointing finger represented in the sludge of Brody's hallucinating mind, among the wyverns and goblins that resided there.

I lifted the finger and pointed it at him. He shrank backwards. "Tell me now," I said quietly. "Right now, Billy."

"Hey, I don't know no . . . no! Wait! Maybe . . . yeah, there was this dame . . . yeah, that must have been the one . . . I don't remember her name. You know, man . . . just a broad, just one of them things, a one-nighter . . . maybe two. Yeah, she was maybe thirty . . . she gave me a couple'a bills."

"How long ago, Billy?"

"Hell, I don't know. Maybe two, three months. I don't keep track." He was moving around me in a circle, his eyes never leaving my hand.

"You're lying, Billy. She was with you longer than that."

"Wait, man! Come on, you know how it is. Time don't mean nothing. Anyhow, she was just another—" He leaped wildly away as I stabbed at him with my finger.

"Say it," I said tightly. "Go on, say it." I moved around the circle with him, closing the distance with every step.

"Hey, Jesus! Please, man, come on. Okay! Maybe a week . . . no longer, I swear!"

"And you don't remember her name," I said softly. I was closer to him now.

"No, I swear! I just don't! Please!"

I took the photo out of my pocket and held it in front of his skittering eyes. "Tell me, is that her?"

He moaned. "Jesus, I don't . . . yeah, yeah, that's her, that's the one."

"Where is she now?"

"Aw, Christ, I don't know!"

I leaned forward and stabbed my finger at his crotch. He screamed and dropped to his knees, his hands crossed tightly between his legs.

I prodded him with my toe. "Where did you leave her, Billy? Last chance."

He rocked and moaned, pressing into the wall. "Jesus! Please. Maybe the . . . maybe the Dolphin Club."

"Why there?"

"I—I saw her . . . week, maybe ten days ago . . . hanging around the Dolphin Club."

I leaned forward and touched my finger to his cheek. He shrieked, winding down into a shuddering moan. I waited.

"If you're lying to me, Billy, I'll be back." I crossed to the door. "The next time," I promised, "I'll beat the hell out of you."

* * *

On the way home I stopped at a hardware store and bought two dead bolt locks. I installed one on the rear door first, and had just finished drilling the holes for the front when I heard his voice behind me.

"Good morning, Mr. Roman. Hard at it, I see."

"Hello," I said. I put the drill on the lawn chair with the remaining lock, and stood waiting as he clumsily dismounted from his bike and walked stiffly up the walk, the halo of white hair giving him a curiously angelic look.

"Just something I've been meaning to do for years. Never could seem to find the time."

"I can certainly understand that," he said cheerily. He shook my extended hand and stood surveying my work. "Installing more security, I see. Well, these days one can't have too much." He eyed me shrewdly. "Not after the fact, I hope."

"No. Nothing like that. But I have been lucky. We've had a lot of burglaries in the neighborhood lately."

"Yes. In our area, as well." He smiled wryly. "You would think an enterprising burglar would avoid the smaller homes. Go where the money is, as it were." He weaved slightly and looked around.

"Here, Mr. Whitecomb, have a seat." I removed the drill and the lock from the lawn chair.

He nodded his thanks and sat down with a grateful sigh. "I'll hold that for you," he offered, taking the new lock and turning it in his slender fragile fingers. "Very well made. Sturdy. So many things nowadays have such shoddy workmanship." He looked up at me. "Please, Mr. Roman, go ahead with your work. Don't allow me to distract you."

"All right, if you don't mind. I'm almost finished. We can talk as I work."

I arranged the template on the doorjamb and carefully marked the location for the locking plate. I selected a small sharp chisel and began working the soft wood.

"I located your daughter's boyfriend, Mr. Whitecomb. I'm afraid they're no longer together."

"I see. You work very fast, Mr. Roman. What did the young gentleman have to say?"

"He's a hard-core doper, Mr. Whitecomb. Nothing is very clear in his brain. But he did give me a lead. I'll check it out as soon as I have a chance."

"My . . . daughter? Did he say how she is? Is she all right?" His voice was dry and hesitant, as if he wasn't sure he wanted to hear my answer.

"He couldn't tell me that. He couldn't tell me much of anything—" I broke off, a brief flex of memory bringing me upright. "Wait—didn't your son-in-law's friend say he saw them just a few days ago?"

"Yes. That's what he told us."

"So he was lying," I said grimly. "I'm sorry, Mr. Whitecomb. That had completely slipped my mind. Brody said he hadn't seen your daughter for weeks. And he was lying like hell. He had another girl in his apartment and I believed him. I'll have another talk with Mr. Brody." I spread my hands apologetically. "I'm sorry. This other thing I'm working on has me tied up in knots."

He made a deprecating gesture. "Quite understandable, sir. Please don't distress yourself. Perhaps I shouldn't have intruded my sordid problems when you have much more important matters on your hands."

"Not more important, Mr. Whitecomb. Possibly more serious. A man's life may very well be at stake." I felt a small flash of embarrassment at my overdramatization.

"Then by all means, sir, do not allow my small dilemma to distract you."

I nodded and went back to work on the door. "I won't. Part of my days are free. I can still devote some time to finding your daughter."

"Excellent, Mr. Roman. I can't ask for more." He struggled awkwardly to his feet. "I wonder," he began, then gave me a small abashed grin. "I hate to take up more of your time, but I wonder if I might have a glass of water."

"Of course," I said. "I'm sorry. I'm not well known for my manners. Please come in. Would you rather have a cold beer?" He followed me haltingly into the entrance hall.

"No, no. A glass of cool water would be fine, sir. I'll just wait here if you don't mind."

He was standing in the doorway to the den when I returned. He looked up and nodded approvingly. "You have a very nice house, Mr. Roman. I was just thinking. The floor plan seems very much like my son-in-law's. His is a much smaller house, of course. Are the bedrooms along that hallway to the left?"

"Yes. Would you like to see the rest of it?"

"No, no. It just seemed so familiar. On a much larger scale, of course." He nodded with an old man's satisfaction at his own perspicacity and drank noisily from the glass. "Ah, that was just right. God's sustenance, sir. Much better than man's brews, wouldn't you say?" There was a twinkle in his blue eyes.

"Well," I admitted, "when you're really thirsty."

He laughed melodiously and made his way back outdoors. "I'll stop again later. Are you home during most of the day?"

"Yes. I sleep a good part of it. I'm usually gone between seven-thirty and nine, and between five and six. Other than that, you can generally catch me."

He lifted one hand. "Don't worry, sir, I won't disturb your rest. I'll make sure you are up and about."

"You can call any time between seven and about eleven at night, Mr. Whitecomb. Nobody's asleep before then."

He climbed on his three-wheeler and peddled down the street. I lit a cigarette and thought about Theron Brody. He had seemed so damned terrified. It was hard to believe that he had been able to maintain a lie the way he had. Maybe there was more to him than I thought. Well, I'd damn sure find out at our next meeting.

I slept later than usual and had to hurry to make the quitting bell at Anne's office. After dinner she cleaned up the kitchen and I sat listening to Warren answer the questions on *Tic Tac Dough.* When it was over I got up and turned off the television set. Warren looked at me in surprise, his face a mixture of indignation and nervousness.

I lit a cigarette and sat back down. "Why didn't you tell me about the coma, Warren?"

"I didn't think it mattered," he said defensively. "That was a long time ago and it couldn't have anything to do with this."

"You let me be the judge of that. You're probably right, but you're in no position to make that kind of judgment. It makes me wonder what else you haven't told me."

He wagged his head vehemently. "Nothing. I haven't told you nothing else." He thought about that for a moment, and his face flushed a dull copper. "I mean . . ."

"I know what you mean. You said something once about having nightmares. You think they could have any connection with the coma?"

"I don't see how."

"What were they about? Do you remember any of them?"

He nodded. "Well. I should, I told them to Dr. Carelton often enough."

"You didn't tell me about the psychiatrist either, Warren."

"I know," he rumbled uncomfortably. "I don't like to tell people about those things."

"I'm not people. I'm the man who's trying to save your ass. Tell me about the dreams."

"Well . . ." He licked his lips and grinned foolishly. He glanced over his shoulder toward the kitchen, then lowered his voice. "Well, there's this one. I have it a lot. I'm on the beach with this girl—or sometimes it's in a bed—and I'm trying to . . . you know, make her. She seems willing and everything, but I keep having this feeling, this compulsion to . . . to . . . just show it to her and brag about how it's a—" He stopped, the foolish grin coming back. "About how it's a missile." He waited expectantly for me to respond, and when I didn't, he looked a little disappointed. "I keep telling her over and over that I'm a missile and . . . and that I'm going to explode in her." He watched me, ready to grin if I did.

"Well, what do you think of that?" he asked seriously.

"Seems like a regular old sex dream to me," I said. "Does anything happen?"

"No. That's it. But I have it a lot. It just ends there, after I tell her a few times."

"Any more?"

His face sobered, all traces of levity vanishing. "The one I have most. I don't know, it's got sex in it too. In a way. But it's . . . well, scary." He wet his lips again. "I'm somewhere with another man. I don't know who. There seems to be something wrong with his face, something that keeps me from seeing it. But still I know who he is . . . but I don't, if that makes any sense." His voice had become a dull monotone. "We're at some big house, somewhere in a woods, or at least there's woods nearby. Me and the man are coming out of the woods, slipping along like. Then all of a sudden we're in the house and I'm alone . . . the house is quiet, a kind of scary quiet, a kind of deadly quiet. I'm afraid for some reason and I want the other man to come back. But he doesn't and I go looking for him. There's a big winding stairs . . . then I'm in a room, a bedroom. There's a man and a woman on the bed. Without knowing how I know, I know that they're dead. I look down at them and I don't feel anything . . . I know I should, but I don't. Then suddenly I'm in another room, and there's another bed. There's a small boy on this one and he's dead too. I can see blood, a lot of blood, and this time I feel like crying. Then I'm in another room, another boy dead on the bed. Older, in his teens. I want to cry again . . . another room, a little girl, maybe twelve. She's naked and bloody, and she's dead too. And I keep saying to myself that this is too much, too much, that this is foolish, that the other man shouldn't be playing like this. And then it's like a game of hide-and-seek.

"I go to two other rooms—two more dead girls, small ones, naked and bloody. I am crying by this time. And then the last room. I'm outside the door, and I hear noises. I know what the noises mean and I feel anger. I go in the room and the other man is in the bed with a girl. She's naked and he's . . . doing it to her. Her mouth is wide open like she's screaming but I don't hear anything. All I can see is his back rising and falling, rising and falling, and hear his grunts . . . like a pig at a slop trough. Then the man gets up and pulls a knife out of his belt. He stands over the girl laughing and raises the knife. I scream at him and he turns toward me and his face is terribly angry. He begins screaming at me . . . some kind of . . . poetry. 'The willow bends when the Chinook blows.' He screams it over and over. . . . I start toward him to stop him from killing the girl . . . and the dream ends. It always ends. I never know whether I saved the girl's life or not."

"Jesus!" I said.

He expelled his breath with a sharp explosive sound and smiled crookedly.

"Well, Doctor, what do you make of that one?"

"Damn, I don't know. That must be a humdinger. How do you feel when you wake up?"

"Scared to death, with the cold sweats. How would you feel?"

"What did the shrink have to say about that one?"

He shook his head. "He's a Freud man. He jumped on the sex part, but he never made much of the rest of it."

Anne had come into the room during his narration and she smiled at him. "Go ahead, War, tell him what he said about it."

"He never really said anything. He just asked things."

"You know what I mean."

"Well." He shifted uncomfortably. "He kept coming back to Anne and me. Wanted to know if we had ever . . . well, you know, done it. Kept asking me if I ever wanted to do it to her, or if she acted like she wanted to do it with me. Crazy stuff like that."

"And you've had these two dreams more than once?"

"Repeatedly. There's one other I have a lot, but it

doesn't amount to much. I'm in some kind of hotel. I register at the counter, a room on the fifth floor. They tell me the elevator is out of order, but that it will be easy to walk up. The rest of the dream is just walking. I pass the fourth floor, and I walk and walk up the stairs, but I can never reach the fifth floor."

"Have you had them lately?"

He shrugged. "I don't keep track anymore. Probably once or twice during the last month. They're so familiar that when I begin, I actually tell myself, Here comes the beach dream, or the death dream, or the hotel dream. It's kinda like watching an old movie you've seen dozens of times before. Even the variations become familiar." He had regained his color, the resonance in his voice. He sat back in the chair. "It's funny," he mused. "There's an aura of terror about all three dreams, a sort of nameless menace, dread, even though the beach dream and the hotel dream don't have a connotation of evil of any sort." He laughed huskily. "At least in the telling."

I nodded. "I know what you mean. I've had dreams with just shadows, or a smiling face even, and wake up with a feeling of horror. It's not a pleasant thing."

Anne said, "I'm one of the lucky ones. I don't dream. Maybe I'm too dumb."

"You dream. You just don't remember when you wake up. Did this Dr. Carelton have anything specific to say about the dreams?"

"Not really. After a year and a half of questions, when he went up to seventy-five dollars an hour, I quit."

"Can't say I blame you."

Warren was squirming restlessly. "I'd like to watch TV if we're finished, Dan."

Anne looked at me and smiled.

"Sure," I said. "Would either of you like a drink?"

Warren looked up, then glanced at Anne and shook his head. She smiled and nodded.

"Bloody Mary okay?"

"I'd rather have orange juice."

"Okay. One screwdriver coming up."

I made the drinks and Anne and I drifted into the kitchen, leaving Warren with his T and A programs and the mindless laugh tracks.

"I've been meaning to ask you. I thought he had a drinking problem?"

"He does. Or, at least, he used to. He hasn't touched a drop for two or three months. I think it was the dreams. I could always tell when he had one of the bad ones. He would be grouchy and hard to live with. He would usually end up on a bender. But he's stopped. I don't really know why."

"I wonder if something could have happened on one of his drunks? Maybe he ran someone down and somebody's trying to get revenge."

"I don't know," she said morosely. "If he did, he didn't do any damage to his car."

"Aw, hell, I'm just guessing. I hate this working in the dark." I took a drink of the Bloody Mary. "It's scary as hell, is what it is."

"I know," she said. She touched my hand with warm fingers. "How's your hand?"

I flexed it and grinned. "A little sore and stiff in the mornings. I did it a lot more damage than I did to your brother's chin."

"Well, you hurt his feelings, anyhow." She massaged my hand idly, her fingers pressing and rolling and probing, her touch almost electric, stirring up a tingle in my hand that somehow transferred itself, as if by magic, into my groin. I could feel the heat growing, expanding, the turgescence building, and after a while, I used lighting a cigarette as an excuse to reclaim my fingers. I glanced at her over the flame of the lighter; there was a tiny enigmatic smile and a faint rosy glow on her face that were quickly hidden as she ducked her head and drank from her glass.

An awkward silence followed; when she could stand it no longer, she finished her drink and leaped lightly to her feet. She murmured something about a shower and a hard day tomorrow, and she was gone.

I finished my own drink and prowled around the house, checking the doors and windows, searching the shadows at the edge of the floodlight's range. Warren looked up and smiled vaguely as I came back through the den. His usual demeanor had returned. He was happily watching reruns of Mary Tyler Moore on Channel 11. I fixed another Bloody Mary and slumped on the love seat. The cushions sank slowly beneath me, and I unclipped the .357 from my belt and laid it on the cushion beside me. Warren lasted ten minutes into the ten o'clock news before he succumbed to boredom and got up and went to bed, totally unconcerned with the weighty and seemingly unsolvable problems of the world. Within minutes his sonorous snoring began to compete with the droning of sounds coming from the television.

I moved to his vacated chair, feeling a familiar restlessness, a tightness in my chest, a faintly irritating, but not unpleasant, tenseness in my loins. It had begun with the touch of soft warm fingers on my skin, and for the hundredth time I wondered disgustedly about my moral fiber—or lack of it. In love with one woman, yet stirred profoundly by the innocent touch of another. But had it been entirely innocent? I remembered the veiled downcast eyes, the rosy glow of freckled cheeks. But, dammit, that shouldn't make any difference. Whether the touch was innocent or deliberately provocative, I should have enough strength of character to resist. I leaped to my own defense. Resist what? A momentary surge of innocent lust. Nothing more. A purely physical response to tactile stimulation, my body acting independently of my reasoning mind. Bullshit, brother. You've wanted her from the time you first saw her, from the first time you glimpsed that soft full mouth, the target zone outlined with the thin red line of lipstick. Well, so what? What was wrong with that? Stimulation was the name of the game. Titillation of the senses from every direction . . .

I was so absorbed in my internal conflict that I almost didn't notice her come in. Without looking at me, she sat down on the edge of the couch, her hands folded almost demurely in her lap, her eyes trained on the television. A minute ticked by on the clock while I watched her, unmoving, a faint stirring of anger building in my chest. "I couldn't sleep," she said faintly, apologetically, and it was her humble tone, as much as the fact that she didn't have on any clothes, that sent my anger blossoming.

"And I'm supposed to fuck you," I said harshly, "and make it all better."

"Yes," she said, refusing to be put off by my crudity, her voice almost inaudible.

"Sorry," I grated, "but I'm all out of charity fucks."

"All right, Danny." Her white hands fluttered in her naked lap like two doves hovering over an empty nest.

I sat frozen, immobile, wondering with something like horror at my own cruelty, suddenly realizing with painful clarity that my anger was not directed at her, but at myself, my own relentless crushing desire.

"All right, Danny," she said again, and rose to her feet, suddenly self-conscious, her hands making a feeble attempt to cover herself, the enormity of the situation, the humiliation of my total rejection seeming to come crashing down on her. She weaved as she walked toward the door, her face colorless.

"Dammit, Anne!" It was an agonized wail, an abject admission of defeat. I lurched to my feet and lumbered after her with all the grace and agility of a charging rhino. I caught her at the door, overcame the token resistance her pride demanded. I held her until she was quiet, the shivering subsided to an occasional tremor. I led her down the hallway to the bedroom, pausing only long enough to close the door on Warren's stentorian rumblings.

She stood stiff-armed and ramrod straight while I slipped out of my clothing. Still caught up in the emotional backlash of my exquisite asininity, it was a while before my gentle touchings, soft words, and softer kisses brought a stirring of response. She moaned, then fastened her hands in my hair and jerked my face down to hers.

"You bastard," she hissed, and her lips meshed fiercely with mine. Once aroused, she was ruthless, relentlessly pursuing the burgeoning demands of her body. I let myself be caught up in the surge of her lust; and only a part of me, a very tiny part, remained aloof, helpless to intervene, watching our twisting bodies with shame and guilt; and even that was gone at the coupling; I sank into the hot liquid velvet of her, a breathtaking splash of quicksilver fire; a time of mindless, grasping searching, a primitive yearning to reach the ultimate deliverance, the eternal siren song of our bodies that is never quite fulfilled.

/8/

Going to work the next morning, Anne was uncharacteristically quiet. She sat demurely against the far door, her eyes gazing straight ahead, her hands folded primly in her lap. Warren, garrulous for a change, leaned an arm on the sliding window and gushed in my ear.

"I think we're finally on to something really important." The declaration was made with all the authoritative pomposity of a first-year biology student announcing that he had just discovered how a frog works.

"How's that, Warren?"

"Well, I can't say anything yet, but it looks like this new technology may be a breakthrough."

I risked a look at his animated face. "Really?" I was only half listening, wondering what was going on under that glossy head of auburn hair that was now leaning against the window.

"Yeah," he said enthusiastically. "A couple of more years and we—"

"Years? I thought you were getting ready to come out with a paper."

"Oh, no! First you have to test it, under strictly clinical conditions, of course, then you have to try it out on mice, then rats, then guinea pigs, then monkeys, then—"

"Won't matter by then, Warren. I'll be too old for it to do me any good."

"Huh?" he said, then realized I was kidding him and blew out my ear with a booming laugh. I thought I saw a tiny smile flicker across Anne's face.

He was still chuckling when I dropped him off a few minutes later. I watched him lumber up the walk and disappear inside the building. I circled the parking lot and reentered the morning frenzy.

"Good morning," I said.

"Good morning, Danny."

"You . . . uh, sleep well?"

"Yes, thank you."

"Going to be a nice day," I said.

"Uh-huh."

We drove quietly for a while; I lit a cigarette to fill up the silence. I whistled tunelessly, and drummed my fingers on the wheel. I fidgeted and fussed until she finally turned her head and smiled shyly.

"There's no need for you to feel nervous, Danny. I was there too, remember?"

"I wasn't sure how you felt about it this morning."

She stretched lazily, brought her black-clad legs up under her chin and clasped her arms around them. "I feel wonderful. How do you feel?"

"I feel pretty good too." Her eyes on my face were almost like a touch.

"Guilty?"

"A little," I admitted. "No, Anne, as a matter of fact, a hell of a lot."

"You don't have to. What happened was just between us."

"That's easy to say. But it never works like that."

She gazed at me silently for a moment. "Are you trying to tell me that it's not going to happen again?"

"Yes, I guess I am."

Out of the corner of my eye I saw her head turn to face the front again. I wanted desperately to see her face, but I kept my eyes resolutely on the traffic ahead of us.

We were turning into her parking lot before she spoke. "It's all right, you know."

"That's great," I said, my voice dry and husky, aware for the first time of my fixed, white-knuckled grip on the steering wheel.

She got out and closed the door and smiled at me through the window. Then she opened the door and said, "It really is all right, Dan."

She closed it again and walked toward the office door, her left hand fluffing her hair.

I debated going by the apartment in Irving again; but I was bone-weary and emotionally bankrupt. I went straight home and went to bed.

After a dinner of spaghetti and half a glass of cloying red wine Anne had found on the back of the shelf in the liquor cabinet, I showered and shaved and spent an hour listening to Warren guffaw and stealing glances at Anne curled up on a corner of the sofa, her chin cupped in her hand, face relaxed and placid, obviously up to her belly button in her own private reverie.

Restive, irritable, I prowled the rooms of the house, checked the locks on the front door, paused briefly at the windows. My station wagon was in Hector's driveway and Rowdy, sitting at his customary place at the gate, saw me at the window and wagged his tail. I waved at him and he twitched his ears in acknowledgment. I detoured through the living room to bypass the den, picked up a can of Coors from the kitchen and exited through the utility room door onto the patio. I wrestled the heavy redwood lounge to where it was facing the open field and the woods beyond.

I lit a cigarette and sipped my beer, gratefully feeling the acrid taste cut through the sweet-heavy residue of the spaghetti sauce and wine. The sun was still an hour in the sky and the shadows from the taller oaks in the woods had just begun their relentless march across the field. Not a great view, as views go, but better by far than the asphalt streets and monotonously stereotyped houses that were sure to come. Already the harbingers of invasion, the little men with their transits and flags, were seen occasionally waving and yelling at each other across the slope of the hillside. The bulldozers wouldn't be far behind.

A squirrel scampered along the electric line behind my fence. He leaped to a tree at the corner of my backyard and I watched his progress through the treetops to the huge oak at the center, to the nest built high in a fork. Another followed, this one tailless, his small body somehow ludicrous and ungainly without the balancing effect of the tail. I had first noticed him early in the spring along with two of his brothers, fresh from the nest, venturing down the trunk of the tree in search of tender new grass shoots. In all my years of hunting and wandering the woods, I had never before seen this phenomenon, and I had wondered about his ability to survive. But over the months I had seen him often, traversing his treetop home as surely and with as much agility as his tailed brethren. I had read once that old bull squirrels often raided the nests of their harem, severing the testicles of baby males, eliminating potential competition. Maybe in haste, or an excess of zeal, some old nervous bull had bitten off the young squirrel's tail instead of his testicles or maybe both.

Another article I remembered reading had stated

with indisputable logic that squirrels would find it impossible to live in the trees were it not for their hairy appendages acting as a counterbalance. So much for expert opinions.

I drank the rest of my beer and jumped as Anne's voice came over my shoulder.

"I had about decided to go back in. You were so still I thought you were asleep." She paused at my side. "Do you mind some company?"

"Not a bit. Here, you take the—"

"No, no! I'll sit over here. Just stay where you are, this chair will do fine." She sat in a padded redwood chair and drew her knees up to her chin. "It's nice out here."

"Yes, but I'm afraid the peaceful days are numbered. I've seen surveyors in the field and woods several times in the last few weeks. Pretty soon all you'll hear out here will be the song of progress, buzzing saws and pounding hammers."

"Maybe not," she said. "Building has slowed to a crawl."

"The whole country's going to be crawling if the White House has its way."

"You're a liberal," she said teasingly. "I never would have believed it."

"I'm not a liberal or a conservative. I'm not anything. But I do have a reasonable sense of justice. And what kind of justice is it when there are lots of people around who spend enough on one dress to feed the poor people of Midway City for a week—or maybe a month."

She shrugged. "It's always been that way."

"That doesn't make it any damn better. It's not so much that they have it, it's the fact that they flaunt it."

"It must be nice," she mused. "Being able to go

into Neiman Marcus and buy what you want and not even consider the price."

"Or the supermarket, for that matter," I said.

She laughed. "That too." She cocked her head and gave me a shrewd glance. "You seem to be doing all right, Dan. You can't be getting rich from your job, if what you say is true about how often you work."

It was such an obvious bit of nosiness that I almost laughed. I grinned instead. "Well, I wouldn't want it to get around, but I have a stable of girls working in Dallas. I push a little pot, coke, a few pills now and then. Nothing real heavy, you understand . . ."

"Okay," she said, her face taking on a tinge of color. "I deserved that."

I laughed and lit a cigarette. "Seriously," I said. "I do have a small supplemental income. From some land my dad left me. Enough to scrape by on if I had to, I guess. Enough to give me the privilege of picking and choosing my jobs."

She smiled ruefully. "You didn't do so well on this one, did you?"

"Oh, I don't know. It's been relatively painless so far."

Her color deepened and her lips quirked in a crooked, mirthless smile. "Even servicing your client's neurotic sister?"

"Come on, Anne. I wanted that as much as you."

Her eyes were dark shadowy holes in the deepening twilight. "I wish I could bring myself to believe that."

"You can," I said uncomfortably. The conversation had taken a sudden turn for the worse, a one-way street with no exit. I had a disquieting feeling that this was where it had been headed from the beginning.

She pressed her cheek against her knees and looked away from me, and there was a heavy oppressive silence. I wondered listlessly if I should break it, but I couldn't think of anything to say.

A zigzag flash of lightning streaked across the horizon west of Fort Worth. I wondered if it was going to rain; I wondered what she was thinking and if my shaky fortifications of resolve could withstand even a moderately heavy assault; I wondered how her breasts would feel through the thin silky material of her blouse.

As if she could read my mind, she uncoiled from the chair and floated toward me, gracefully elegant in the dusk. She lifted my crossed feet off the lounge and placed them carefully on the concrete, one on each side; she sank down between my legs and slid backwards into the V, her head coming to rest on my chest, just beneath my chin.

"Hold me, Dan," she whispered. "Please, just hold me."

"Okay," I sighed, "I'm on hold."

She chuckled and I felt a tremor pass through her body. Then again the heavy silence; but it was no longer oppressive. I was suddenly aware of a tiny flicker of strangeness in my mind, elusive and fleeting, nagging, like something momentarily forgotten, something important that you had promised yourself you wouldn't forget. There was a sharp pungent smell in the air, the odor of ozone after a summer storm. I tightened my hands and felt the bastions trembling, the ramparts beginning to crumble.

We sat for what seemed like hours before Warren stuck his head out the door. "Anne? What are you all doing out there?"

"We're just talking, War. Are you going to bed?"

"Yes."

"Get out of the light, Warren."
"Okay. Good night."
Anne squirmed and sighed. "This is nice, isn't it?"
"Uh-huh."
"You about to go to sleep?"
"Not quite."
She chuckled, low and throaty, then threw her arms around my neck and gave me a soft kiss.
"Jesus, Anne, I can't stand that."
"I know. See? I'm as ready as you are."
"I see," I said thickly. What was it I was supposed to remember?
"Do you want me?"
"No."
"Liar!"
"Pathological."
"What?"
"Nothing."
"Right now? Do you want me right now?"
"Whenever," I said indifferently. "You know what they say," I whispered, hearing the far-off boom of the last parapet falling, "there's no time like the present."
Her low laugh was soft and sibilant. "Well, if you're going to argue, forget it."

It was the time for silence, tranquillity; the time for cuddling and a restorative cigarette. Anne sighed mightily and wiggled into a more comfortable position; I smoked and watched the brilliant display of summer lightning slowly working closer, listened to the drumroll of faraway thunder. I desperately needed a can of beer, but I hated to disturb the contentment of the time, the lassitude and serenity that comes from lovemaking well done.

I basked in the glow, trying not to think of the time when the guilt and self-disgust would start. I smoked another cigarette and debated the advisability of asking Anne to get me a beer; then the telephone took the decision out of my hands.

Anne stirred. "Oh, no," she said grumpily. "Let it ring."

"Might be important."

"Want me to answer it?"

"No. I'll get it."

I caught it on the fifth ring. "Hello."

"How was it?" It was a smooth voice, resonant, a southern accent, but not Texas.

"I beg your pardon?"

"How was it?" he repeated.

"Look, pal, I think you have the wrong number."

"I don't think so, Mr. Roman. And I'd really like to know. How was it?"

"Look, buddy, I'm too tired to play games. What is it you want?"

"I can imagine. From where I sat, it looked like it was great. Was it?"

"Would you like to clarify that?" But I thought I knew, and I felt a prickly stirring on the back of my neck. A faint chill.

"Aw, come on, Mr. Roman. Okay. If you want to play it dumb. Was that a good piece of ass you just got out on your patio?"

"About as good as it gets."

He laughed, a low husky sound. "I just wanted you to know, Roman. We could have taken you any time we wanted the last few days. But we don't want a lot of hoopla. All we want is the big buffoon."

"Why?"

"You give him to us and we'll tell you."

"I'll bet you would. Why don't you come and get him, asshole?"

"No need to get hostile, Roman. It's all a game, right?"

"Yeah, right, a game."

"Okay, look, give it a few more days. Make a few bucks. Then I'll call and we'll talk. It could be worth a couple of big ones. Okay?"

"Sure. Why not? Everybody's got to live. Right?"

"Three hundred a day's not worth getting killed for, cowboy."

"Depends on the fringe benefits."

"Okay, cowboy, be a wiseass. Way I figure it, they're going to run out of money before long. Three hundred a day adds up. They don't have that kind of cabbage."

"For a chance to meet you, peeper, I'd work for nothing."

"Okay, cowboy, I gave you a chance. From now on I'd do my lovemaking indoors. And everything else. Next time you stick your nose out, we're gonna nail your ass."

"Happy hunting, shitbag."

There was a moment of silence. "By the way, Roman. That was a cute little doll I played with at your place the other day. I'm going to enjoy that, especially since she's your daughter."

"I don't think you can do anything when you're dead, asshole."

He spat out an obscenity before he could stop himself. My calm conversational tone was getting to him. He had expected bluster, ranting and raving, fear, anything but what he was getting.

"All right, you bastard," he railed. "Ready or not, we're coming after you."

"Bang! You're dead," I said, and hung up the receiver.

I let out my breath slowly, drew in another one, deep, fighting the searing rage that was running through me like a fever. I stepped into the den and leaned against the wall by the sliding door. I stood there a moment until the shaking subsided, then I opened the door.

"Time to come in, Anne."

"Aren't you coming back?"

"No. Come in. Now!" The anger and the fear made my voice harder than I meant it to be. She almost ran to the door, her eyes wide, alarm building in her face.

"Danny! What . . . ?"

I shut the door and drew the drapes. "It's all right, Anne." I forced my voice to be calm. I turned to face her.

"We had an audience out on the patio. Probably someone with a night scope."

"You mean . . . you mean someone was *watching* us?" The freckles stood out against her suddenly ashen skin like splotches of brown paint. "But . . . but how could they? It was dark!"

"A scope gathers light. There was enough."

"How do you know? Was it the phone call?"

I nodded.

"That's . . . that's sick!"

"They're sick all right, but not the way you think. There was a gun under that scope."

"Oh, no."

"It's the same ones," I said, answering the unspoken question in her eyes.

"Oh, God!"

"I'm sorry, Anne, but you have to know how serious it is. We'll have to tighten up. Stay off the patio. Stay away from lighted windows. Any one of us could be a target now. They'll have to think I'll go to the cops, so they don't have anything more to lose."

"Oh, God, Danny!" Her eyes filled, began to leak over the edge. "For the . . . for the first . . . time, I . . ."

"I know," I said gently. "I was still having a little trouble believing it myself. Even after that business with Susie, I kept thinking there might be a mistake, mistaken identity . . . something. But there's no doubt now. They want Warren and now they'll go through us to get him. I think they've been holding off, hoping I'd get careless, give them a chance at him alone. I think they wanted as little noise, as little attention as possible, but now . . ." I hesitated. "Do you think you could talk him into going into protective custody?"

"You mean in a jail cell?"

"That's how it would have to be. They couldn't spare the manpower to watch him around the clock."

"He'd never do it, Danny. He couldn't stand being locked up."

"He might have to," I said grimly. "We'll talk to him tomorrow."

I prowled restlessly the rest of the night. Not that I really expected them to come so soon, but just on the off chance they might think that way and come anyhow. I spent a lot of time at the kitchen and utility room windows. Despite the fact that the floodlight on the rear corner of my house reached to the fence, there were a lot of trees and a lot more shadows. I had to believe that was the route they would take. The front was well illuminated from yard lights and a light on the corner. The south end where the bedrooms were was semidark, but Rowdy slept at the driveway gate, and nobody was likely to get past him. The north end of the house was blind, in deep shadow, but that was the garage end, solid brick, and there were no windows except in front. And even if somehow they should manage to get into the garage, there were two doors to come through: one with a lock and an inside jamb bolt, the other a shiny new dead bolt. That would be noisy, and noise was their enemy.

The most vulnerable spot from the standpoint of quick entry was the sliding door in the den. The lock was relatively flimsy and could also be brought crashing down with a well-placed blast from a shotgun. But that would be noisy also, and they would still have to come through the draperies. So if they came, they would have to come shooting. That meant noise—a lot of noise. If I stayed halfway alert and they didn't bring an army or a tank, I should be able to take them. It was a vaguely reassuring thought, but I started carrying one of my three twelve-gauge shotguns with me on my rounds. The other two, loaded with buckshot, were located at strategic positions near the rear of the house. At close range a twelve-gauge shotgun loaded with buckshot is damned hard to beat for deadly.

Anne and Warren both were up early the next morning. Even though it was Saturday, he wanted to go to work. It was only after I promised him I would commit bloody atrocities on his hulking body that he stopped his whining and plopped sullenly in front of the TV to watch cartoons. I made Anne promise to watch him and get me up by noon. I crawled gratefully into her side of the bed, still warm from her body, and went immediately to sleep.

/9/

"And in case you couldn't find yours to take it off, I brought my own tools." Homer Sellers stood grinning at me while I raised the garage door.

"You're really gonna take the damn thing?"

"You bet. I been doing your work for you for years. About time I got something out of it. Besides which, you don't ever use the damn thing. Told me so yourself. Hell, look at this. Dust an inch thick on it."

"I've used it a few times," I said defensively.

"Yeah, how long ago?" He opened his toolbox and selected a box wrench. He grinned at me again. "Say, you heard about the guy going to the doctor with somethin' wrong with his pecker?"

"Probably."

"Well, this guy goes to the doctor, see? He says—"

"You're gonna need two wrenches, Homer. Those bolts been on there a long time."

"Well, this guy goes to—"

"Use a socket on the top, Homer, and an open-end on the bottom. Don't you know anything?"

"Okay. This guy says to the doctor, 'Doc, there's somethin' wrong with my pecker. Every time I feel of it like this, it feels funny.' And the doctor says—"

"—then let me feel of it, I need a good laugh," I finished for him, grinning wolfishly.

"Dammit, Dan, whyn't you tell me you'd heard it?"

"Been so long ago, I'd forgotten."

"Yeah? I thought it was a new one." He finished removing one of the bolts and started on the second.

"When you finish stealing my drill press, how about coming inside and helping me talk that blockhead Stillwell into protective custody?"

"Okay. You gonna give me the bolts, too?"

"Hell, yes, Homer. Anything else you see you want?"

"I'll look around. Anything else happen?"

"I got a call last night. The asshole tried to be real cool and smooth, but he was putting off real evil vibrations, Homer. I have an idea he's a hired gun, a pro."

"You ain't found out why they're after him yet?"

"Nothing. I'm as much in the dark as I was in the beginning. Maybe more. It gets more confusing as time goes on."

"How so?" He grunted as he worked the second bolt out of the hole.

"Stillwell. He's a paradox if I ever saw one. Bastard's smart enough to get a bachelor's, a master's in physics, and a doctor's in mathematics in seven years, yet most of the time he talks and acts like a ten-year-old. He watched cartoons all morning."

Homer looked at me blankly. "So?"

"So? Jesus Christ, Homer! Do you know how long it takes the average person to get a doctor's degree—not to mention the master's in physics?"

"Yeah, I understand about that. But what's wrong with watching cartoons?" He walked off grinning, the drill press dangling from one hamlike hand.

I followed him out to his car, watched him stow the drill press in the trunk. We went into the kitchen, and while he washed his hands, I pulled the tops off two cans of beer.

"Light beer?" he asked incredulously, mimicking

the commercial. "Whoever heard of drinking *light* beer?"

"Take it or leave it," I said, not really in the mood for levity.

The television was going full blast. Warren was hunched forward in my chair watching gaily colored cars crash into each other at full tilt. There was a vacuous grin on his big mouth and his eyes were dancing.

I did the only thing I could do to get his full attention: I turned off the set.

He looked at me, annoyance and petulance crossing his face in that order. "That was *Destruction Derby*," he said mildly.

"Yeah." Homer grunted. "I've seen that. Russian roulette with cars."

"Warren, this is Captain Homer Sellers. He's with the Midway City Police."

Warren struggled to his feet and shook Homer's hand. The two big men stood eye to eye, and except for Homer's thinning hair, bifocals, and forty pounds of extra tonnage, they were uncannily similar.

Homer turned away first, took the chair on the other side of the fireplace facing him. "Hear you been having some trouble, son," Homer said.

"Well, not lately," the big man said. He threw me a hurt look. I shrugged and lit a cigarette.

"Wanta tell me about it?"

Warren pushed back in the recliner, crossed his legs at the ankles, and folded his hands. "I'm sure Dan has already told you."

"I'd like to hear it from you." Homer gave him a friendly, big-toothed grin. "Straight from the horse's mouth, as they say."

Warren gave me another aggrieved look; he cleared his throat. "Well . . ." he began, then broke off as the telephone rang.

"Go ahead," I said. "I'll get it in the bedroom."

I met Anne coming down the hallway. "It's for you." She made a small face. "It's her," she said, then added with a small apologetic smile. "Your girl."

I swatted her on the butt as I went by.

"Hello, darling." There was a tiny thread of coolness in her voice.

"Hi, Susie, how's my girl?"

"She taking your calls for you, too?" There was just a trace of emphasis on the *too.*

"By golly," I said jovially, "if I didn't know better, I'd think you were jealous."

"You better believe it, mister. Mean and vicious along with it."

"That don't sound like the sweet little girl I know . . . and love."

"Maybe the sweet little girl has gotten smarter." There was a faint sound of laughter in the background and a burst of rock music.

"How's your grandmother, honey?"

"Fine." A muted sound of voices and jangling, discordant rock, loud and brassy.

"You have company?"

"No. Why?"

"I thought I heard laughing a minute ago."

"Oh, that was the TV." The coolness had gone from her voice, replaced by something that could have been anxiety.

"Let me speak to Lucille."

"Uh, oh, she's not here, Danny."

"Where is she?"

"Shopping." She was talking too fast, a defensive note in her voice.

"Okay, Susan, what is it? What's wrong?"

"Wrong? Why do you think anything's wrong?"

"All right, Susie. If you're not going to tell me, I'll just keep calling back until I get Lucille."

There was a tiny exasperated sound, then a long, long moment of silence.

"Danny?"

"Yes."

"You won't be mad at me?"

"Tell me, Susie."

"Danny, I just couldn't stay there any longer. I called Mr. Proctor and he said I had to come back to work by Monday or lose my job. I just couldn't—"

"Where are you?" I was fighting to keep the anger out of my voice, under control.

"Danny, please don't be mad. I'm at Marsha's . . . you know, Marsha Calder. Remember, Danny, you met her and her husband . . . he's a cop too, Danny, so I'll be all right . . ." She was chattering, almost gibbering in her effort to get it all said before I could interrupt. ". . . and they said I could stay here as long as I wanted." She broke off on a breathless note, took a deep breath, and waited. I let her wait.

"Danny?" She let her voice trail upward plaintively.

"All right, Susan," I said quietly.

"You're not mad?"

"Would it make any difference?"

Another silence that seemed longer than it was. "Yes, it would, and you know it. I don't like it when you're mad at me. It upsets me terribly." She allowed a little sultry warmth to creep in.

"Not enough to do what I tell you."

"I did what you told me," she protested indignantly. "I just couldn't stay any longer. You know how boring—"

"Uh huh, now we're getting to it, aren't we?"

"No, I really did call Mr. Proctor and he said he really needed me back Monday."

"Where are you?"

"Fort Worth. Not very far from Seminary South. I'll give you the address."

"Never mind, I won't be coming over there."

"Danny!"

"It's too dangerous, Susie. And I don't want you coming around here until I tell you. Understand?"

"Oh, yes, I understand. Probably more than you think I do." Reverse psychology again.

"You don't understand anything, hotshot. If you did you'd have stayed in Waco."

An injured silence. "That's not fair. After all the time I spent with that cute policeman making sketches."

"When was that?"

"Two—no, three days ago."

"Was he going to send them to Homer?"

"I don't know. He just said the Midway Police Department."

"Homer's here, and he didn't say anything about it."

"Well, at least *that's* not my fault." Now that we were safely past the point of my being angry, she was working back around to the part of the wronged woman.

"All right, Susie. Now that you're here, I guess it can't be helped. Just don't be going anywhere alone, okay? Be careful."

"The least you could do," she said icily, "is say you miss me."

"Oh, I miss you, honey. Most of all that sunny good nature."

Another of her pregnant pauses. "Oh, brother," she promised darkly, "are you going to pay for *that*." And I was listening to a dial tone.

There was silence in the den when I returned. Homer was rocking back and forth and there were dull red spots high on his cheekbones. Warren sat sullenly examining his hairy hands. I glanced at Anne standing in the kitchen doorway. She grimaced and shook her head.

"Well," I said cheerily. "That was Susie. Everything's fine with her. Anybody want another beer?"

Homer shook his head. He was a simple man, his emotions always close to the surface, easily readable. And he had been a cop too long to have much patience or finesse.

"I'll get you a beer, Dan," Anne said brightly.

"Sure, why not? Homer, you sure?"

He ignored me. He stared hard at Warren. "I was just trying to figure out what kind of charge I could hold your friend on. Maybe obstruction of justice."

I glanced from him to Warren. "Okay, what's going on here?"

Homer shrugged. Warren examined his nails. "I ain't going to no damn jail cell," he muttered.

"You might," Homer said thinly.

Warren abruptly rose to his feet and walked out, his face stiff with childish defiance.

"So what happened, Homer?" Anne brought me the beer and sat down beside me.

Homer scowled, then let his face relax into a sheepish grin. "Sucker called me a lead-footed flatfoot."

I laughed. Anne giggled, then said, "Now be fair, Captain Sellers. He didn't call you that."

"Midway City Police Department, same thing."

Anne turned to me, smothering a smile. "War was being critical of the police for not finding the man who tried to set the bomb."

"Come on, Homer," I said. "If you got this mad every time somebody criticized the department, you'd be dead from apoplexy by now."

He ran a hand through his thinning hair. "He just has a way of getting under my skin, is all."

Anne solemnly looked from Homer to me and back again. "Well, what are we going to do?"

I shrugged. "Just keep on doing what we've been

doing. Unless you have any suggestions." I caught the look in her eyes and the beginnings of a blush, and looked away.

"I could hold him for seventy-two hours on suspicion of something or other. But it wouldn't solve anything, wouldn't solve his problem in the long run." Homer was watching us shrewdly, his expression suddenly different around the eyes. He was an excellent judge of character and very little went on around him that he didn't see.

He slapped his hands on the arms of his seat and pushed himself to his feet. "Well, got to be moving along. Nice seeing you, Mrs. Lawrence. Dan, you want to walk out with me?" There was a peculiar inflection in his voice that I recognized, and I had the distinct feeling that I was suddenly on his shit list.

He waited until he was sitting in his car, the key in the ignition. There was a deliberate sneer in his voice. "You're sorry, boy," he said coldly.

"Come on, Homer, you're just guessing. Anyhow, it's none of your damn business."

"That woman in there is in love with you. You just had to go to bed with her, didn't you? What about Susie? Make you feel proud? Make you feel like a man having two women in love with you? What are you going to do when this is over? Have her move in with you too?"

"Homer," I said evenly, through clenched teeth, anger fed by guilt ballooning like putrid gasses inside me, "just butt the hell out! You're my friend, not my damned conscience."

He started the car and shifted into reverse. "You're sorry as hell, boy," he repeated contemptuously, "and I'm sure as hell not proud right now to be your friend."

"Go to hell!" I yelled, as he backed out into the street and revved his motor; but it was unlikely that he heard me over the roar of his faulty old muffler.

Dinner was a dismal affair. Anne tried; she waxed eloquent over the spareribs, gave us a glowing synopsis of the latest Robert De Niro movie, tried her best to draw us into the one-legged conversation with bright-eyed observations about the federal deficit and, last but not least, a brand-new theory of evolution, based on monogenetics, espoused by a Harvard professor. As catholic as her subjects were, they elicited only monosyllabic replies from Warren and me, and finally she literally threw up her hands.

"Listen, you two," she said, a mock-ferocious grin on her face, "I can't carry this conversation alone. You've got me chattering like a magpie, and I hate chattering women."

"You're doing great," I said. "That one-cell theory was interesting as hell."

"Yeah," Warren said, giving her the affectionate look of a benevolent Saint Bernard. He sucked the marrow from a rib bone. "Them was good ribs," he added happily, knitting one more strand in the fabric of his image as a doctor of mathematics. He licked some stray sauce off his thumb and looked wistfully at the empty platter.

"Next time we'll have a whole roast pig."

He grinned at me sheepishly and wiped his hands on his faded Levi's. "I always been a big eater," he declared.

Anne gazed at him fondly. "I saw him eat two whole chickens at a picnic one time."

"Dead or alive?"

Anne gave me a quick reproachful look, then

broke up laughing, her ladylike chortle immediately drowned by Warren's raucous bellow. He reached over and almost dislocated my shoulder with a swipe of one big paw. "That's a good one," he boomed. I flexed my shoulder gingerly; well, at least they were having fun.

"That wasn't very nice," Anne said, still chuckling, a few minutes later when Warren was ensconced deep in my chair in front of the telly.

I grinned. "Aw, he's a good kid, he didn't mind."

"That's how you think of him, isn't it? A kid?"

"Pretty hard not to sometimes." I hooked my head toward the den, where he was enthusiastically calling out the answers to questions on a game show.

"Lots of people do that."

"By themselves?"

Her eyes flashed, but she giggled. She laid one of her hands on mine. "I don't guess we can go out on the patio tonight," she said, a mischievous light in her eyes.

"I'm afraid not."

She squeezed my hand. "Well," she began softly, her face beginning to soften, her eyes melting, "we can . . ." But I was on my feet, reaching for a cigarette.

"If I hurry, I can make a round outside before it gets too late." I went into the den and took down a 30.06 from the rack. I worked a cartridge into the chamber and turned to find her in the doorway watching me, her face expressionless except for two pink spots high on her cheekbones. "What are the neighbors going to think," she said lightly, "you running around with all that artillery?"

I checked the scope and wiped an imaginary spot off the barrel. "The Ellstons won't be able to see me and it won't make any difference to Hector. He thinks

I'm a combination of James Bond and a soldier of fortune now. I wish my life was half as exciting as he seems to think."

I picked up a pair of binoculars and brushed past her on my way out the utility room door. It was all a show and she knew it; and she knew that I knew she knew. But since I was there, I went across the patio to the corner of the bedroom and scanned the line of trees through the binoculars. I didn't expect to see anything, and I didn't. It was far too early; too many people out jogging, cycling, or just plain walking. Besides, the kids who lived in the houses bordering the woods on the other side used it as a playground. And kids are notoriously curious about men with guns, particularly long guns.

No. They wouldn't be there until after dark, probably long after, but it gave me an excuse to get out of the house for a while.

I went back inside before dark. I checked all the doors and windows, and just to be doing something constructive, I took down the twin .38s and loaded them. I pushed one between the cushions on the love seat and carried the other to the mantel. I arranged pictures of Susie into a rough U shape and slipped the gun behind them.

I slumped on the love seat, waiting patiently for the ten o'clock news and Warren's departure for bed. I was soul-weary and bone-tired, and a hell of a lot more melancholy than I wanted to be. Losing my best friend and a lover in one day was something of a record, even for me.

The call came at two o'clock, jerking me out of a half-doze, out of my chair and to the telephone before I was fully aware of what was happening. I shook my head to clear out the sawdust.

"Yes?"

"Mr. Roman, this is Captain McNary of the Texas Department of Public Safety. Do . . . ?"

"Highway Patrol," I said stupidly.

"Yes. Mr. Roman, there's been an accident—a very bad one, I'm afraid. Identification found on one of the victims lists you as next of kin. A young female, Susan . . ."

A loud roaring in my head drowned out his voice. *Victims? Accident?*

"Susie? Where—was she . . . ?" I choked on the hard knot in my throat.

"She's alive, Mr. Roman . . . but it looks serious. . . . She's on the way to John Peter Smith Hospital at this moment."

A ball of ice formed in the pit of my stomach and sent chilling tendrils of fear along my veins.

"Where did . . . are you sure it's Susie?"

"Yes," he said dully.

The line sizzled emptily. "I'm sorry, sir, but if you want to see Miss Roman alive . . . ?" His compassionate voice seemed to come from the bottom of a well. I leaned my head against the wall by the phone, helpless under a sudden wave of weakness.

"Mr. Roman? Are you all right, sir?"

"Yes. Yes, I'll leave now." I reached to hang up the receiver, then brought it back to my ear. "Captain McNary? Could I have your badge number?"

"Of course. It's 6492, Mr. Roman. My phone here is 298-2543. I'll call ahead if you like . . . tell them you're on the way."

"Yes, please. Thank you." I broke the connection, dialed the number with a trembling hand.

"Department of Public Safety, can I help you?"

"Captain McNary, please."

"I'm sorry, sir, he's tied up at the moment. Could I help you?"

"No. No, thanks. Never mind." I sagged against the wall.

"Danny! What is it? What's wrong?" Anne was suddenly beside me, her strong hands under my arms. "My, God, Danny! Are you sick?"

"It's . . . it's Susie," I said tonelessly. "A car accident. She's hurt . . . badly hurt. I've got . . . got to go to her."

"Oh no! Where . . . ?"

"I don't know where it happened. She's on the way to the hospital. The Highway Patrol . . . they just called." I pushed away from her, stood looking wildly, helplessly, around the room. "I've got to go," I repeated.

"Of course, Danny. Do you want me to drive you?"

"No. There's Warren . . . look, Homer's home number is on the list in front of the phone book." I was moving toward the door as I talked. "Call him. Tell him what's happened. He'll send somebody to stay until I get back. In the meantime, if you hear anything, see anybody . . . anybody, understand? Call the police emergency number on the side of the phone. They can be here in two or three minutes."

She nodded vehemently. "Okay, Danny. Please go. Don't worry about us, we'll be fine."

I crossed the utility room and opened the door to the garage; I hit the buttons on the garage door opener and turned back to her, pale and lovely in the green robe, her eyes dark and troubled. "I'll call," I said. "Now go, Anne. Call Homer."

I was in the truck with the motor turning over by the time the door reached its zenith. I gave the pickup all it could handle and made the turn into the street on two wheels, a block away before I realized I hadn't turned on the headlights, two blocks away before I could decide the quickest route to take.

I was a hard tight bundle of muscle and nerves behind the wheel, my mind working again, my whole being concentrating on driving as I careened around the cutoff into Highway 157 heading south to the old turnpike.

Almost calm now, I went over the conversation with McNary, searching for some thread, some shred of something that could give me reason to hope.

... an accident, a very bad one, I'm afraid ... a young female, Susan ...

Oh, God! I gripped the wheel even tighter as I dropped over the hill in the Trinity River bottom.

... she's alive ... but it looks serious ...

Serious? That didn't sound too bad!

I'm sorry, sir, but if you want to see Miss Roman alive ..."

Miss Roman? Miss Roman? But Susie's name wasn't Roman ... Susie's name was Farley.

A cold chilling wind crawled up the back of my neck. Suddenly I was cursing savagely, tromping the brake. The pickup swerved, lurched sickeningly as the right wheels hit the gravel shoulder, then the rear end was sliding and I was coming around in a shuddering one-eighty-degree turn, horn blaring a shrill warning at the lone car approaching. The car screamed to a stop and I was heading back the way I came, the rear end of the light truck fishtailing as it fought for traction to match the grinding thrust of the engine.

I was burning up, choking, cursing my stupidity, cursing the Bloody Marys that had fogged my brain. Suckered like a damned rookie! Fooled by a trick as old as time—lure away the shepherd and the lambs were there for the taking. But the cold bastards were smart. I had to give them that. Using a captain's name, a real one—on duty at the time—was a master touch. The badge number was probably genuine also. They had to believe I might check, call back to verify just as I had done. Or had the number been a fake? But captains have screens, people between them and the public, people to weed out the nuts, the cranks. People to decide whether the caller has a captain-level problem. They had known that also, counted on me not wasting the time to work my way through the screens once I had verified that the captain existed, was on duty at that time. Clever, insidiously clever, and even if they had failed, they had nothing to lose.

But they hadn't failed. I had gone for it like an angry bass after a flashing spoon. I pounded the steering wheel savagely, held my foot to the floor, closing my ears to the whining, screaming protest of the engine. The cab vibrated violently, the front tires trying to wrench the wheel from my hands at every bump. Cold sweat trickled down across my stomach and into my groin.

Another block and I was approaching the corner, my heart hammering in my ribs, my breath coming in short harsh gasps, my hands aching from their death grip on the wheel. I slowed, released my right hand, flexed it to restore feeling, circulation.

Around the corner; there was a car, dark and silent, across, and fifty feet down the street. I could see the dark outline of a head through the rear window, but it was the two men crossing the walk, stopping at the front door that brought my breath bursting outward in a hissing sound of relief.

In time! They had waited too long! They weren't so damned smart after all! I was still a half block away and slowing, but the dead bolt would stop them. I got the gun out of the glove compartment and let the pickup coast, leaning low over the wheel, then straightening and staring with disbelief as the door opened, a brief flash of light knifing into the darkness. They slid through and the light disappeared.

God! I gunned the truck and swerved up and over the curb, the tires digging up my neighbors' turf. I slammed into the waist-high hedge at the edge of my driveway, then was out of the truck and running as the thick wall of Ligustrum held, bouncing the front of the truck high in the air and killing the motor.

The front door was ajar, and I stopped long enough to slip off my boots. I was easing the door open when the voice reached me, rough and strident. "Just put it down, sister. I don't want to use this."

I slid across the entryway tile; he was standing in the den, the black gun with the thick black cylinder on the barrel pointed at Anne in the kitchen doorway. I slid my arm past the doorjamb.

"Hey," I said softly. He came around without hesitation, bringing the gun with him, and I had one quick glimpse of his openmouthed face before my bullet turned it into a dead thing, falling limply, the rear portion dissolving in a shower of red, the bits of blood and brains and hair mixing with the roses on the den draperies.

Anne screamed; but I had already turned away. There was another one, and I knew where he would be.

I stopped beside the coat closet in the entry hall. There was no sound from the adjoining hall; but then, I hadn't expected any. I eased the closet door open, gathered an armload of coats and sweaters. I rolled them into one large bundle and tossed it into the hall.

There was the sharp flat splat of a silenced gun; another hard on its heels. I felt my lips peel back in a tight involuntary grin as I followed the bundle of clothes, leaping spread-eagled on top of them, my eyes catching a glimpse of him before I landed, my gun sending him a message even as the breath whooshed out of my lungs. He was crouched against the wall a few feet from Warren's closed door, tall and thin and dark, long arm extended like the finger of doom. I couldn't tell if I had hit him, and I squeezed off two more; but somewhere in the thunder of my shots, the splat of his gun was lost and I felt a split-second thrill of surprise as the world exploded around me, and I went hurtling headlong into blinding white light that rapidly evaporated into soft, infinite darkness. . . .

/ 10 /

Everything was white, I noticed that first; the ceiling, the walls, the cloth of the uniform a few inches from my face, even the hair and narrow cadaverous face of the man standing silently a few feet away, his hands tucked under folded arms, his gray eyes studying me critically. "He's awake," the face said.

I was face down on a white table and somebody was doing something very painful to my head. "Don't move," the somebody said, generating even more pain and promising in a cheery indifferent voice: "I'll try not to hurt any more than I have to."

My head felt hollow and extremely large. It would have to be to accommodate the volume of the ringing noise passing back and forth between my ears.

"If you're cutting into my brain," I croaked, "shouldn't I be out?"

The cadaverous face laughed, showing even more white. "He's just stitching you up a little, Mr. Roman. All on the exterior surface, I assure you."

"Just one more minute," the stitcher said. "One or two more. You shouldn't be feeling anything, we gave you a local." Another biting, stinging pain. "Okay, I'm covering you up." I heard the snip of scissors, a faint dull pressure, the scissors again, then the stitcher stepped out of my line of vision. "There you go."

The tall cadaverous man hooked a stool with his toe and sat down on it. He rolled toward me. "I'm Dr. Whittaker, Mr. Roman. You were brought in with a gunshot wound to the head." He smiled cheerfully. "I must say you're a very lucky man."

"You bet. I haven't had one for a long time."

He laughed. "I didn't mean that, exactly. You're lucky you're lying there able to talk to me."

"It's just been a lucky day for me all around."

He ignored me this time. "I'd give a lot to see that bullet. Unless it passed through something, some relatively hard object before striking your head, I don't understand what kept it from shattering the occipital portion of your skull." He gazed at me thoughtfully, his lips pursed. "You have a half-inch-wide furrow from here to here." He demonstrated on his own head. "The bullet followed the curvature of the skull. By all rights this portion should be gone." He touched a pear-sized section of his head with extended fingers.

"That's very interesting," I said hollowly.

"Yes, isn't it?" He pursed his lips again. "Well, strange things do happen." He smiled wryly. "I'm afraid the gentleman who shot you wasn't so fortunate." He slapped his knees and got to his feet. "Well, you don't have a concussion, Mr. Roman. That's the very least I would have expected from such a traumatic occurrence." He sounded slightly aggrieved, as if I had just demolished all his medical precepts in one fell swoop.

"I'm sorry," I murmured.

"Yes. Well, there's a Captain Sellers outside. Do you feel up to talking to him?"

He swung toward the door. "Don't try to get up just yet, Mr. Roman. Lie there for a bit. You might want your family doctor to see that within a day or so. Gunshot wounds can be a nasty business." He stopped with his hand on the door, reluctant to leave. "I just don't understand it."

"Maybe I've just got a hard head," I offered, but he was finally gone, to be replaced seconds later by Homer Sellers's scowling face. He stood over me, his hands on his thick hips, a dead cigar jutting from his jaw; the stereotype cop, tough and cynical.

"Well, you've gone and done it again, dummy."

"Don't pick on me, Homer, I'm wounded."

"Wounded hell! Ain't nothing but a scratch. I've got worse working my garden."

"How many times you been shot in the head?" I lifted my head indignantly, then lowered it quickly as somebody behind me began pounding on it with a hammer. "Jesus! That hurts."

"Just be glad you can feel it. That's more'n them two other fellers can do."

"Got both of them, huh?" I asked hopefully.

"Yeah, you got both of them."

"How's Anne?"

"She's all right. A little hysterical maybe."

"Warren?"

He nodded. "Okay. Mad as a wet hornet."

"Mad?"

"Yeah. I got his ass in jail. That's where it's going to stay for a while."

"You can't hold him, he didn't do anything."

"The hell you say. I can hold him as a material-damn-witness. You just watch me."

"Crap, Homer. You must know what happened."

"Yeah, I know. The girl told me. But that don't mean I have to close the case right away." He grinned evilly. "They sucked you in, huh?"

"Not for long. Not long enough." I swung my legs over the edge of the table and gingerly raised my head. Homer reached out a big hand and steadied me.

"Think you ought to get up yet?"

"Hell"—I grinned painfully—"it's just a scratch, Homer."

My head was whirling, but the jackhammer had died to a dull steady throbbing. I touched a tentative finger to the bandage on my head. "They weren't quite as smart as they thought. They believed all along that Susie was my daughter. He made the mistake of calling her Miss Roman. And I damn near didn't catch it. All her identification has Farley on it, but she does have me listed as next of kin. If they had taken her name from her ID, then he'd have known her name was Farley." I fingered my scalp. "How much hair did they cut off?"

"Place about as big as my hand."

"Jesus Christ!"

"Looks gross," he said.

"You should have heard that doc telling me how it should look. He painted a pretty damn graphic picture. What kind of loads was that guy using?"

"Hand loads, thirty-eight caliber. Homemade dum-dums. I think he shaved them too thin. They hit your hard head and flattened. If he'd hit you anywhere else, he'd bored a hole the size of your fist."

"You run a make yet?"

"Working on it. Both of them were clean."

"Sounds like pros."

"Wouldn't be surprised."

"Anything on a third man? There was a car two houses down across the street with somebody in it. Looked like a Ford or Chevy, late model, dark color."

"First I heard about it."

"Did Anne call it in?"

He grinned. "Guess who? Your neighbor, Hector Johnson, of course."

"Good old Hector."

"If there was a third man he might have saved your ass. He called it in when he saw you get out of his truck and run across your lawn with a gun. The patrol car was only a couple of blocks away. The driver says he heard at least two rounds fired as he came around the corner."

"He use his horn?"

"I imagine so, why?"

"If the third man heard him, he wouldn't stick around."

"That's so, but what's your point?"

I slid down off the table. Other than a slight dizziness and a feeling of nausea, I felt pretty good. "The guy who called me the other night. I don't think it was the skinny guy in the hallway. I only got a quick look, but the voice didn't seem to fit him, somehow. That's why I'm sure there was a third man. They had to get there somehow. If you didn't find transportation, that cinches it." I sighed. "That also means nothing has been solved. Whoever wants him dead is still out there."

"Yeah," he grunted. "And that's why I'm gonna keep them in jail until I find out something."

I was walking around in a circle, trying out my legs, and almost missed it.

"Them? You've got Anne in jail too?"

"Yep," he said, his face flat and expressionless.

"Dammit, Homer, you can't keep her in there."

"Wanna bet? Material witness, protective custody."

I gave him a long hard look. "You're doing this to keep her away from me," I said hoarsely. "You bastard!"

He rolled his beefy shoulders. "Don't get horsey with me, son. I can put your ass in there too, you know."

I shoved my face close to his. "Do it, Homer! Come on, dammit, do it!"

"You killed two men tonight . . ."

"So-damned-what? They were in my house with deadly weapons threatening the lives of my clients. They fired on me and I killed them in self-defense and you damn well know it."

"Don't make no difference at this point," he said belligerently. "Law says you got to be arrested. It's not up to me. It's up to—"

I glared at him, eye to eye. "You arresting me, Homer?"

"I already have," he said gruffly. "I'm just releasing you on your own recognizance. You'll be notified when to appear and I'll need a statement too," he said mildly.

"To hell with your statement."

"Come on, Dan. You know the drill as well as I do."

"To hell with your damned drill, too." I yanked open the door and ran into the arms of a hefty young nurse with a mass of blond hair, a striped cap, and a pretty red face.

"My, my," she clucked, "you gentlemen are talking rather loud."

"I'm just leaving," I said. "Who do I see about paying?"

"If you'll go to the cashier's office, sir, I'll be there with your chart in just a moment."

* * *

He was waiting at the front door when I came out.

"You'll need a ride home."

"I can get a damn cab."

He looked at me levelly, his face beginning to get red. "Get in the damn car, Dan."

I got in.

We rode without talking, the silence growing heavier and more oppressive with each block. He chewed the cigar butt, worked it from one side of his mouth to the other, a sure sign he was upset. It wasn't something that happened very often.

He threw the cigar butt out his open window with an air of finality. "It's for their own damn good, Dan. Yours too. You can't keep riding herd on them forever. Next time you may not be lucky."

"You can't keep them in jail forever either."

"Don't mean to." He glanced at me. "Give you a breather. Give you a chance to do some real work on this thing."

"Such as?"

He shrugged irritably. "You're a detective. Used to be a good one. Use your head. Somebody wants to kill somebody else, there's got to be a reason. This'll give you a chance to find it. Hell, I don't have to tell you. Backtrack him. Somewhere in his past something happened—to somebody."

"He says no. So does his sister."

"Bullshit, Dan! Dammit, wake up! You're letting that girl . . . well, never mind that. We've decided these guys are pros. Okay. Someone's hiring them. That makes it a good reason. Nobody's gonna spend the kind of money this guy's spending just because some nut cut him off in traffic, or some dumb thing. He wants Stillwell bad. And that kind of action is going to leave tracks somewhere."

I listened to him talk and let the crisp morning air bathe my head, ease the burning that had begun with the cessation of pain. He was right, of course. I'd known all along that guarding them was a stop-gap measure, that there would have to be a day of reckoning. I watched the houses slip by in the gray dawn light and wished I had a drink, wished Susie was waiting for me at home, wished I'd never heard of the Stillwells and their problems, wished I'd never . . .

"The coma?" I said.

"What?"

"Coma. He was in a coma for two years. That's what he said. Two years, 1971 to 1973. It don't smell right, never did."

"How come?"

"It's all too vague. An automobile accident; a small military hospital in California that he doesn't remember anything about. Walter Reed. He was transferred there a month or so before he was released from the army. He was due for discharge in 1971 when the accident happened. But there are no scars. Seems to me there should be scars."

"Not necessarily . . ." he began.

"Don't argue with me, Homer. This was your idea, this backtracking." I lit a cigarette and watched the wind suck the smoke out the window. "Can you get me a copy of his military records, Homer? Maybe we can take a shortcut."

"Reckon I could," he said slowly. "I got this nephew in the Pentagon . . ."

"And a copy of his medical history. Walter Reed must have something on the coma."

"That might be a little tougher, but I reckon I could. What are you going to do?"

"While we're waiting for the records I can be checking United Labs. Make sure there's nothing there. His school years, his ex-wife. Don't worry, Homer, I'll stay busy."

"Good." He grunted. "Keep you off the streets."

He eased to a stop at the curb in front of my house. "Still a mess in there. I'm curious about something. What was all them coats for you were lying on in the hall?"

"I needed something soft to land on," I said, and he nodded as if that made perfect sense.

"What happened on that other thing?"

"What other thing?"

"The motorcycle make—some guy looking for his daughter, you said."

"Nothing happened, Homer. I guess now nothing will. It's a shame too. He was a nice old geezer."

I crawled out of the car, then held the door and looked back in at him. "Can I get someone in to clean this place up?"

"Probably. Let me check when I get in. I'll call you."

I closed the door and lifted my hand in a wave. Someone, probably Hector, had moved the pickup into my driveway. I walked over and examined it; other than a few scratches on the right fender panel, it was undamaged.

The phone was ringing when I opened the door. I closed the door and locked it and took my time getting into the kitchen, hoping the damn thing would stop.

"Hello," I said tiredly.

"Next time, cowboy," the smooth voice said softly. "Next time you go with him."

"Why didn't you come yourself, shitbag?"

"I was there, cowboy. That cop hadn't been looking down my throat you'd be cold meat on a slab."

"Like your buddies?"

"Just like them."

"I'm here now," I said. "Cowboy."

"Next time," he said, and hung up.

"Piss on you too," I said into the dead phone.

I've always had the notion that I drank for pleasure, a simple harmless pastime. Something to do when time hangs heavy on the hands, when the mind begins to atrophy, to enhance the conviviality of good conversation with boon companions. But never because I needed it. People who needed it were drunks. And drunks drank for different reasons than I. Drunks drank to forget, or maybe to jog their memory; for lost love or because they never had it; to seek oblivion, or to clear their head in order to understand what it was they were drinking for in the first place. Whatever the cause, drunks had a compelling reason. I had no such compulsion; I could take it or leave it.

I looked at the bits of hair and blood and brains, dried now, on the fireplace brick and the draperies, and decided that at long last I had a compelling reason.

I stepped carefully around the taped outline on the floor, the glutinous pool of smeared blood. The man's face came unbidden unto my mind, the openmouthed look of astonishment when he looked into my gun and saw death. I wondered what his last thoughts were in that split second before yawning eternity: pain? fear? horror? Or maybe relief.

I sloshed scotch into a glass and went back into the kitchen for an ice cube. I sat at the kitchen table, my back to the den, and watched the squirrels out for an early-morning romp. The tailless one was quicker and more daring than the others, darting and leaping and scampering, as if in compensation, as if he too had something to prove.

Rowdy was sitting in the corner of the Johnsons' yard, watching through the chain-link fence. He yawned with the casual indifference of old frustration, only the twin spires of his alert ears betraying him. The squirrels pranced enticingly close, and one sat on the top rail above him and chattered abrasively, tail curled high over its back, flicking and whipping impudently. Rowdy yawned again, and when the tailless one scampered to within a yard of him, sat insolently watching with bright beady eyes, he tested the wire with a tentative hopeless paw, then rose to his feet, shook himself, and trotted away with majestic dignity, his own tail curled high in complete and total disdain. The squirrel on the top rail barked after him in gleeful derision.

The telephone rang. I jumped. Homer telling me to have the mess in my house cleaned up, I thought.

"Yes."

"Hi, honey."

"Hi, yourself," I said, trying not to let her know how delighted I was to hear her voice.

"It's Sunday."

"So it is."

"I haven't seen you for a week."

"It's been a week for me too."

"Do you miss me?"

"Fiercely."

"I'll bet," she said derisively, but I could tell she was pleased.

"What are you doing up so early?"

"Oh, I couldn't sleep. I was wondering what you were doing."

"Getting ready to go to bed."

"Oh," she said, the one syllable speaking volumes. "Is Miss—Mrs. Stillwell up yet?"

"No," I said, "and it's Lawrence."

"Whatever," she said coolly.

I thought it over swiftly and decided there was no good reason why I shouldn't tell her; she was going to hear it on the news later in the day anyhow.

"She's not here, Susie. Her brother either." I hesitated. It wasn't as easy to tell as I had thought. "Two men made a try for him last night."

"Oh, Danny, no! What happened? Did they . . . did . . ."

"I stopped them, Susie."

"Are you all right?"

"Yes, I'm fine."

There was a long moment of silence and then she asked it. "What . . . what about the two . . . men?"

"They're dead. They were trying to kill us, Susan."

I heard the sharp intake of her breath, the soft sibilant sound of expulsion. "As . . . as long as you're all right, Danny. That's all that matters."

"Yes, that's all that matters."

"Then I can come home."

"No, Susie, not yet."

"But . . ."

"There was a third man, honey. The two I . . . stopped were just hired hands. Nothing's changed."

"Oh, God, Danny." There was quiet desperation and the sounds of weeping in her voice.

"I'll be all right, Susie," I said, as gently as I could.

When she spoke again, her voice was toneless, hollow. "Danny. I—I don't know. This kind of . . . thing. I don't . . . it terrifies me, Danny. I don't know if I—I can take . . . can stand it . . ." She let it fade into muted sobs, and I had a terrible crushing feeling that something wrong was about to happen, that Chicken Little had read the signs correctly for once and the sky was about to fall. The silence grew while I sat with a thick tongue and a dry mouth, knowing that I should be talking, saying words of wisdom, meaning, saying something for a change that really mattered. But instead I lit another cigarette, sipped my scotch, and filled my voice with indifference.

"Maybe we should think about it for a while, Susie. What do you think?"

"Damn you, damn you," was all she managed to say before she hung up the phone.

I walked out onto the patio with another scotch. The squirrels darted for the safety of the trees. Rowdy paused in his pilgrimage and gave me a friendly bark and a wag of his tail. I wagged back.

Crisp, fresh, almost clean, seventy-degree Texas air; you can't beat it with a stick. I took a deep breath, coughed, and leaped wildly backward as the Mr. Smoker on the table beside me exploded with a jangling crash. I heard the flat crack of the rifle a second later, but I was busy crawling by then, and when the second bullet grooved the concrete under my belly, I didn't even flinch. A third one shattered a brick at the corner of the bedroom as I rolled into its sheltering shadow. I scuttled back against the brick wall, discovered I still had the glass and most of the scotch. I drank it gratefully and drew the .357 Magnum. I looked at it, then shrugged and put it back. Too damn far. Five hundred yards to the woods, the spot the bullets must have come from. I was safe for the moment, protected by the projecting corner of the bedroom. Unless the shooter moved down the line of woods. But that was unlikely. It was Sunday morning; people were up and about, and even in a world inured to violence against others, someone in Sunset Gardens was bound to wonder about rifle fire in the woods behind his home. Or so I hoped the shooter would believe.

I lit a cigarette and waited five minutes and told myself that surely he was long gone. Sharing my narrow triangle of safety was a redwood lawn chair. I slipped out of my jacket and fitted in around one of the cushions. I placed it on the concrete and gave it a shove with my foot, watching in horror as it twitched and jumped a second before the sound came. The bullet ricocheted from the brick to my right and whined off into the distance. The slug had grooved the concrete again and I realized with a small tingling shock that the line of flight was different.

The angle of trajectory had changed; the cool son of a bitch was moving down the woods!

Reflex action more than conscious thought brought the .357 into my hand again. I stared at it stupidly for a second, then pointed the barrel into the air and jerked the trigger three times. I waited thirty seconds and did it again. The echoes had barely died when I heard the yell:

"Mr. Roman! Mr. Roman!" I could picture Hector's Adam's apple sliding up and down his neck as he yelled. "Dan! You want me to call 'em?"

"Yes," I shouted. "Do it now, please."

I crawled back into the corner as far as I could get and arranged the redwood chair in front of me. It wasn't much protection, but it might screw up the bastard's sight picture, and maybe the two-by-fours of the frame would slow down a bullet.

My head was splitting sharp bright flashes of pain, and I had somehow torn the skin on the palm of my left hand. I drew my knees up to my chin and locked my arms around them, feeling helpless and incredibly vulnerable, confused in mind and wounded in spirit. I squeezed my knees harder and whimpered a little as I pictured the rifle barrel being laid against a sturdy tree, a cold eye dispassionately judging the distance, assessing trajectory, casually but expertly adjusting the crosshairs . . .

The sound of the siren was amazingly close by the time it penetrated the clutter in my head. I heard the squeal of brakes, then Hector's excited babble—but I stayed where I was. I edged into a tighter ball and wished they would just go away and leave me. The confusion was back and my head was pounding in sync with my frightened heart. I heard the scrape of cautious feet on the patio, a murmur of voices. Then a single one, rough, with an edge of excitement and maybe compassion:

"Mr. Roman? You all right, sir?"

/11/

United Labs, Inc., was housed in a low, flat, rectangular brick building with all the esthetic appeal of a scuffed shoe box with swinging doors. I spent thirty minutes sharing the reception room with a cold-eyed brunette in a wine-colored dress of some fuzzy material that looked like brushed velvet. She had the longest fingernails I had ever seen, and used them to expertly spear chocolate-covered cherries from a box on the corner of her desk. She was a tad more than pleasingly plump, buxom, and she chewed each of the chocolates savoringly with an expression of mystical exultation, of almost religious ecstasy. She ignored me until something buzzed on her desk, then gave me a stingy smile.

"You can go in now, sir. Just down the hall. The door at the end."

Dr. Marvin Wilder was a small man with a handshake like a stevedore and a voice as deep as Tennessee Ernie Ford's. Five-two in gleaming high-heeled cowboy boots, he had a narrow lined face, tiny eyes, and inordinately small hands and feet.

"Mr. Roman. Very sorry to keep you waiting. But Monday mornings are one of our worst times. Particularly first Mondays." He waved me to a chair and scampered back around his desk. He arranged himself in a high-backed cavernous chair and regarded me with bright-berry eyes. "If I understood correctly, your visit concerns our Dr. Stillwell? I must say that if Dr. Stillwell had not called early this morning to explain that he would be unavoidably detained for a few days, I would not have taken time to grant you this interview. I must say also that curiosity plays a major role, since Dr. Stillwell would not comment on the reason for his absence. I assumed you might be able to clarify things a bit." He folded his hands and gazed at me expectantly.

"Yes I can. He's in jail."

He couldn't have been more shocked if I'd offered to fondle his genitals. His little eyes stretched wide and his mouth literally fell open. "Jail? Dr. Stillwell? My God, whatever for?"

"No fault of his own, Dr. Wilder. He's in protective custody as a material witness. The police are trying to prevent someone from killing him."

"*Our* Dr. Stillwell? Dr. Warren Stillwell? My word! I can't imagine anyone wanting to kill Dr. Stillwell."

"He can't either, Dr. Wilder. That's one of the reasons I'm here. There have been four attempts on his life during the last three months. Someone wants very badly to see him dead. Can you think of any possible connection between that fact and his work here at United Labs?"

"His work? Goodness no! Warren's work is eminently satisfactory. In fact . . ."

I couldn't stop a smile. "I didn't mean that exactly, sir. I thought maybe something in the personal relationships between Warren and other employees . . . someone perhaps who might possibly be after his position . . ."

"Oh, heavens no! Warren is by far the best researcher we have."

"That's what I mean," I said patiently. "Is there someone who might be jealous of Dr. Stillwell's ability, his position?"

He nodded his understanding. "I see what you mean. But no, I wouldn't think so. Our work here, Mr. Roman, is divided into four categories, four different sections, if you will. Dr. Stillwell is in charge of one section. Other than a secretary, he has four research assistants, all technical people. It would be preposterous for one of them to aspire to Warren's position. They are technicians, nothing more."

"How about their relationships? Is he a tough boss, demanding, arbitrary? You know what I mean."

"No! No indeed. Quite the contrary. They all like him exceedingly well. They consider themselves fortunate to be assigned to Dr. Stillwell. He is an exceptionally gentle man, easy to work with and for."

"The other three sections you spoke of. Is it possible one of the other section leaders could be jealous of Warren's section? Someone envious of his accomplishments? Someone who considers the research Warren's group is doing to be more important than his own?"

He smiled politely, condescendingly. "You don't understand, Mr. Roman. My four section leaders are experts in their own fields. Accordingly, each considers his or her own endeavors to be of paramount importance. Warren's current assignment, for instance, is concerned with the application of nonsurgical and nonpharmaceutical techniques to the treatment of certain malignancies. Ultrasonics, lasers, certain magnetic principles are involved, just to mention a few. He is considered something of an authority in the fields of optics and electronics, you know."

"Those too, huh?"

"Yes indeed. Sometimes his capacity for acquiring and retaining knowledge is . . . well, almost frightening."

"Total recall, maybe. A lot of people have that."

The condescending smile had almost become a sneer. "Memorization by rote, sir. There is considerable difference between that and the assimilation of useful knowledge, the extrapolation of that knowledge into the mainstream of existing knowledge to arrive at—"

"You don't have to sell Dr. Stillwell's accomplishments to me, Dr. Wilder. It took me six years to get a bachelor's in business."

"Indeed."

"To be frank, Doctor, I'm grasping at straws. Warren has no idea why anyone would want to kill him. Particularly someone with such obvious determination."

"The whole thing is totally ridiculous." He patted the side of his carefully styled hair, then laid one baby finger alongside his chin. It was an utterly feminine gesture, and a light went off in my head.

I lit a cigarette, ignoring his disapproving frown, then leaned forward and grabbed his bright little eyes with mine.

"Is Warren a homosexual, Doctor?"

To my surprise, he didn't quiver an eyelash. His lips pursed thoughtfully and it was a while before he answered. Obviously he hadn't connected my question with his own feminine mannerisms.

Finally he shook his head. "No, I wouldn't think so. I happen to know that he has dated one of the technicians in another group a few times, and if you can believe the office gossip, they . . . made out. I believe that's the current euphemism."

"Why did you hesitate?"

He said coolly, "Because I am, Mr. Roman, and while I can usually recognize a kindred spirit, so to speak, Warren is somewhat difficult to . . . categorize."

"Doesn't it strike you as odd that he is so brilliant, and yet so childlike in his behavior?"

He lifted his lips in a facial shrug. "No, not particularly. In some respects Warren is a genius, and genius, like any other great gift, has its own negativisms. Einstein was shy, retiring, at least at an early age. I think Warren's behavior in personal relationships stems from both his great size and great mental abilities. I believe it to be overcompensation. Judging from his moderate grades in high school and earlier years, I think Warren has been overcompensating all his life because of his size." He finished with an ironic smile. "Perhaps that's why I'm gay. It solves the problem of female rejection, wouldn't you say?"

"Napoleon had Josephine."

He laughed, a deep booming sound. "A specious analogy, Mr. Roman." He pushed away from his desk and I got up and tapped an inch-long ash into his wastebasket.

"I appreciate your time, Dr. Wilder."

"Not at all. I just wish I could be of help. But I think you'll have to look elsewhere, sir. While there are always minor disagreements in any research environment, everyone here likes Dr. Stillwell, and what's more important, respects him."

I shook hands with him again, and on my way out I stopped beside the unfriendly receptionist long enough to whisper in her ear: "You're fat."

The Dolphin Club took its name, I supposed, from the fact that it was quite close to White Rock Lake, and while there aren't any dolphins in White Rock Lake, there are a lot of sailboats, boats, and sailors, and sailors and dolphins have long been known to have an affinity for one another. It was a combination restaurant and bar, the two facilities distinctly separated for the convenience of those members who wanted to bring their families to dine, and quite possibly because of Texas law also. To either drink or dine you had to be a member; to become a member you had to give them your name, an address, and a dollar bill. In return you received a small gold card, embossed with the club's name, that entitled you to the use of the club's facilities on that occasion only. I learned that fact when they took the card away from me on my way out.

Armed with my card and a bow tie supplied by the front desk, I went into the bar. It was a long narrow room with tables spaced more or less evenly along one wall and a fake mahogany bar stretching the entire length of the other. Not too surprisingly, considering the time of day, I was the only customer. That the place was brightly lit was surprising. But not for long. There were two men working behind the bar, and one of them looked up as I entered. He walked along the bar shaking his head and dragging a rag along the polished surface as he came. His head was covered profusely by tightly curled black hair.

"Not open yet, sir. Bar don't open till two."

I gave him a friendly grin. "They didn't tell me that when I gave them my dollar."

He grinned back. "They wouldn't. Restaurant's open though. If you're desperate."

I stopped at the corner of the bar and took the picture of Sherry Bascomb out of my pocket. "It's a little too early," I said. "But I would like to know if you've seen this lady around here."

He wiped the bar in front of me out of habit. "Kinda thought you might be a cop."

"Can't fool a barman or a taxi driver," I said admiringly.

"See a lot of 'em in my business." He gingerly picked up the photograph by the edges. He looked closely for a minute, then laid it back down gently. "Nope. Don't believe I've ever seen the lady." His grin came back. "Not much about her to make me remember either. What's she done?"

"Not a thing. Just some routine questions. She may be a witness in a case I'm working on."

"Nope. Sorry, can't help you." He turned and yelled down the long bar. "Hey, Pete, come here a minute. Officer here looking for a woman."

Pete was short, fat, and had a pockmarked face. He was also surly. He glanced at the picture without picking it up, then looked at me. "Ain't seen her."

"That was pretty fast," I said pleasantly. "Why don't you take a little closer look?"

He opened his mouth to say something, then thought better of it and closed it with a snap. His eyes burned feverishly. Jesus Christ, another nut, I thought. Somewhere along the line, Pete had run afoul of the law.

"Ain't seen her," he said sullenly, but he picked up the photo and looked at it again. "Naw," he said. He dropped it back on the counter, and without looking at me again, stomped back down the bar.

"Not too sociable."

The black-haired bartender laughed. "That ain't the half of it. You should have to work beside the asshole all night."

"You and him the only ones working here?"

"Yeah. We spell each other some along, but it makes a pretty damn long night."

I lit a cigarette, reluctant to leave. If I left here empty-handed, it would probably be the end of the trail.

"How about waitresses?"

"Yeah, we got two—had two," he amended. "One quit a couple days ago. Her replacement starts today."

"How about the other one? Know where she lives?"

He shook his head. "They maybe could tell you out at the desk."

"She comes on at two?"

He nodded.

I slid off the stool and took out a ten-dollar bill. I laid it on the counter. "Have one on me when you open up."

His eyebrows lifted. "Never saw a cop hand out any money before."

"Private," I said. "Ex-cop though. You weren't too far wrong."

The bill had already disappeared. He swiped at the bar and winked. "Next time you're in, the house'll buy one."

I started to turn away and his low voice stopped me. "Hilda. Hilda's her name. She lives at the Lakeview Apartments. Apartment 16. Don't give me away. We ain't supposed to do this."

"Do what?" I asked. We exchanged grins and I got out of there.

* * *

Apartment 16 didn't answer the bell, and neither did the door marked MANAGER. A girl about eight came skating down the sidewalk and held out her hands for me to stop her. I grabbed her wrists and slowed her down.

"If you're looking for an apartment, there ain't any," she said.

"There ain't, huh? How do you know?"

"Because my mama's the manager, that's why." She had pigtails, a dirty sunsuit, and two front teeth missing.

"Why aren't you in school?"

"I'm sick." She eyed me warily. "Why? Are you the truant officer?" She was drifting slowly away down the slight slope, her knees splayed, her balance uncertain.

"Yep."

"No, you're not."

"Yes, I am. And you know what I do to little girls who pretend to be sick and skip school?"

"No, what?" She had a gap-toothed grin of delicious anticipation.

"I eat 'em for breakfast!"

She squealed in mock terror and skated awkwardly away, enthusiasm partially compensating for her lack of grace. I watched her go windmilling around the corner, then walked back toward Apartment 16 and my car.

I had the motor running and was lighting a cigarette when the small gray Ford whipped around the corner from the alley and zipped into the slot marked No. 16. I shut off the engine and got out.

She was a tall, big-boned, healthy-looking woman with thick dark hair and a face that would have been pretty ten years before. But there was a pinched look about her, lines at the edges of her mouth that could have been caused by either dissipation or bitterness, or both. She had large eyes, dark and clear, but underneath there were plum pouches.

"Hilda?" I asked, as she backed out of her car with an armful of packages.

She jumped, startled. "Oooh, you scared me!"

I smiled. "I'm sorry, I thought you saw me."

"Do I know you?"

"No, ma'am. We've never met. My name is Dan Roman. I was at the Dolphin Club earlier and they told me where you lived."

"I see," she said, waiting quietly; the way of people who have reason to regret past encounters with wily salesmen and wilier bill collectors.

I held the photograph up so she could see it. "I'm trying to find this lady. I have reason to believe she may have been in the club lately. I thought perhaps you might remember her."

She shook her head slowly. "I don't think so. No, I'm pretty sure I've never seen her."

"She wouldn't necessarily look like this photograph. Hair could be different, even another color."

She looked at it again, intently; shook her head again. "No. I can't be one hundred percent sure, of course, but I certainly don't recognize her."

I sighed. "All right, Hilda. I apologize for calling you that, but I don't know your last name."

"It's quite all right, Mr. Roman." She smiled crookedly. "It must be a frustrating thing, looking for someone. Are you a detective?"

"Yes. Private. And you're right, it is very frustrating at times. I'm sorry I took up your time."

"Not at all. Wish I could have been of some help."

She was still standing there watching me when I drove off the parking lot. And I wondered, as always, if she could have been lying for some damn devious reason of her own. Or the bartenders at the club. Or Theron Brody. That was the biggest problem with being a detective, any detective, it made you paranoid eventually. One of the first things you learned was that all people were not basically honest as you had been led to believe; another, a great portion of the population would rather lie than tell the truth, particularly if lying would in some small way benefit themselves. On the other hand, being paranoid in my fashion has its compensations; while it results in excessive wariness, on those occasions when I do encounter verisimilitude I get such a rush, a pleasant glow that usually lasts until my next question.

Homer bent a few rules and let me talk to Warren in his office. Oddly enough he was in a good mood and seemed glad to see me.

"Are they treating you okay, Warren?"

"Aw, it's not so bad. Not as bad as I thought it would be. They treat me pretty nice. I always thought being in jail would be something awful. Kinda like they show it on TV sometimes."

I laughed. "Being in protective custody isn't exactly like being a con, Warren. At least you know you won't be in here long."

He cut his big cow eyes at me. "I dunno. You don't seem to be making much progress in this case."

"I'm working in the dark, Warren. And you sure as hell haven't been any help."

"I dunno," he mumbled again. "Seems to me you oughta be doing something. I can't stay in here forever."

The old familiar bubble of anger was beginning to form in my gut. "You want out of here, buddy? Okay, then tell me something I can use. But let me explain the facts of life to you first." I took a deep shuddering breath. "Nobody but nobody can be protected from a dedicated killer. Not unless he locks himself in a sterile room and stays there. Somebody wants to wipe you out and if he's got the time to put into it, well, buddy, you're gonna get wiped . . ."

His head moved, raised, and something surfaced in his eyes, a glimmer of intelligence, a spark of cold fire that flashed briefly, then slowly died, leaving his habitually vacuous look.

"What is it, Warren?"

He ducked his head. "I dunno. That word you just said . . ." He let it trail off vacantly.

"What word?"

"You know, *wiped.* For just a minute it seemed to have . . . seemed to be . . . I don't know . . . significant, or something."

"Significant in what respect?"

"I dunno," he said irritably. "I just felt funny when you said it. Like . . . like it meant something . . . bad."

"It did. I was using it as a euphemism of *killing.* That's as bad as it gets."

He wagged his shaggy head in frustration. "That's not what I mean. I—I can't explain it, but it's happened before . . . with other words . . . things. Like a flash of light, sorta, like a word has a different meaning than I know it has, but I don't know what that meaning is. I oughta know, but I don't. Like when somebody's name is on the tip of your tongue and the harder you try to remember the more you seem to forget. Like that."

"Maybe it has something to do with when you were in a coma. Some coma victims can hear and feel and understand what's happening around them. They just can't communicate. Did Dr. Carelton try hypnotherapy on you?"

"Yes."

"Do you know if he tried to regress you to your coma years?"

"Yes."

"Well, what happened? Did he learn anything?"

"No. I'd just come out of it."

"Out of hypnosis?"

"Yes. We could go back to before the coma and after it, but every time he tried to penetrate it . . . I'd just wake up."

I leaned back in Homer's chair brimming with frustration, my usual reaction to a talk with Warren. He somehow had the unique ability to highlight my inadequacies. If a trained psychologist couldn't accomplish anything in eighteen months, what kind of chance did I have?

"Wiped!" I said.

He looked at me and a fleeting grin flashed across his face like a puff of smoke in a windstorm.

"Didn't do anything?"

He shook his head faintly.

"Okay, Warren." I sighed. "I'll see you again in a few days. Why don't you tell that sergeant that brought you up here to send up Anne?"

"What for?" he asked, his face taking on a slight copper hue.

"I want to talk to her, that's what for."

"I don't think so, Dan." He was avoiding my eyes, his jaw clamped stubbornly.

"Why not, Warren?" I asked softly.

He looked up then, his face set. "Because of what you two been doing."

"You mean fucking?"

"Yes." The color was climbing higher, becoming deeper.

"Why does that bother you? Your sister is a grown woman. She's thirty-six years old, for pete's sake."

"I don't think it's right for you to take advantage of her like that."

I very nearly laughed at that one. "Aside from that, Warren," I said quietly, another one of those lights flashing in my head, "does it bother you that she fucks at all? Did it bother you when she was married? I seem to remember Anne telling me you didn't like her husband. Was that the reason? You think maybe that's why Dr. Carelton kept coming back to incest?"

"That's not the reason." There was a sheen of perspiration on his wide brow and he fidgeted nervously in his chair. I decided to press a little harder.

"That's it, isn't it? You want to fuck Anne yourself. Or maybe you have. Did you, Warren? Did you ever—"

He caught me flat-footed, completely off guard; not that it would have mattered much one way or the other. One moment he was sitting in the chair wiping his brow, the next he was across the desk, his huge hand knotted in my shirt, the other one somewhere at the juncture of my neck and shoulder—and the lights were going out. I could feel my life draining away . . . a swift blanket of darkness descending. It was almost like fainting, but somehow different, as if everything was closing down, stopping, seconds away from ending . . . and his eyes were two cold bright blue flames burning . . .

He was patting my face; light timid blows that rocked my head, his worried face peering at me through a red haze that slowly began to break into jigsaw patterns and fade away.

"Dan," he said so faintly I almost couldn't hear it. He said it again and it was louder and I realized the problem wasn't his voice but the roaring in my head.

"Dan?"

"What the hell happened?" I asked weakly.

He cleared his throat with a horrendous noise. "I dunno, Dan. I was . . . I just . . . I dunno."

I touched the side of my neck tenderly. "Son of a bitch! That hurts!" I reared back in Homer's chair and looked up at him. "Damn, man, you almost killed me."

He was wringing his hands, his broad face ludicrous, close to tears. "No! I didn't mean . . . I didn't even know what I was doing. . . . I—I'm sorry . . ."

"Shit, you oughta be, you big ape. What did you do, anyhow?"

He danced around nervously, his face a study in copper-toned bewilderment. "I dunno, Dan. I don't know what . . . what happened. You—you just made me mad, I guess."

"Remind me never to do that again. Christ, Warren! I was trying to provoke you, I'll admit, but I was only going for a little reaction. A little reaction! Jesus!"

"You want me to have Anne sent up?" he asked eagerly, anxious to be gone, to be away from the source of his confusion, pathetically anxious to please.

I worked my head in a circle timidly. "No, I don't think so. I'll see her later. I'll see you later too, Warren. Much later."

Through the slits between the venetian blinds on Homer's office windows I watched him shuffle off behind the small red-haired sergeant. He was slump-shouldered and stooped, an unsuccessful effort to diminish his size. I wished I had a drink, but Homer's right-hand bottom drawer was empty. If he kept a spare, I didn't know where it was. I rubbed my neck and wondered if I might be the victim of a monumental put-on. My instincts told me it wasn't possible: the sudden incredible metamorphosis from bumbling buffoon to cold-eyed efficient killer—and back again in a matter of seconds. There was, after all, a limit to my credulity. A very low limit, as a matter of fact. I had the nagging feeling that I was a gullible pawn in a much more complex game than I could have imagined. And I wasn't even being allowed to peek at my hole card. I was being jacked around and I damn well didn't like it. Intimidated, my woman molested, shot, ambushed, and now, almost killed by an idiot-genius who was either the world's best actor or the reincarnation of Jekyll and Hyde. And I was worried about being paranoid?

12

I woke up Tuesday morning with a hangover and a neck with a charley horse in it. I forced myself into the shower, cursed and sweated through a bandage change on my head wound, then ended up in the kitchen listening to my stomach revolt at the thought of food. I needed something, so I fixed a Bloody Mary, omitting the Tabasco and salt. I was lowering myself into the den recliner when the doorbell rang. Too dispirited and numb to even bother cursing, I struggled back to my feet and weaved unevenly to the door.

Lionel Whitecomb's face, distorted and blurred by the wide-angle optics of the peephole, stared back at me patiently, an apologetic smile already in place.

I opened the door.

"Mr. Roman. Good morning. I sincerely hope I didn't get you out of bed?"

"Not at all," I said, returning his smile. "I've been up for hours."

"I know I promised not to bother you unless I saw you up and about, but I may be out of town for a few days and I thought perhaps I might touch base with you before I left."

"Quite all right. Won't you come in?"

He hesitated. "Well, perhaps just for a moment. If you're alone, that is. I certainly don't want . . ."

"Come in, come in. Nobody here but us chickens, as the saying goes."

He laughed politely, his eyes studiously avoiding the bandage on my head.

"Ran into a barbed wire fence," I said fatuously as we settled in the den. I wondered vaguely why I was lying and decided with a righteous glow that it was out of consideration for the old fellow's feelings. The shock of the truth might well do the fragile old boy in.

He nodded solemnly, not believing it for a minute. "I read in the papers that you were attacked. I daresay I was relieved to hear that you had defended yourself quite well. Yes, very well indeed," he added with twinkling eyes and a small approving smile. The old man was made of sterner stuff than I had imagined.

"The media tends to exaggeration," I said. I had successfully managed to avoid reporters and cameras, and their stories had been a combination of sterile police reports and overactive imaginations. The television accounts had been even worse. I came out sounding like a combination of Dirty Harry and Marshal Dillon.

He nodded, not entirely convinced. "I'm sure that with all that's happened, you haven't had an opportunity to pursue my daughter's disappearance. I mainly wanted to pay my respects and satisfy myself that you were all right."

"I appreciate that, Mr. Whitecomb. Other than assorted bumps and bruises and the gouge in my scalp, I'm doing fine."

He cleared his throat, looked embarrassed. "I was wondering, Mr. Roman, if this . . . what has happened, might mean that your responsibility in that other matter was at an end?" He lifted a thin bony hand and added hastily, "I'm not trying to pry, you understand. I merely thought if that were so, that quite possibly you could devote all your time to my daughter . . . at your full fee, of course."

"Mr. Whitecomb." I stopped, not certain how to say what needed to be said. "I don't think there's much more I can do to locate your daughter. I have been working on it, but I've run into a stone wall, a dead end, and I'm not sure there's anywhere to go from here."

He sat quietly, his thin shoulders seeming to slump without moving. He nodded, and a small smile came to his face. "I quite understand, Mr. Roman. I realize that this is just your kind way of telling me that you can no longer spare the time from your other commitment . . ."

"No, sir. That isn't it. The people I was guarding are in protective custody, and my investigation of the case is at a standstill for the time being. I could probably spare another day, possibly two, to finding your daughter, but I think it's useless to continue. A waste of your money."

"The money doesn't matter."

"I'm sure it doesn't, sir, but the lead, the only lead, I had has dried up. Brody barely remembers your daughter, if at all. He's a doper, Mr. Whitecomb, into the heavy stuff. He chews up women like we do oranges. He squeezes them dry, then kicks them out and remembers them about as long as it takes to close the door. I think he was probably lying to me to get me off his back. I could go back to see him all right, dance with him a little, but I don't think it would matter in the end." I paused and softened my tone as much as I could. "Mr. Whitecomb, it's been my experience that runaway women your daughter's age don't come back. Not decent women who've left in an indecent way. Pride, shame, deep remorse . . . whatever the hell it is, won't let them. They feel dirty, contaminated, not worthy any longer of the regard of so-called decent people. Right or wrong, that's the way it is. And if they do return it usually doesn't work out. It takes a hell of a big man to forget and forgive. Not many men are near big enough. And those that are generally spend the rest of their lives making the woman pay in one way or another. It's a no-win situation, sir, the worst catch-22 of them all. I don't enjoy having to say this, but I think it needs to be said."

"She could live with me," he said stiffly.

"Yes, she could. I knew that. That's what made me take the case in the beginning."

"You make it sound so hopeless."

"Yes," I admitted.

He studied his clasped hands, his narrow face pale and still, sadder than it ought to be. I lit a cigarette and let him think about it. I looked longingly at the Bloody Mary I had left on the bar.

He cleared his throat again, and lifted one thin shoulder in an apologetic shrug. "I'm sorry, Mr. Roman, I can't let it be," he said simply.

"All right," I said promptly. "I'll get back into it this afternoon . . . and tomorrow, if I can. But I have to tell you, Mr. Whitecomb, I'll have to break away if anything happens with my other case."

"Excellent!" His smile was bright with relief. "I can't tell you how much I appreciate this, Mr. Roman." His pale face had regained some of its color and his blue eyes were dancing.

I shook my head. "I'm still at a dead end. I have one small lead. A waitress that used to work at a place your daughter was seen. If I can locate her . . ." I let it fade away.

"Fine! Fine! I'll leave that to you." He rose to his feet with something approaching alacrity. Then his knees gave way and he caught hastily at the arms of the chair. "It's all right, all right," he said testily, waving me back into my seat. "Just the old bones refusing to cooperate."

"Can you make it all right?"

"Oh, yes." He moved toward the door, awkwardly at first, then with greater ease as his kneecaps began to mesh properly.

"I'll be gone for two days," he said, as we shook hands on the porch. "I'll check with you when I return, if that will be all right."

"That'll be fine."

The small Ford looked lost and lonely in parking space 16. I pulled in next door, climbed down out of the pickup and crossed the handkerchief-sized yard. The front drapes on apartment 16 were closed, but almost immediately after I pushed the bell, I heard muted footsteps. They approached the door and then there was silence, and I realized that it was my turn to be distorted and blurred through the eye of the peephole.

I tried to look friendly; I must have succeeded: there was the sound of a chain sliding, then falling.

"I didn't recognize you at first," she said, holding the door wide. "You're the one from yesterday, the one looking for a lady."

"Yes," I said, somehow inordinately pleased that she had remembered me. "I was wondering . . ."

"Won't you come in?"

"Thank you. I won't take much of your time."

"Time is only important when it is gone." There was a hint of Scandinavia in her voice, but the cast of her jaw and chin were distinctly Slavic, as were her deep-set eyes. "Could I get you something to drink?"

"No, thanks, I don't want to be a bother."

"No bother. Some wine perhaps? Or a beer?"

"Beer would be fine."

"Good." It sounded almost like "goot." "Please have a seat, Mr. Roman."

So she had remembered my name too.

I found a seat by an ashtray at the end of a salt-and-pepper couch that looked new. As did the rest of the scanty furnishings. Cheap but new, slightly incongruous in the small square room with its dirt-streaked walls and faded brown rug. A portable TV sat quietly on a stand in front of the single large window, and there was a single red rose in a vase on the coffee table. A rocker-recliner covered with imitation leather sat across from the television, a magazine rack filled to overflowing waiting nearby. It was a bland room with no identity, nondescript, the red rose the only feminine touch.

"Here we are," she said cheerily. She had the air of someone making the most of an infrequent visit by a very special person. She deposited a small round tray containing a bottle of beer and a glass at my elbow; a brand I had never heard of.

"Thank you." I poured half the bottle into the glass and took a polite sip. Bitter, a little heavy on the hops.

She seated herself in the rocker-recliner and sipped

from her glass of wine. "Now, Mr. Roman, how may I be of help?"

"I understand there was another waitress working at the Dolphin Club with you until just recently?"

"Yes. Gracie. Gracie Carter. She quit her job two days ago."

"Do you know where I might find her?"

She raked strong blunt fingers through her thick hair. "I'm sorry, Mr. Roman. Gracie left for Los Angeles this morning. I took her to the airport myself. If you had only said something yesterday."

I nodded glumly. "The story of my life. A day late and a dollar short."

She laughed as if she had never heard it before. Maybe she hadn't.

"Perhaps you will find your lady anyway."

"Maybe," I said. I drank the rest of the beer in the glass, trying my best to repress a shudder.

"I have only been at the Dolphin Club for a month. Perhaps your lady visited there before then."

"No. It was supposed to be recently. A few days ago, maybe a week."

"I don't think so. Not in the bar."

I nodded and got to my feet. "Thanks for the beer. And your time."

"You're quite welcome."

At the door her eyes twinkled. "Did your lady friend hit you on the head?"

I laughed. "No, it's not that kind of relationship."

She laughed with me, but the leaving was an awkward moment and her laugh eroded to a smile. "Come back anytime, Mr. Roman." Her voice was suddenly warm and vibrant.

"Yes. Well, thank you again for your trouble."

I walked down the path to my car, feeling the weight of her eyes on my back. I didn't know what her invitation meant, and I decided I didn't want to know. My life was more than complicated enough the way it was.

"Be careful." Her voice carried easily across the tiny yard. I waved to her as I backed out of the parking space, and she was still framed in the doorway when I turned the corner. She didn't wave back.

There was no answer at the Brody apartment, at least no one came to the door. And there was no motorcycle in the parking lot at the end of the building, so I assumed they were gone. I stood on the steps for a moment debating the practicality of another assault on the vicious little bastard in the manager's office. Common sense told me it would be another exercise in frustration and I didn't need that. But there was a part of me that wanted to do it; confront the evil little snipe, poke his coals, and watch him burn. The same part that hated sloppy waiters, indifferent store clerks, and petty government officials.

But in the end I said to hell with it and drove straight home.

There was a message on the telephone recorder from a disgruntled Homer: "Why in hell don't you ever stay home, boy, and tend to business? I got them records you wanted, but I don't reckon they're gonna do you much good. Leastwise I didn't get much out of them."

I got a can of beer and went in the bedroom. I lay across the bed and dialed his number.

"Midway City Police, Captain Sellers's office."

"Hi, Mitzi."

"Oh-oh, he's mad at you again."

"No kidding? I can't think why."

"Since when does he need a reason?" She giggled, and I heard a click.

"Sellers."

"What've you got, Homer?"

He grunted and I heard the rasp of his lighter. "Got them records on Stillwell."

"Service and medical both?"

"Yeah. Don't do anything for me though."

"Anything in there about the coma?"

"One dinky statement. Says he was hospitalized from May 1971 through August 1973. Period."

"I'll be damned!"

"Yeah. I got one other thing. A photostat copy of his Walter Reed record. All it says is he was received there June 1973, discharged August 1973. Lists some medication, sleeping pills, pain pills, stuff like that."

"And that's all?"

"Can't tell you what ain't here . . . just a minute. There's a notation on the bottom: 'transferred from Greenville Military Hospital, Greenville, California.' Then there's a printed line here that says 'Transfer authorized by,' and that's got a name typed in: J. L. Mittleton, M.D. That's all there is, boy, there ain't no more."

"J. L. Mittleton. He must have been Warren's doctor while he was in the coma."

"Maybe, maybe not. He might just be the one signed the transfer order."

"What about the two years? There must be something in his medical record about that time, the treatment, daily records, stuff like that."

"Just what I told you, Dan. Nothing like that here. Must be we didn't get it all."

"Hell, Homer, everything's supposed to be in your medical jacket."

"Complain to your congressman. It ain't here."

"Okay, Homer. I'll stop by and take a look later."

"What's the matter, you think I can't read?"

"Not too well," I said. "Spell that doctor's name for me, will you?"

I wrote it on the pad by the bed. "Well, thanks, buddy. I'll see you later."

"Hey, wait. What're you planning on doing?"

"Only thing I can do. See if I can get in touch with this Dr. Mittleton."

"How you going to do that?"

"Hell, I don't know. You got any suggestions?"

"You're the detective."

"What the hell are you, Homer, if you're not a detective?"

"I know about killings, boy. I ain't up on all this fancy stuff like finding people."

I was beginning to get suspicious. I could read a satisfied smirk in his voice. He was holding out on me.

"Okay, you've had your fun. Now, what are you trying to tell me in your own cute little way?"

I've always wanted to tell Homer that when he giggles he sounds silly as hell; and this time I almost did. I waited patiently until he flushed it all out of his system.

"Okay, little buddy," he said, his voice fading in and out. I could picture him wiping his big owlish eyes. "Like I always tried to teach you when you worked for me, the first thing you always do when you get a name is run a make on it. Right?"

"Right, Homer."

"Okay. I run your doctor friend through D.C. What do you think?"

"He's not my friend, and I don't like guessing games. Come on, Homer."

"Well, he hit the bricks about eight months ago. He did a little over seven years of a five-to-fifteen in a California penitentiary. How's that grab you?"

"What the hell for?"

"Murder. Second degree. Seems he sliced the throat of his boyfriend."

"You mean that literally?"

"Yep. Guy worked for him. Cut his throat in a park rest room. It don't say, but maybe he caught him cheating."

"If he did time in the state pen, that means he wasn't in the military then."

"I'd say so."

"Well, he had to be in the army in 1973 or what the hell was he doing signing a transfer order for Warren?"

"Don't ask me questions I can't answer, boy."

"And what the hell would all this have to do with Warren anyhow?"

"I told you not to ask . . ."

"I was just thinking out loud."

"You still going to see this Mittleton?"

"Sure. Why not? Have any idea where I can find him?"

"Only relative listed is a sister. She lives in southwest Indiana. Evansville. That's about a hundred and fifty miles from Saint Louis, if that means anything. Chances are you'd find him thereabouts, don't you think?"

"You have her address?"

"Yeah, got a pen? Okay. Her name's Mittleton, too. Must be a spinster. Lives at 10150 Burkett Road. Nina May Mittleton."

"Got it."

"When you going?"

"Tomorrow maybe."

"Well, good luck."

"Yeah. I'm sure going to need it. Particularly since I don't even know what I'm looking for."

"You'll think of something, boy. I got faith in you."

"What do you think about this now, Homer? You know about as much as I do."

"I been giving it some thought," he said soberly. "One possibility I came across is so damn outlandish it just might come close to the truth of the matter."

"What's that?"

"Well," he said gruffly. "You're probably gonna laugh, but this business of the coma. That just don't go down right. There ain't enough information here about it."

"I agree with that. Go on."

"All right. Supposing he wasn't in a coma after all? What does that suggest to you?"

"Well, he was still in the army. Then that would probably . . . hell, I don't know."

He laughed. "You don't want to say it either. A cover story of some kind. Right?"

"Okay. I'll buy that. What?"

He drew in a deep breath. I could hear the air whistling between his big teeth. "An agent of some kind."

I started to laugh, stopped, suddenly remembering Homer's office, a big man who moved with the speed and grace of an attacking cat, a damn big cat. Suddenly remembering cold eyes . . .

"You're not laughing," Homer said.

"No, I'm not. I want to, but somehow, I can't. It's a mind-boggling thought, but it might explain something that's bothered me all along."

"The two men at Grapevine Lake?"

"Yeah." I hesitated. "But why didn't he kill them?"

"Maybe he did—one at least. How do we know what happened?"

"Something else it might explain."

"What?"

"Why somebody's trying to get him."

"Well, that's the purpose of all this, ain't it? To find that out?"

"Aw, shit, Homer, it's too absurd. Anybody but Warren."

"You got any better ideas?"

"Not at the moment."

"When you leaving?"

"First plane out tomorrow."

"Better wear your long johns, it's cold up there."

/13/

Homer was right: it was cold in Evansville. Cold and damp and rancorous. A fitful, blustery wind clawed at me with gleeful savagery as I followed the boy to the rental Ford. He tossed my bag into the trunk, handed me the keys, then whirled away with the wind, my dollar tip clutched in his hand, his pale handsome face wearing a contemptuous sneer that would have made a New York taxi driver envious.

It was a dark blue Ford Mustang, and I climbed in still in a mild state of shock. It had been three years since I had last rented an automobile, and the prices had doubled.

From high in the air Evansville, Indiana, had appeared as a huge brown leech, tail curled in ecstasy as it suckled with wild abandon at the umbilical cord of an unseen giantess. From the surface it was a curious mixture of the old and decaying and the bright and shiny new. Tired, sagging, shotgun-frame houses stood in the shadow of towering monuments to man's eternal optimism. Brick and glass and plastic and steel, relentlessly functional, without regard for aesthetic appeal. There was an air of sad decrepitude about some of the old houses, a kind of monumental patience, a haughty, if somewhat tawdry, grandeur.

I followed the red-lined route the girl at the rental agency had marked for me. It was a city map and about five miles out the line ran off the edge.

"You'll have to stop and ask directions," the girl had said. "That will be outside the city limits, in farming country. But everyone knows everyone else out there, so you won't have any trouble."

The last house number I saw before leaving the city limits was 6051, and judging by the distance already traveled, I estimated another three miles to number 10150. Outside the city the houses thinned rapidly, seemed to gradually fade away from the highway, become tree-studded oases in fields of brown drooping corn and green soybeans.

A mile farther on I stopped at a small grocery for directions. A few feet from the elevated front porch there was a long narrow oval of raised concrete that had once supported gas pumps. The pumps had been ripped out, but the bolts remained, poking forlornly through the cement like skeletal fingers of forgotten dead.

The proprietor was a short plump man with swept-back thinning hair and a mouth speckled with gold fillings. His welcoming smile died an abrupt death when he learned I wasn't buying.

"Mittleton? Never heard of 'em. Where do they live?"

"That's what I'm trying to find out," I said affably. "Their number is 10150."

"Numbers don't mean diddly-squat out here.

Names on the mailboxes. That's what counts." He spoke swiftly, his tone nasal, his tiny eyes gleaming maliciously.

Jesus Christ, I thought, they're everywhere.

"Well, thanks anyway."

His voice caught me at the door. "Read the boxes, sonny. That's where you'll find them."

I stopped again a mile farther on; a mobile home fifty feet from the highway. A woman hanging clothes on a line at the end of the trailer in spite of the glowering sky.

"Oh, sure," she said. "Nina Mittleton. We go to the same church." Her voice was filled with the rich rhythms of the South, soft, almost shy. Her smile was warm, her face lined, and her eyes had seen more than her share of troubles. She wiped her hands on her apron as if she thought I might want to shake one.

"Do you happen to know if her brother is there?"

"John? Yes, he's there. He never attends church, so we don't see much of him." She hesitated a moment, blushed a little at her own temerity, then asked it anyway. "Are you kin?"

"No, ma'am. I know John from his military days."

"Oh, yes. Poor man. Dedicated his entire life to his country. He's only been retired less than a year now."

"Poor man?"

She blushed again. "I shouldn't be going on this way. It's just that he seems so frail . . . so tragic somehow." Her voice was thick with sympathy, her eyes cloudy with feeling, a woman who understood the meaning of compassion beyond the facile lip service emanating from the pulpit and the politician's dais.

"Yes, ma'am. Do they live nearby?"

"Oh! Oh, yes, of course. Go down the highway about a mile. You'll see their lane. You can't miss it. There's two large oaks at the corner of the pasture."

"And a mailbox, I'll bet."

She gave me a funny look. "Yes. A mailbox."

"Thank you." I turned away, then turned back. "Tennessee or Georgia?"

She blushed and smiled shyly again. "Tennessee," she said. "Five miles from the Georgia line."

I smiled. "Go back," I said. "This cold Yankee country is no place for a nice southern lady."

Her laugh warmed me all the way to the car.

Texas can be a harsh, hostile country: from the flat, dusty Great Plains region to the warm moist dripping nose of the bear, from the dry hellish heat of El Paso to the choking flora and fauna of the Big Thicket and all the variations in between. And with the possible exception of the Rio Grande Valley, no match for this fertile black loam in the bottomlands of the Ohio River. But as I turned into the narrow gravel lane, nothing more than a tunnel between rows of withered brown-and-green cornstalks, I found that I was homesick already. Tired of this dour humorless land with its red-painted barn roofs, its drab faded houses that leaned slightly into the wind. A land of pragmatic people, tunnel-visioned with practicality.

It was a large house, badly in need of paint. Two-storied, it had high gables and a steeply pitched roof covered with green asbestos shingles. A broad fireplace chimney of stone extended up one wall, and across the front there was a covered porch with metal lawn chairs and a wooden swing.

I pulled into a hard-packed graveled area close to the porch. Above me, its trunk considerably larger than a fifty-gallon drum, a giant red oak towered sixty feet into the air.

A door at the end of the porch opened and a woman came out. She was wearing a white calf-length dress with red flowers and a man's bulky leather jacket that reached to her knees. She came to the edge of the porch and stopped.

"Mrs. Mittleton?"

"Yes. I'm Miss Mittleton." She spoke pleasantly enough, with clipped precision and the faintly harsh nasal intonation I had come to associate with native Hoosiers.

"My name is Dan Roman, Miss Mittleton. I wonder if I might speak with your brother?"

"John?" Her eyes widened as if in surprise, and her thin features were suddenly more pointed, wary. "What's your business with John?" she asked harshly.

"Mine, I'm afraid, Miss Mittleton. Is he home?"

She looked shocked. Her mouth tightened in anger; the colorless hand, holding the jacket together in front, twitched. I waited patiently while she glared at me, gauged my intestinal fortitude, my stick-to-itiveness. I must have made some kind of impression.

"He's here," she said grudgingly. "But I don't want him upset, you hear me?"

"I'll do my best."

She still didn't like it, and I could see she was considering her options. Finally she pointed off to the right. "He's patching the roof on the corncrib. That's the second building past the barn."

"Thank you." I turned back toward my car. She came down the steps.

"You'll have to walk. Too muddy down there for an auto."

"Okay." I gave her a cheerful grin. "Just straight on down the lane here?"

"Yes. Wait a minute. I'll change shoes and take you."

"No, thank you. That won't be necessary." I gave her a friendly wave and walked off before she could argue.

The barn was a hundred yards from the house and incredibly old. It had a metal roof, painted red, and plank siding that was grooved and pitted by age and the elements. The entire structure canted noticeably to one side, and one of the huge doors was missing. Inside I could see the outlines of a tractor and several other pieces of large farming equipment. There were other pieces of rusty equipment scattered about the barn lot, and a general air of neglect hung over everything like a dirty old horse blanket.

Beyond the barn there were two other buildings. The first one, smaller, in much better repair, sported a shiny new padlock and I assumed it to be a tool building of some sort. The third building was as old as the barn, and through the cracks between the boards I could see the yellow shine of corn on the cob. There was a ladder propped against the front and John Mittleton sat on the sloping roof. He appeared to be resting, his knees pulled up and locked by his crossed arms, his right cheek pressed against his kneecaps, his head sideways, facing the other way. There was a large gray cat perched on the third step of the ladder. It watched me pick my way across the muddy compound, then leaped down as I approached. Tail lashing, the cat walked sedately to the side of the building and sat down a few feet away from the rifle.

It was lever action, .30-.30 by the look of it. A few feet closer and I caught the gleam of the gold trigger and I knew for certain: a Marlin .30-.30 lever action. I had one exactly like it.

I stopped near the foot of the ladder and looked up. He was still in the same position. I fished out a cigarette and my lighter. He didn't move until I snapped shut the cover on the Zippo lighter. I saw the almost imperceptible jerk of his head.

"Dr. Mittleton?"

His head moved, began slowly to raise; the first thing I became aware of was his eyes: they were a brilliant blue, so bright they looked artificial, and for a moment I wondered if he was wearing contacts. His face was long and thin, with a large nose, curved gently at the center. His skin was the color of half-baked dough; he was completely bald.

"Yes." His voice was soft, melodious, with none of the rasping abrasiveness of his sister's.

"Dr. Mittleton. My name is Dan Roman. I'm from Dallas, Texas. An old friend of yours who lives in Dallas asked me to look you up."

"Oh," he said politely. Not a question, his tone left no doubt concerning his lack of interest.

"Yes," I said. "He's a doctor also. Warren Stillwell."

He was sitting close to the edge, his toes hanging over the eaves, his face no more than six feet away, but I was unable to detect the slightest change of expression. A minute went by and he continued to gaze at me.

"Maybe *friend* was the wrong word. He used to be a patient of yours. Greenville, California. An accident victim. He was in a coma for two years. You signed the order having him sent to Walter Reed for discharge." I paused, waited for a reaction. None came. "Fifteen years ago. Long, but not long enough to forget somebody like Warren, Doctor."

The silence grew. Somewhere behind me a crow cawed raucously, and there was a rustle of sound from the corncrib. The cat rose to its feet and slipped quietly through the door. Mice, I thought. That's why he's so fat. Another sound above me brought my eyes back to the doctor. He had rolled over on his knees, was climbing slowly to his feet. He came carefully down the ladder, cautiously testing each step before applying his weight. He reached the ground and turned toward me, his hand outstretched. The wry beginnings of a smile on his thin bloodless mouth.

"I'm sorry, Mr. Roman. I didn't intend being rude. Of course I remember Warren Stillwell. I was remembering just then. Woolgathering. I tend to do that at times. I hope you'll excuse my bad manners."

He towered over me by at least five inches, thin to the point of emaciation. Up close I could see that the startling coloration of his eyes was his own.

"Certainly, sir." I shook his hand, a dry bundle of sticks.

"Warren is still alive then?" He said it as though he was mildly surprised.

"Of course. Is there any reason he shouldn't be?"

He shook his head. "Before we go any farther, Mr. Roman, perhaps you should tell me what your connection is with Warren."

I took out my billfold and handed him my ID card. He scrutinized it carefully, then handed it back and looked at me curiously.

"A private detective. I've seen a lot of them on television, Mr. Roman, but you're the first I've ever met."

"Maybe you've just been lucky up to now."

He smiled politely and leaned against the ladder. "If we've going to talk I'm afraid I'll need to sit down. I'd invite you into the house except my sister tends to become agitated around strangers. Perhaps we could go into the barn. I have chairs there and it'll get us out of this damp air." He turned and started across the barn lot without waiting for an answer, a stork of a man who could easily have been the inspiration for Ichabod Crane.

"You want to bring your gun, Dr. Mittleton?"

He stopped and looked over his shoulder. "It'll be all right," he said indifferently.

"The moisture is bad for it, sir."

"Very well, bring it if you would."

I caught up with him halfway to the barn. "Are you a deer hunter, Dr. Mittleton?"

His laugh was like the dry rustle of windblown leaves. "No. I use it occasionally for varmints—but mostly for the rats."

"Rats? Isn't that something of an overkill?"

"Yes, I suppose it is. But, you see, it's the only gun I have. I load my own, sixty-grain bullet and about half the charge."

"That should do it."

"They are very large rats. Over the years they have become very cunning. They have learned to leave the poison alone. Why shouldn't they? They have a whole crib of corn to choose from."

He flipped a switch as we entered the barn and a weak overhead light came on. I leaned the rifle against a post and looked around while he looked for the chairs. Surprisingly enough it was relatively tidy. Except for a narrow alleyway down the center, every available inch of space had been utilized for the storage of hay. Neat even bales that reached almost to the ceiling on either side. There was a tractor near the door, a hayrake, and two other pieces of equipment I didn't recognize. At first glance the rear wall of the building appeared to be covered with junk, and maybe it was, but it was the kind of junk a true Americana buff would have found fascinating: old saddles, bridles, hames, hand-forged bits, ancient hand tools, and an intricately carved wooden corn sheller that looked as if it might still work. Higher up were wagon wheels of varying sizes and a hand scythe that could easily have come over on the *Mayflower*.

"That's fascinating stuff," I said, as the tall thin man came toward me dragging two heavy metal chairs.

"A hundred years' accumulation. And that's only a small part of it. Most of the good things went to various museums around the area."

"Must be nice to have that kind of roots."

"My family has owned this land well over a hundred years."

I nodded toward the hay. "You run a lot of cattle?"

He shook his head. "No. I sell it. This will all be gone before Christmas."

He was leaning forward, his elbows on his knees, long bony fingers interlaced. He slid back into his chair and crossed his legs. The gesture had an air of finality about it.

"You wanted to know about Chinook."

"What did you say?" Somewhere deep in the bowels of my brain something stirred, surfaced for a fleeting second, then was gone. "What did you call him?"

He waved his hand limply. "I beg your pardon. Chinook. It was his code name. That is the only way I think of him."

"Code name?"

"Yes. We weren't supposed to know their real names. Only the code names. I only knew Warren's because I brought him into the program."

"Code name? Program? I'm afraid you've lost me somewhere."

His hand lifted again. "Yes, of course, you wouldn't know. The Titan program. Warren was a part of it. The best part, I might add."

"Titan? Isn't that a missile?"

"Yes, so it is, but that has no bearing on our Titan program. That was simply one of Dr. Burchwalder's little jokes. Titans are giants."

"Dr. Burchwalder? Giants?" I was beginning to feel like a parrot.

"Dr. Mason Burchwalder. A truly great man. A genius in his own way. I worked with him for six years."

In spite of my frustration, I felt a tiny tingle of excitement. "Doing what?"

He smiled. "It's not something you can describe in a word. It was a very complex procedure. The fascinating thing was that the results were never exactly the same. There was always that element of suspense, you see."

"What did Warren have to do with this Titan program?"

"Warren *was* the Titan program. He and a few others very like him." He paused and closed his eyes as if deep in meditation. "Warren was Level Five. Only three others achieved that distinction. Chinook and Willow and Shadow and . . ." He stopped for a moment, then clucked his tongue in exasperation. "Who was the fourth one? If only I still had my journal. But they never gave it back to me after the trial."

His eyes caught mine for a second and he stirred uneasily. "That's the only reason they caught me. I left it in Albert's car. You do know about the trial?"

"Yes," I said absently, my mind elsewhere. Chinook and Willow. Where had I heard those words? The small creature deep in my mind stretched, yawned, and rolled over and went back to sleep.

"They wanted me to destroy him, you see. But I couldn't do that. He was the only one left after Willow was killed. Dr. Burchwalder was dead by then . . . his procedure lost in the fire . . . I just couldn't do it. All of our work . . . the sacrifices, the failures. It was unthinkable to destroy what we had worked so hard to achieve. Dr. Burchwalder had given his life . . . I, six years of mine. So, I convinced them I could wipe him, restore him completely." His voice rose, lost some of its didactic quality. "I buried him instead. Oh, I knew its effectiveness, you see. We had used the technique before on some of the failures." He sighed. "But I required assistance with the machines. I chose Albert. He was competent enough, but otherwise quite barren intellectually. He was also a queer. That's why I had to . . . kill him, you see." His final words were almost apologetic.

"Dr. Mittleton . . ." I began, but he was talking again. He was rambling, reweaving the fabric of his past randomly. But sooner or later he was going to say something I understood.

"They were in a panic. That Watergate mess in Washington. It had them scared out of their wits. They began frantically to cover all their tracks. And then when the fiasco with Chinook and Willow occurred in Poland, or Hungary . . . or was it Czechoslovakia? Damn, if only they had let me keep my journal. I was never involved directly in that end of it, but I kept an account of what information came my way. A form of instinctive self-preservation, I suppose." He paused and stared musingly at the wall behind my back.

I leaped in before he could start again, "Dr. Mittleton. What do you mean by *buried*?"

He moved a long-fingered hand listlessly. "Posthypnotic suggestion, essentially. There was more to it, of course. But that is its essence."

"And you buried . . . Chinook?"

He looked annoyed. "Yes, of course, I thought you understood that. It was necessary. The only alternative was to destroy him. I told you. They wanted all traces of Titan eradicated."

"Who are they?"

"I was never sure. Some government agency. They funded us. Dr. Burchwalder handled it. Either the CIA, Army Intelligence, or the National Security

Agency. One of the three, I'm almost certain. I never knew which. It never mattered. Only the project mattered."

There was a sudden rattle of scattered raindrops on the metal roof of the barn, then almost immediately a steady drumbeat of rain.

He looked upward at the roof and nodded his head with satisfaction. "Good, we need the moisture."

"Dr. Mittleton. Exactly what was the Titan project, and how did Warren fit into it?"

He nodded and smiled, eyes squinted reflectively, small bits of blue as deep and shiny as Montana turquoise. "I brought Chinook into the program—I think I told you that. It was an accident . . . I mean it was as the result of an accident. He was driving a supply truck, more than a little drunk. He rammed a Jeep and seriously injured an officer and his driver. I treated Chinook myself. A light concussion, no more. But he was truly an amazing physical specimen. He aroused my interest immediately as a possible candidate for our program, a simple uncomplicated boy in a man's body. I interviewed him extensively before I made my proposal to Dr. Burchwalder. He was opposed in the beginning, but when he realized my enthusiasm, he relented. The real problem was Chinook himself. We got along well. He was an affable, good-natured boy who wanted to please, but I could not get him to volunteer for our program. He was interested only in women and drink and a good time." His gaze was centered on the wall again, a small indulgent smile on his lips. "Then the army came to my aid. They were going to court-martial him because of the accident and his drinking on duty. I convinced him the least he would get would be a dishonorable discharge. We promised to get the charges dropped if he would come into Titan. Eventually he did, of course. It was quite an accomplishment. He proved to be even better than Willow." He pursed his lips in a soundless whistle, then shook himself like a dog coming up out of water.

"Better at what?" I asked, irritation and frustration nibbling at me like minnows around a pair of hairy legs.

"Oh, everything actually. His capacity for expansion, growth, was far superior, for instance. Physically, there was no comparison." His eyes glittered mischievously. "That's how I chose their names. Chinook was as strong as the wind; Willow was . . . well, Willow." He stopped and frowned, then looked at me accusingly. "Chinook made one mistake, though. He said Willow was dead. But he is alive. He was here not more than six months ago. Here at this very farm. Imagine that, after more than fifteen years. He wanted to know about Chinook. How he was, where he was. Nostalgia, he said. They were the only two survivors. But I don't know . . ." His voice trailed off.

"Did you tell him?"

"His name only. And that he was from Texas. That's all I remembered about his background . . . if I only had my journal . . ."

"Were they friends, Chinook and Willow?"

He tugged at his chin reflectively. "I never really thought so. They were competitors, more or less. Friends? I never had that impression. I could have been wrong. They worked well together. They were paired at least twice before the last assignment, the one where Willow was killed . . . or supposed to have been."

"What kind of assignments?"

He shook his head. "I had nothing to do with that. Assignments came from our funding agency. But Chinook told me about the last one—" He broke off, his head cocked, listening. I heard it too, the faint sounds of a car motor, the engine racing intermittently as the tires fought for purchase on the rain-slick ground.

He glanced at his watch. "That will be Fats Williams. He buys hay for his milk cow." He walked to the big door and looked out. It was still raining, a slow steady downpour. He lifted a yellow slicker from a hook beside the door. "This won't take but a minute, Mr. Roman." He pulled the hood over his bald head. "I hope he doesn't get stuck," he muttered, and stepped out into the rain.

I could hear him over the beat of the rain, splashing through the mud, swearing as he slipped and slid. I heard the rattle of a chain on the door at the side of the barn, saw flickering light patterns across the rafters as he swung it open, and heard him grunt as he lifted the first bale. The sound of the car came closer. He grunted again and then made another sound that was more like a squeal, a squeal that was punctuated by a muted rapping, the short staccato sound of a woodpecker pounding on a hollow tree—but there were no woodpeckers, and no trees, and I was up and running before the sound had died.

He was sprawled facedown in the mud, arms outflung, his right leg bent at an awkward angle, his foot propped against a bale of hay. The car was backing away, accelerating rapidly, the front end fishtailing as the rear end fought for traction. I reached automatically for my gun, felt the emptiness, and in the same instant remembered the rifle and cursed savagely. But it was too late to go back: the car had reached the parking area in front of the house. It lurched into a ninety-degree turn onto the gravel, then came roaring out, rear tires spraying mud and rocks as it headed for the blacktop a half mile away.

I didn't have to touch him to know he was dead; the back of his head was gone and the two neat holes in his back stood out against the yellow slicker as obtrusively as roaches in a plate of vanilla ice cream.

14

The sheriff of Henderson County was a tall rangy man with tightly curled blond hair and a body that was rapidly going to fat. He had too-red lips and a babyish pouting look that women would probably find irresistible, and that I eventually found nauseating. He kept at it far too long under the circumstances. I wasn't even an actual witness to the shooting and he had one: Mittleton's sister. She had come out onto the porch when the car drove by the house and she had watched them shoot her brother.

But Sheriff Hotchkiss had himself a stranger, a private cop to boot, and he wasn't about to let go. He hurled questions at me, staring at me steely-eyed across his desk; he drank from the water bottle in the corner, staring at me steely-eyed through the glass; he stared steely-eyed out the window, then whirled to catch me off guard. I got the idea that somewhere along the line some admiring sycophant had told him he had steely eyes. His favorite seemed to be walking around me in a loose circle, steely eyes fastened on mine, occasionally nudging the gun butt of the long-slung Colt .45. Carrying a gun in a room with a suspect would have been enough to get him kicked off the force in my town.

But he let me go finally. After a written statement and an oft-repeated promise to return for the inquest, which we both knew I wasn't going to keep. There was no way he could break my story that I was an old friend of Mittleton's and had just stopped by for a friendly visit—being in the neighborhood, and all. By the time he got around to comparing notes with Mittleton's prostrate sister, I intended to be long gone.

He could have held me for seventy-two hours on suspicion alone, and I suspected the only reason he didn't was that he had called Homer Sellers as I had suggested. One thing about Homer Sellers, I thought fondly, he could always be depended on in a pinch—well, almost always.

On the way back into Evansville I stopped at a Texaco station with a phone booth at the edge of its apron. I talked the surly attendant out of twenty quarters for a five-dollar bill and called Homer.

"Goddamn, boy," he rumbled. "What're you doing back there stirring up them Yankees? You're too damn mean to turn loose in the world."

"I take it Sheriff Wyatt Earp called you?"

"Yeah, he called. Had a good notion to tell him I'd never heard of you. Do you good to spend some time in one of them Yankee jails eatin' sauerkraut and wieners."

"Much as I hate to admit it, Homer, you hit the damn nail on the head. That coma shit was just that. Stillwell was involved in some kind of government didoes. Only thing is, he doesn't know it."

"What do you mean, he doesn't know it?"

"It's been wiped out of his mind—or, I guess *buried* is the word he used. Hypnotized, posthypnotic suggestion."

He gave me the Texas version of the Bronx cheer. "Hypnotized, my ass. Nobody stays hypnotized for fourteen, fifteen years."

"He's not hypnotized now, Homer. It's posthypnotic suggestion. There's other things involved. Some kind of electronic voodoo. But it fits, Homer. That could explain his weird dreams he keeps having over and over."

"Bullshit! I have weird dreams all the time. I never been hypnotized in my life."

"Listen. This is costing me money. They got Mittleton before he got around to everything. He rambled so damn much—but he kept talking about a journal. It was involved in his trial in Greenville, California. I think maybe what we want to know is in there. He never got it back, so the police in Greenville must still have it in their evidence storage room."

"Not necessarily. Old evidence is a closed case. Probably deep-sixed it a long time ago."

"Maybe not. They'd have kept it past time for any possible appeal, anyhow. Maybe I can find out something. I don't have much choice, do I?"

"So?"

"So I'm going out there. I want you to call them and pave the way. We need that journal, Homer. I found out a lot from Mittleton, but not enough."

"Greenville, California, eh? Where's it at?"

"Hell, I don't know. You've got a map. Look it up."

"You going to California from back there?"

"As soon as I find out where it is and can get a plane out."

"Just a minute, I'm looking it up."

"Don't bother, Homer. I can—"

"Here it is. Just hold your horses a minute. Looks like about forty miles north of Los Angeles. Yeah."

"Okay. You'll call them, right?"

"I'll think on it," he said laconically. "You be careful out there in the big city. Country boy like you ain't got no business—"

The operator cut in. "Please deposit two dollars more."

I hung up and walked away from the booth grinning, wishing I could see Homer's face when the operator tried to get him to accept the overcharges at his end. The telephone was still ringing insistently when I climbed back into my car and drove away.

Dallas freeways are no slouches, and sometimes at the right time of day you can spend a lifetime on one of them during a half hour's drive; but at their worst they can't hold a candle to Los Angeles freeways for downright scary. Human nature being what it is, the folks around Dallas tend to exaggerate the speed limit a little on occasion, but five minutes into the Ventura Freeway I would have given ten-to-one odds that the idiots in Los Angeles had never heard of a speed limit.

I had slept like the dead all the way from Evansville on the plane; even during the two stops they were supposed to make. But I was still whipped, groggy from lack of sleep and jet lag, and in no condition to be playing freeway hockey with a mob of resentful nine-to-fivers being goaded beyond endurance by a swarm of doped-up kamikaze eighteen-wheeler pilots.

I told myself I could stand anything for an hour. I caught a death grip on the wheel of the little rented Chevy, picked a lane not too far from the center, and hung there, watching them streak by on each side of me, hoping the blur wouldn't make me nauseous again.

Finding Greenville might have been a problem, since there was nothing but solid city on each side of the freeway, but there was a sign on a bank high up on the side of a hill and I turned in to the next exit ramp.

The police department was housed in a small

squat stucco building two blocks off the freeway. Knowing Homer, I figured he had started at the top. So did I.

"My name is Dan Roman. I wonder if I could speak to your chief of police."

The man behind the desk was short, fat, and red-faced. He had red hair and freckles and marbled eyes. He had pink palms and sergeant's stripes on the sleeve of his tan short-sleeved shirt. He put down the magazine he had been reading. He had almost no eyebrows and it gave him an owlish look. Not wise, owlish.

"You're the guy from Texas."

"Yes. Captain Sellers called."

"That journal must be pretty important, you come all the way from Dallas for it."

I shrugged. "I wouldn't know, I'm just the carrier pigeon."

He opened the drawer in his desk and took out a clear plastic bag. There was a leatherbound notebook inside. He opened the bag and took out the journal. He riffled the pages, then looked at me and smiled thinly.

"You don't look much like his sister."

"Not a whole lot," I agreed.

"This thing was tagged that his sister would pick it up when we released it. She never showed."

"I guess not."

"We had a lot of trouble finding it," he said aggrievedly. "Had to move a lot of crap to get to it."

I started to ask him how they knew where to look, thought better of it.

"Couldn't make much sense out of this crap," he said.

"Code, maybe," I said agreeably.

He riffled again. "Bending the rules giving this thing to you, you know that, don't you?"

"Appreciate it," I said, beginning to wonder if he was angling for a payoff.

"I remember this guy, Mittleton. I was riding a black-and-white then. Asshole never would have got caught if he hadn't left this in his sweetheart's car with his name on it."

"No kidding?"

He put the book back into the bag and zip-locked the top. "Well, chief says to give this to you. It's his ass, I guess. Need for you to sign this."

He handed me the bag and pushed a slip of paper and a pen at me. I scrawled my name and gave them back.

"Thanks."

"Don't mention it, Tex," he said. He picked up his magazine and gazed at me over the top. "Have a nice day," he said.

Inside my car, I resisted an impulse to take out the journal and read it. I could see "J. Mittleton" in large enbossed letters on the outside, and I knew if I started I would be sitting there until I finished.

There was a noon flight to Dallas and I had planned on taking it, but my body had been sending me rude messages ever since I got off the plane. I decided I had pushed myself enough. I drove back to the highway and stopped at the first motel I found. I needed a drink badly, but I needed sleep more. I also needed a shower, but I flopped on the bed to rest my eyes for a moment first and that was the last thing I knew.

I was waiting for Homer when he came into his office the next morning. I was seated at his desk going over some of the passages in the journal again. I had read it through on the red-eye flight from L.A., but there were holes in the fabric, chunks missing that I hoped I might have skipped over in my first hurried reading. With what I had learned from Mittleton's rambling discourse in the barn and a considerable amount of reading between the lines, I now felt I had assimilated enough information to present a fairly accurate picture of what had occurred during Warren's "coma" years. I knew much of what had happened, why, and a certain amount of the how; what I didn't know was how it was going to help me in the present. If pressed, I could make an educated guess as to who was trying to kill Warren, but I had no idea why. And even if I was right, I hadn't the slightest idea how to go about finding him, or even who he was in the real world. I was neck-deep in the mire of my quandary when Homer came in.

"Chilly out there this morning, little buddy." He was rubbing his big hands together, his shoulders hunched forward in the thin suit coat.

"Forty degrees. Little early for this crap." I got up and moved to his visitor's chair.

"Happens sometimes," he said absently. He was standing over his desk looking at the journal. "This is it, huh?"

"That's it."

He picked it up and riffled the pages, glancing at one or two and wincing. "This guy's got lousy handwriting."

"Not too bad once you get used to his *r*'s and *w*'s."

"You already read it all, huh?"

"Some of it twice. You were right for once, big fella. Warren—as ludicrous as it seems—was an agent."

"You mean like in spy?"

"I don't know. Mittleton was involved mainly in developing Warren. He didn't have anything to do with what the government used him for. There's a couple of scraps of information about two or three of his missions. But it's incidental stuff, probably what he overheard or Warren told him. They were pretty good buddies according to Mittleton."

"Developing? You mean Mittleton was making spies?"

"No. Mittleton worked for, and I guess with, another doctor named Burchwalder. A really sharp cookie according to Mittleton. The way I understand it, this spy stuff was an offshoot, a by-product, of their real work. And it came about because they were funded by a government agency, CIA, NSA, or Army Intelligence. Mittleton wasn't sure which."

"And what was their real work?" He was watching me over the rim of his glasses.

I lit a cigarette and thought it over for a moment. "I don't know if they had a name for it. If they did, Mittleton never mentioned it either to me or in his diary. But I kind of made up my own name for it while I was reading."

He leaned back in his chair and folded his hands on his stomach, his heavy features solemn, his eyes keenly intent.

"For lack of something better, what I call it is . . . mind development."

He crashed forward in his chair and slapped the desk top. "Aw, shit! I thought you was gonna hand me something real science-fictiony, or something." He rolled his head in disgust. "Crap. That's what they're supposed to be teaching in the schools . . ."

"No. Wait. It gets better. Not exactly that kind of mind development, Homer. Maybe *development*'s not the right word. Maybe mind . . . expansion would be better."

He snorted. "Same damn thing. That's just semantics."

"Will you listen for a damn minute? I'm not talking about learning, for Christ sakes! I'm talking about expanding the functional capabilities of man's brain by mechanical, chemical, electronic, and psychological means. I'm talking about increasing the functional capability of a man's brain from the estimated ten to fifteen percent we now use to . . . sixty, seventy . . . hell, I don't know, maybe a hundred damn percent!"

A laugh had been building deep in his diaphragm as I talked; it came bubbling out and just as suddenly stopped. His face sobered.

"By God, you're serious!"

I nodded. "As serious as sin."

"That's pretty science-fictiony after all. Man, that's hard to swallow."

I shrugged. "I couldn't believe it at first, either. But I kept coming back to Warren. It takes a slightly better than average intellect to get a doctorate in mathematics, and both a bachelor's and a master's in physics in less than seven years and all at the same time. You explain that."

"Maybe he's just a late-blooming genius. Hell, look at Einstein . . ."

"Yeah, I know. Couldn't talk or some such shit until he was five. So what? I don't see any parallel here. Warren got mostly C's in high school. Anne said he had some trouble maintaining that. According to his military record he scored a little less than average on his vocational tests. Supply school—average. Then all of a sudden, after six years of very undistinguished service in the army, he becomes a great intellect? Come on, Homer."

He smiled weakly. "Yeah. It is a little hard to buy, ain't it?"

"Don't give me that dumb act. You're smart as hell and we both know it. Why this sudden obstinacy? You don't usually have a closed mind. All of a sudden you're the devil's own little advocate. Remember, you were the one started me on this track, all that talk about agents."

"Yeah," he said uncomfortably. "But we're talking something different. We're talking about a . . . a . . . an intellectual Frankenstein."

I nodded. "Maybe more than you think," I said grimly. "Maybe the real thing too."

"What's that mean?"

"This whole Titan project. They had a total of twenty-five volunteers—they called them volunteers. I wonder how many were recruited like Warren. Given what he thought was the lesser of two evils. They were going to court-martial him. He was almost sure to get a dishonorable out of it at least. Mittleton sucked him into the program by having the charges dropped. At any rate, according to Mittleton's journal, out of the twenty-five who went into the program, at the end of 1973 Warren was the only 'viable' one remaining. His word, *viable.* There was one other, but at the time they thought he was dead. His name was Willow—code name. Only four out of the twenty-five achieved Level Five—"

"What the hell is that?"

"Achievement designator of some sort. Level Five was the epitome of their developmental yardstick. Mittleton called the others misfits. Euphemism for failures, I imagine. The poor bastards probably ended up in some fruitcake farm somewhere—or dead. I know the other two in Level Five were killed. He mentions it in his journal. Some assignment by their control agency."

Homer unwrapped a cigar without taking his eyes away from my face. "What did you mean a while ago when you said 'the real thing'?"

"It seems there were some . . . undesirable side effects. I'm not sure exactly. He referred to it as a . . . a misalignment of spirit." I smiled ruefully and held up my hands at his expression.

"Don't look at me like that. They're his words, not mine. He was a great one for euphemisms."

"What do you think he meant?"

"I'm not sure, Homer. What's the spirit? Soul? Conscience? What? Smart men have argued that one for centuries." I lit a cigarette and went on slowly. "I have a theory, a feeling about what he meant. I think that maybe while they were expanding these people's intellects, that maybe they took something away. Maybe they went too far. Maybe there has to be a balance . . . a kind of compensating factor involved. Kinda like adding water to good scotch: you get more volume, but you reduce the quality of what's already there."

"All this is in the diary?"

"Some of it. Some he told me. I just didn't know at the time what the hell he was talking about. In view of what I know now, most of what he said makes sense."

"And you really believe Warren doesn't remember any of it? That this guy hypnotized it out of him?"

"Yes. Not exactly that, but it comes close. Mittleton told me himself that he buried Chinook—that's Warren's code name—and I later decided that *buried* means hypnotized. Another one of his damn euphemisms. Hypnotic block, hypnotic amnesia. Warren remembers it all, it's just been buried under a layer of hypnotic control. And since the controller is dead, it might never be removed. It's like a certain portion of his memory is sealed off, a small room that's under lock and key. If you don't have the key you can't unlock the door. Maybe it could be done by an expert hypnotist, but it would probably take a long time. Warren's doctor, an analyst named Carleton, tried to penetrate the two years he was supposed to be in a coma. I suppose, to find out if Warren remembered anything at all. But Warren said each time they approached, from either direction, that he just woke up. Bingo. Just like that, he would come out of it."

"How come you know so much about hypnotism all of a sudden?"

I smiled sheepishly. "I bought a book before I left L.A. It's a fascinating subject once you get past all the bullshit you've heard about it over the years."

"Like what?"

"Like you can't get a hypnotized person to harm someone if they weren't homicidally inclined in the first place. That's baloney. A lot depends on the hypnotist. If he's completely in control he can make you do anything—even kill yourself."

He shook his head dogmatically. "I don't believe that."

"Just don't bet your life on it. It's true. It's been proven, documented. Sometimes a little misdirection may be necessary."

"Like what?"

"If I wanted you to kill someone, I'd tell you, in a hypnotic state, that he was . . . say, a spy, and that he was going to kill you. You'd do it in a second."

We sat looking at each other, smoking in silence. After a while he screwed his face into a frown.

"Something here I don't understand. Accepting that they could do what you say they could, why would they want to . . . to bury Warren's memory?"

"Fear. Mittleton told me the agency suddenly got cold feet, wanted Chinook destroyed one way or another. Wanted his brain wiped—restored, I guess he meant. But according to his journal, all their attempts at restoring someone to their original state failed completely. They became misfits. Warren was their greatest success. He couldn't bear to see him either killed or made into a vegetable. So he blocked his memory. It was evidently a combination of posthypnotic amnesia and some type of electronic stimulation or repression. I don't know. But he needed assistance. Someone on the electronic equipment, he said. That was Albert, the homosexual he killed years later to keep him quiet about what he had done. Who knows? Maybe Albert had grown tired of their relationship and threatened to expose him. Or maybe it was blackmail. Mittleton evidently reported to the agency that he had taken care of Warren as they had requested. Then the authorities picked him up for Albert's murder and sent his butt to prison. He's only been out eight or nine months."

"So where does all this leave us? We still don't have a clue on who's trying to kill Warren."

"I think we do," I said.

He cocked his head. "Oh, yeah. I must have missed something."

"No. It's something I haven't told you. Willow. I think it has to be. Mittleton said Willow came to see him about six months ago. He wanted to know about Warren, his address. Mittleton didn't know anything except Warren's name and that he was originally from Texas. The attacks started about two and a half months ago. That would give Willow three and a half months to locate Warren. Enough time if he had the money to do it right."

"There's some holes in that. Why did he wait all these years if he wanted him dead?"

"I don't know. I do know that Chinook and Willow went on a mission, the last mission before the whole thing blew up, and Chinook came back and told Mittleton that Willow was dead. Something must have happened on that mission. Why he's waited so long . . ." I shrugged. "There could be a lot of explanations for that."

"You think this Willow killed Mittleton?"

"Yes."

"Don't make sense either. Why didn't he do it six months ago? After he got his information?"

"I don't know that either, dammit. I don't have a crystal ball, Homer. But I think it makes a lot of sense, and there could be logical explanations for your holes."

"Okay. Who is this guy Willow?"

"That's a biggie."

"It's not in the diary?"

"No. Mittleton didn't know his name. Warren happened to be the only one he knew. Only because he brought him into the program. Evidently Burchwalder was the only one who knew all the names. He died in some kind of fire, and his records went with him."

"So how in holy hell do we find out?"

"Charles Chapman."

His head snapped upward and he stared at me in disgust. "Who in hell is Charles Chapman? Dammit, Dan, you keep coming up with these names from out of . . ."

"From out of the journal," I said, grinning.

"Okay." He sighed. "What's his line?"

"I'm not sure. He's mentioned three times in the journal. I know, because I went back and counted. Twice it was in relation to progress reports on their program. That was in 1971. The last time was mid-1973. A simple notation: 'C. Chapman upset over Poland failure—bastard.' "

"That's all?"

"Yes. Mittleton said Chinook's last mission was in one of the Iron Curtain countries—he thought Poland, but he couldn't remember."

"So?"

"So, I think Chapman was the agency control. They

had to have someone. Normally he dealt with Burchwalder, but maybe he contacted Mittleton when Burchwalder was gone."

"Hell of a lot of maybe."

"You got anything better?"

He grunted.

I picked up the journal and walked to the door.

"You get that name, Homer? Charles Chapman."

He didn't answer. His head was sunk onto his chest, his face empty of emotion: classic pose of deep meditation. He spoke without raising his head. "Dan, you really believe all this shit—I mean about the mind-expanding thing?"

"Yeah, Homer, I do. I believe it's the only explanation for Warren. You can't hide the kind of mind he has for so many years."

"That business about the . . . souls? You believe that, too?"

I shrugged. "He's different. I know that much." I lit another cigarette and told him about the snake and the bird in my backyard.

"It's a small thing, but in its own way a terrifying thing. I saw his face. It was empty. No expression of any kind, except maybe curiosity. He could have stopped it, but I don't think it even occurred to him. I think they raped his mind, Homer. Whatever they did with their drugs, their electronic probes, their hypnotic surgery, I think they cleaned him out. Maybe they gave him a superintellect, but I think they robbed him of most human emotions in the process. Mittleton said the results were a little different each time. That's one reason he was so fascinated with the work. Maybe it's nature's way of telling us to lay off, to stay out of the bailiwick. I don't know. But I do know that Warren exists on a very rudimentary level emotionally. I think he gives lip service to basic emotions like affection, compassion, empathy, but I don't think he really feels anything."

"You make him sound pretty hopeless."

"I think he's a loaded gun. I damn near found the trigger here in your office the other day. I was prodding him; I pushed a little too far. He almost killed me. I mean in seconds, Homer. He knows the ways, there's no doubt about that. But he doesn't know he knows until something happens, something that penetrates the layer of gook in his brain. I believe that's what his weird dreams are all about. I think it's his subconscious, his memory trying to break out. It can't fight the conscious-level control, so it tries to sneak out when he's more or less defenseless. His dreams have more continuity than any I've ever had." I moved to the door again. "Let me know what you find out on Chapman, will you?"

"You gonna be home?"

"Probably in a couple of hours. I'm going to give that guy Brody one more shot."

"Brody?"

"The guy with the motorcycle. The one who ran off with the old man's daughter. I'm hitting that a little every chance I get, but it's about petered out. I don't think she has any intentions of coming back. But I kinda like the old geezer."

"Yeah." He grunted disinterestedly, reaching for the telephone.

"Okay, I'm going. I can take a hint."

/ 15 /

The drapes were open but there was no answer at the Brody apartment. I was turning away when the door in the next apartment opened. A tousled head poked around the doorjamb and a small pert female face regarded me with annoyance.

"You might as well stop leaning on that bell, mister. They've moved."

"Sorry if I disturbed you. You have any idea where they moved to?"

"Back East somewhere."

"The young lady went with him, I suppose."

"You mean his wife, Betty? Sure. What else?"

"Oh, they got married?"

Perplexity replaced the annoyance. "They've been married for two years. She's four months pregnant." Her frown came back. "I saw you here the other day. Aren't you a friend of theirs?"

"Not as much as I thought," I said.

The frown smoothed out into a blank expression of indifference. "Well, they're gone." She terminated the conversation by abruptly closing the door.

I tried to sort it out in my mind on the way home, but the sieve kept getting clogged. A married junkie who hustled older women for money, that was something of a twist. Not unknown, but unusual. An understanding wife? Or another addict like himself? The quick glance I had at her that day hadn't told me a thing, except that she looked young and fresh. But that didn't mean much. She could be into heavy stuff right along with him. Maybe he brought his women home while she visited with friends—or maybe she didn't bother leaving. That had been known to happen also. What's this damn world coming to? I wondered.

At home I dug out the local telephone book. There were three Bascombs listed, but only one in Sunset Gardens. I sat down at the telephone with a can of beer and a cigarette. I dreaded making the call, but there was no use delaying the inevitable. I had known from the beginning that nothing was going to come of it, and I had tried to tell the old man that, hadn't I? But the stubborn old coot wouldn't listen. Okay, so I wasn't going to take his money. I had known that from the start also, but it didn't make it a damn bit easier. But letting the old man fret and hope wasn't going to help matters either.

I drank some of my beer and picked up the receiver and dialed.

"Hello." The voice sounded garbled, drugged from sleep.

"Could I speak to Mr. Whitecomb, please?"

There was a strangled sound that could have been a choked-off yawn.

"Why are you doing this?" The voice was alert now, filled with quiet outrage.

"I don't understand. I—"

"This is sick! Look, the man is dead, why won't you let him rest in peace?"

I was stunned, tiny ripples of shock vibrated along the surface of my skin.

"I didn't—" But the man had hung up.

I replaced the receiver slowly. Dead? I backtracked to when I had seen him last. Almost three days now. I tried to remember if he had looked different, sicker.

Maybe the two days he had talked about were for a visit to a hospital. Maybe . . . but what the hell was the point of conjecturing? He was dead; that ended it for me. I wondered what funeral home had his body, wondered if maybe I should send flowers. I wished Susie was home. She knew how to handle things like this, what to say, do. I never had.

I carried my beer into the den, tasted it, then got up and poured it into the sink. I slopped scotch into a water glass and slumped in my chair, morosely pondering the futility of it all. If what the old man had was all there was at the end, then why bother? Artificial teeth, weak knees, and a shrunken ass; then sudden death through no fault of his own. That was the final indignity: not to have any say in when or how. Maybe that old guy in *Soylent Green* had the answer: a peaceful, painless passing in an atmosphere of your own choosing, a time of your own choosing. Who knew better when it was time? Certainly not some doctor with a golf ball for a heart and a country club conscience.

The phone rang and I leaped about a foot in the air; thinking about death always did make me jumpy. I let it ring, but when it stopped and started in again, I straggled into the kitchen and answered it.

"Hi, Danny!"

If I hadn't known her so well, I would have believed her voice and thought she was outlandishly happy, but somehow it rang falsely in my ears.

"Hi, Susie. How you doing?"

"Terrific, Danny! Are you doing all right?"

"Sure. I'm fine as peach fuzz."

"Did you notice I was by there?" There was a puzzling hesitancy in her tone.

"No. When was this?"

"Yesterday. I—I picked up the . . . the rest of my clothes, Danny."

"Oh?" I said it quietly, in spite of the sudden knot in my throat.

"Yes. I left you a . . . a note. You didn't see it?"

"No."

"It's . . . it's on the telephone recorder in the bedroom."

There was a moment of silence, an awful dead silence while I fumbled for something light and airy to say. Nothing came.

"I have to go now, Danny. I—I'll see you."

"Sure, kitten," I said. "I'll see you."

Dear Danny:

I came by to pick up the rest of my clothes. Tom and Marsha came with me so don't be mad. I called Captain Sellers and he told me you were in California on business, and I guess it's just as well you're not here right now. It would be so much harder to tell you this in person. I want to stay away for a while, Danny. I have to think things out. Please don't misunderstand me. I don't need to make up my mind about whether I love you or not. I know that already. Only too well. What I have to decide, Danny, is whether I can make you happy, and myself, when I don't know if I can handle what you do. I suppose I'm a coward. I like a quiet peaceful life and I don't know if you and I could have that.

I'm miserable away from you, but it's much easier to think. What we do will be your life as well as mine, so please do some thinking of your own. Take care, my darling, and please understand why this is necessary. And please don't be mad at me.

I love you,
Susan

* * *

"Charles Lucus Chapman," Homer intoned. "United States Army, retired. Full colonel. Two hitches in 'Nam as a line officer. Shoe box full of medals, including the Silver Star. Last sixteen years assigned to Army Intelligence. I guess that answers your question about which agency."

"It sure does. You said retired. Not in Florida, I hope.'"

He rumbled out a laugh. "You lucked out on this one, boy. Lives right here . . . well, not right here, but close enough. Lives up at Lawrence. Probably one of the new subdivisions by the sound of it."

"That's a break. I've had my fill of foreign countries for a while."

He laughed again. "You mean anywhere outside of Texas?"

"Yeah. How long has he been retired, Homer?"

"Last year. Had his thirty. Looks like he's sixty-two."

"Nothing in there about the Titan—naw, there wouldn't be."

"He served two years on Guam, three in Germany, and the rest of the sixteen in California. Detached duty. You know what that means?"

"No. Probably that he wasn't stationed on an army base. I don't know much about the army. I was a flying man, myself."

"Yeah," he said sourly. "Up above it all, huh?"

"Not quite. I flew helicopters, not jets. We had to go down in some tacky places sometimes."

"Sometimes when I've got a couple of days I'll let you tell me about it—again."

I laughed. "You ain't got no patriotic loyalty, Homer. I was over there getting my ass shot off, and you was—"

"Yeah, I know. I was over here beating up on flower

children and hippies and stomping me a few protesters and card burners."

"I can't help it because you had flat feet. Come to think of it, that's probably why they made you a cop."

"You was a whole lot funnier last year. Look, I'd really like to sit here and be your whipping boy all day, but I got work to do."

"Sure, Homer. Look, old buddy, I appreciate this."

"Yeah," he growled, and hung up.

He was a little miffed and was letting me know it. As usual, I had jabbed him a little harder than I intended. There weren't many things he was touchy about, but being rejected by all three branches of the military was one of them. He had been a sergeant when I joined the Midway City Police Department, a happy carefree bachelor, sloppy in his personal habits, but a perfectionist and something of an old mother hen when it came to his job. Midway City had been a very small city then, the entire force totaling not more than fifteen people. Out of a lack of proper equipment, we had been forced to use a lot of unorthodox methods and to fly a lot by the seat of our pants. Homer and another sergeant, Clay Hollister, now the chief of police, had taught us well. As the city grew so did the department, and Homer had risen to captain, and I had been a lieutenant in Homicide when I left the force for good. Homer had been my captain as well as my best friend, and the relationship had grown rather than deteriorated after I quit.

I dug through a stack of maps and found one for Lawrence before I realized that Homer hadn't given me Chapman's address. I sighed and dialed the phone.

"Midway City Police, Captain Sellers's office."

"Mitzi, without disturbing the bear too much, could you get me the address of the guy he was calling me about a few minutes ago? Charles Chapman."

She giggled. "Hold on."

She was back a moment later. She giggled again. "Here you are, Dan. He just growled when I said who it was. Something about always doing your damn work."

"Sounds right."

"It's 121 Starr Drive, Dan. Lawrence, Texas. Okay?"

"You bet, Mitzi. Thanks, hon."

"Any time."

I put down the pen and fixed me another scotch. I sat down at the kitchen window and looked out into the gray day. It was mid-afternoon and my resident squirrels were nowhere to be seen. Probably too much sense to be out on a day like this. It was a heavily overcast day, thick dark clouds glowering on the horizon like a dirty old gray blanket. There was enough moisture in the air that everything was dripping, but not enough to call it rain. Rowdy trotted down to the corner, gave my yard a casual scrutiny, and trotted away again bored. No more than me, I thought, feeling as gray and as empty as the sky. Without Susie, the house had become a prison, cold and dark and lonely, and for the first time in many years, I felt totally abandoned and alone. I finished the scotch, went for another, brought the bottle back with me. A good drunk might help. Why the hell not? Nobody gave a damn anyway. I smiled a little at my childish self-pity, a moment later feeling sorry for myself again. I was suddenly overwhelmed by the enormity of the chasm Susie's departure had left in my life. I contemplated the dreary days ahead and the endless nights, and toasted my fearlessness in the face of such dire adversity. I drank a toast to an old man with weak knees and kindly eyes, and another to his daughter I had never found; I drank a toast to a junkie and his pregnant wife and wished them well; I drank a toast to a tall thin man with turquoise eyes who had died without reason; I drank a toast to the refrigerator and sink, and another to Rowdy and the squirrels. And when I ran out of toasts, I drank straight from the bottle, and next to the last thing I remember was standing and watching with amazement while the kitchen tile came flapping up off the floor and smacked me in the face; the very last thing a pool of vomit laced with blood, and something wet and salty that stung my eyes and tasted suspiciously like tears.

Unlike many small towns that had become moribund with the advent of the great population shift to the urban centers, Lawrence, Texas, had grown steadily in the late sixties and seventies. A great deal of its popularity as a bedroom community stemmed from its location. Within easy commuting distance of both Dallas and Fort Worth, it still managed to maintain some semblance of its former easygoing small-town character. Bordered on the north by Lawrence Lake and on the south by Interstate 35, it boasted both diversified recreation and speedy access.

Charles Chapman's home was located in a subdivision with the somewhat fanciful name of Comanche Crossing. It was a nice enough house. Probably something over a hundred thousand dollars in today's market. A three-bedroom brick, it had an attached front garage that somehow destroyed the desired Spanish effect of the small walled entrance courtyard of lava stone, white gravel, and cactus.

I rang a bell that touched off the chorus notes of a familiar marching song. The door popped open almost immediately and I heard the sweet young voice before I saw the sweet young face. "Hi, honey!"

The face followed hard behind the voice and I was treated to one quick glimpse of a lovely sanguine face a brief second before a tanned hand was slapped over an open mouth.

"Ohmigod!"

"Hi," I said.

"Oh," she said. "I thought you were my boyfriend. He wears a jacket just like that."

"I'll be more than happy to stand in for him," I said gallantly.

She was giggling helplessly, her hand back over her mouth, and she was young enough and pretty enough to get away with it.

"Oh, I'm so sorry!"

"Don't be, I don't usually get called anything near that nice."

"Who is it, Sharon?" The male voice was close behind her, and Sharon backed away from the door still convulsed, giving way to a tall sturdy man with a neatly trimmed Orson Welles beard and almost no hair.

"Can I help you?" he said, his tone noncommittal, but his level gray eyes telling me I had better not be a peddler.

"Mr. Chapman?"

"Yes."

"My name is Dan Roman, sir. I wonder if I might talk to you for a few minutes?"

"That depends," he said, his lips working into a small smile. It was a faintly condescending smile, but not abrasive enough to take offense at.

"I'm a private investigator, Mr. Chapman. I'm making inquiries on behalf of a gentleman named Warren Stillwell." I had always wanted to say that, ever since I heard it in an English movie.

Nothing moved in his face; maybe his smile was a trifle wider. "Warren Stillwell? I don't believe I know the gentleman."

"Greenville, California, sir. Dr. Burchwalder. Does that ring a bell?"

The smile was becoming strained. "Yes. I was stationed at Greenville. And, yes, I knew Dr. Burchwalder."

"Perhaps you might remember Stillwell better under his code name: Chinook."

There was a twitch in the soft dark tissue under his left eye; nothing else moved.

He nodded. "Who are you, Mr. Roman? How do you know about Chinook?"

"I told you, Colonel Chapman, I'm a private investigator. Chinook is my client."

"How does that involve me?"

"It may take a while to explain, sir."

"All right." He stepped back and held the door open. "I wonder if I could see your identification, Mr. Roman?"

"Of course."

He read my ID card as he led me across a short entry hall into a large airy room that was probably similar to a million other family rooms in the Metroplex area. The good life, Texas style: a large brick fireplace that used up more than half of one wall; a wet bar canted across one corner, complete with back-bar mirrors and cabinets to store the booze; a large picture window and a sliding door. And to give it that homey touch, two large ceiling fans twirling lazily; the very latest in fad-fashion.

He gave me back my card. "Something to drink, Mr. Roman?"

"Scotch would be fine, sir." He had the damn bar, might as well let him use it.

For such a large, obviously expensive house the room was sparsely furnished. One small sofa with matching love seat and chair, one plastic recliner and no television that I could see. Two end tables with lamps that matched and an ottoman in front of the recliner that didn't, did little to offset the barnlike quality of the room.

"Here you are, Mr. Roman. Please have a seat."

I chose one end of the couch near an end table. He turned the recliner around to face me.

"Chinook. It's been a long time since I've heard that name. I'm very surprised, Mr. Roman, that you know it."

"Dr. Mittleton, John Mittleton. Do you remember him?"

"Yes. He was second in command of the Titan program. Arrested for murder some years later and sent to prison, I believe. Some sort of homosexual thing as I remember."

"Yes. He was released eight or nine months ago. He was killed less than a week ago."

"That's too bad," he said politely, as if I'd just told him I had to have a tooth pulled. His gray eyes gazed back at me calmly.

"Did you also know a man named Willow?"

"Willow." He nodded and took a sip of what looked like bourbon. "Yes, Willow was another of Burchwalder's patients." He shook his head and clucked softly. "Very sad case. I seem to remember that he finally managed to do away with himself."

"You mean he committed suicide?"

"Yes. Hanged himself as I recall. But then they were all suicidal. That, of course, was one of the primary reasons for their being there."

I stared at him, feeling a fine mist of perspiration oozing out onto my forehead.

"I'm not sure we're talking about the same thing, Colonel. The people I'm talking about were volunteers in an experimental program called the Titan Project."

"Of course." He drank some more of his bourbon and watched me without expression. He had very pale skin, exceptionally fine for a man, like the belly of a channel catfish. He pushed back to the first position on the recliner and propped his booted feet on the footrest.

"Although," he said musingly, "I don't think the word *volunteer* is quite correct. These men were all certified psychopaths. I think *committed* would be a more appropriate word."

I could feel the skin on my face drawing hot and tight. "What exactly was the Titan Project, Colonel?"

His eyebrows arched. "Oh, I thought you knew."

"So did I. Obviously I don't. So tell me please."

He rolled the glass of amber liquid between his fingers. "I don't think I can put a specific name to it. Basically it was an experimental program organized and headed by Dr. Burchwalder and funded by the U.S. Army. Its main purpose, of course, was aimed at the possible cure or remission of psychopathic disorders suffered by U.S. Army personnel. Dr. Burchwalder had developed a course of treatment that was considered to be the most advanced in the field."

"I see," I said, returning his bland smile. "And was Dr. Burchwalder's treatment successful?"

He shrugged. "I can't possibly quote you numbers on his percentage of success. I think, if memory serves me, that it was, as a matter of fact, rather low."

"Do you recall, Colonel, what the level of security clearance was on the project?"

He waved one hand airily. "I don't recall offhand, no, but I would think rather low. Confidential, if that."

"And yet everyone and everything about the project had code names. Doesn't that seem odd?"

"Not at all. Everything in the army has a code name. Particularly anything connected with

Intelligence. They thrive on it." He laughed indulgently.

"Then you're saying the Titan Project was nothing more than a medical research program aimed at a particular type of psychosis, or psychopathic behavior?"

"Essentially that's it. Of course in the army there are never absolutes." He nodded for emphasis. "There may have been a schizophrenic or two who slipped in by mistake." His laugh this time was heartier, with a trace of contempt. I was proving to be a very unworthy adversary.

I laughed with him, leaned back in my seat, and lit a cigarette. I crossed my legs and looked at him . . . and looked at him, and let the seconds tick away. The silence grew and he returned my look with placid equanimity. He wasn't buying; he had been down this road before, and he was finding me amusing. I let it draw out a minute longer, until I had finished my cigarette. There was no ashtray.

I smiled at him and stubbed the cigarette on top of the end table to my left. Nothing changed in his face, not an eyelash, not a muscle moved. I mashed the cigarette carefully, working the hot ash into the wood.

"You're lying to me, Colonel," I said conversationally. "You're lying like hell, and you're sitting there right now with your insides tight wondering how much I know, wondering how far I'll go to make you tell me the rest." I got up and moved to the love seat beside the other end table. I lit another cigarette.

"You have marvelous control. As good as I've ever seen. They probably used to call you the Iron Man. The only trouble with that is, it makes me want to find out what it takes to break it. Brings out the competitiveness in me, you might say." I smiled and knocked ashes on the carpet.

I waited for him to answer, then after a moment, I went on. "I know it all, Colonel. All except for one thing. One small thing actually. If you don't mind, I won't tell you what that one thing is right at this moment. It adds a bit of suspense, you see."

I took a final drag from the cigarette and mashed it on top of the table. "There," I said. I smiled at him, brushed my fingertips, and leaned back.

"Project Titan. Initiated sometime during the mid-sixties, brainchild of Dr. Mason Burchwalder, funded by the U.S. Army, Intelligence Divison. You were the control officer—at least during the time I'm interested in. The purpose of Project Titan? To create, by chemical, electronic, and psychological means, a superintellect—no, *create* is not the correct word—Dr. Burchwalder did not create anything. He was attempting to expand the existing intellectual potential of the human brain to its highest limits. I have no way of knowing what Dr. Burchwalder's motives were. I assume scientific curiosity, possibly an honest desire to advance science, to help man achieve his highest potential. At this point, it doesn't really matter, does it?"

He continued to watch me over the rim of his glass, as still as stone, unblinking, a calculating, clinical scrutiny; the way an old-time gunfighter might have sized up a potential opponent. There was something there, a gleam that could have been intense anger or building fear. I became aware of the low throbbing beat of rock music somewhere in the house.

"Shall I go on, Colonel?"

I lit another cigarette.

"I have no illusions regarding your interest in Project Titan, Colonel. Chinook and Willow and Shadow and—how many others, Colonel? How many of the misfits from the lower levels were you able to utilize? Or were they throwaways? Kamikaze operations that posed no risks because beyond the immediate imperatives of their missions they were blank canvas, unreadable, expendable." I puffed on the cigarette until it was a tiny blazing ember. I leaned forward and laid it on the edge of the pecan coffee table in front of me, the coal an eighth of an inch from the wood. I leaned back and smiled at him through the thin wavering column of rising smoke. I produced a new pack of cigarettes from my pocket; I stripped the cellophane and let it drift to the floor; I tore off the small section of foil and tapped out another cigarette; I lit it.

"Level Five. Chinook, Willow, Shadow, and Mirage. Shadow and Mirage killed in Laos. Chinook and Willow sent into Poland—only Chinook returned. What happened on that mission, Colonel?" I followed his eyes to the smoldering cigarette on the table; the fire was into the wood.

He raised his eyes and stared at me; I leaned forward and carefully stubbed the cigarette in the center of the coffee table. I leaned back and lit another.

He expelled his breath through his teeth, a faint hissing sound like the susurrus of car tires on a wet street.

"Please." It was almost a whisper, a painful declaration of defeat, submission.

"Then tell me," I said brutally.

"You are a crude man, Mr. Roman."

"But effective." I lifted the still-burning cigarette from the table, leaving a half-inch charred groove at the edge. I crushed the fire between my fingers. It hurt like hell. The one in my mouth I stubbed against the edge of my heel and dropped the butt into my pocket.

"Colonel?"

"All I have is my retirement pension. I have a wife, and a daughter still in high school." He let his eyes travel around the big room. "I have a mortgage you wouldn't believe. I have developed a heart murmur and cannot work, my wife is a semiinvalid, and my daughter is pregnant. I served my country well for thirty-two years and I have a pension that grows smaller each month. If they find out I have talked about classified information, I won't even have that."

"They can't touch your pension."

"They can do anything they want."

"The world is a hard place, Colonel. You came into it naked and squalling and nobody promised it was going to be easy."

"You're asking me to risk everything I have. For what?"

"A man's life."

"Chinook's?" His eyebrows lifted sardonically. "Chinook is a monster."

"If he is, you had a hand in making him that way. Now you're going to help undo what you've done."

"I don't think so," he said softly. "I'm sixty-two and I can't fight you. I can't afford to replace the tables you've ruined, but I can have them repaired. You won't kill me no matter how tough you pretend to be. It's better than the alternative."

I smiled wolfishly. "Colonel, you don't have an alternative. I know enough to make them think you talked your head off. I know more than enough to bring the whole stinking Titan Project out into the fresh air, and you, pal, are my source."

All the fight went out of him; like a slowly deflating balloon he seemed to shrink. But I had to admire his control. Only a brief flash of a tiny flame deep in his eyes reflecting what must have been happening inside him.

"What was it you wanted to know?" It was an affable, almost friendly question in a conversational tone. He might well have been replying to a request for directions.

"I want to know what happened in Poland."

"All I know is what Chinook told me when I debriefed him. Willow went out of control and exceeded the . . . dimensions of their objective."

"What was their objective?"

"Why is it necessary that you know that?"

"It's necessary."

"There was a visitor in Poland, a high-ranking member of the Communist Party in Moscow. A member of the Politburo. He and his family were visiting the second in command of the Communist Party in Poland. He received a directive to . . . expel him."

"You mean kill him?"

He shrugged. "Chinook and Willow drew the assignment. A plan was drawn. Simple, direct, a relatively easy assignment for men of Chinook and Willow's caliber. They were dropped at night near the Polish official's summer home: a small rural community not far from Warsaw. A few guards, but that posed no great problems. It went like clockwork, exactly as planned. Willow was to do the actual elimination, Chinook to provide assistance and maintain rearguard action. But Willow got caught up in it, went rogue, killed everyone in the building with his knife—everyone except one. He was raping her when Chinook found him." He paused. "Chinook wouldn't say what happened, but he came back alone. My guess was he killed him." He paused again, and smiled thinly. "Not out of humanitarian considerations, as one might think, but because Willow had destroyed the integrity of their assignment, placed the success of their escape in jeopardy. They had lost valuable time. A change of guard was due. Chinook barely got out in time. The hue and cry was enormous, much more than if only the visiting official had been killed. That kind of thing was a fact of life in the Iron Curtain countries. What's one more fat-cat official more or less? But an entire family of six plus their host and hostess and one or two children of their own? That's another matter entirely. Willow committed the cardinal crime of the assassin: he regressed into impulse killing."

"But Willow wasn't killed. Mittleton saw him six months ago."

He shrugged eloquently. "He was a very resourceful man. Who can say now what happened?"

"Willow can."

He smiled faintly. "Yes, I suppose he can. Why don't you ask him?" His eyes gleamed mockingly.

"That's the other thing I don't know. Who is Willow, Colonel?"

"I can tell you his name, but that probably won't help you. I don't imagine he goes by that now."

"What?"

"Peter Strobow."

"Describe him."

"About as tall as you. Not as heavy. Wiry build, muscular, but long flat muscles rather than bulging. Black hair, a lot of it, thick, but fine. Exceptionally fast, liked the knife versus guns. Black belt in karate, and master of at least two more of the oriental martial arts."

"How about his voice?"

"Soft, as I recall. No perceptible regional accent. Something like one hears from native Californians."

"Would you describe it as smooth, almost silky?"

He looked amused. "I suppose you could, yes."

"I think I've talked to him." I said. "Twice."

His eyebrows lifted inquisitively, but he didn't speak.

"How did his intellect compare with Chinook's?"

"His final exam, so to speak, consisted of reading the Bible, both Old and New Testaments. He could quote them, chapter, page, and verse."

"Total recall. That's not a measure of intellect."

"It is when you can advance infallible arguments both for and against your subject, present constructive comprehensive analysis of all or any part of the material in question."

"You called Chinook a monster. Do you consider Willow one as well?"

"Yes. In a somewhat different way. They were freaks, both of them. All of the Level Five graduates were soulless freaks."

"You used them."

"They made excellent agents. Perhaps the best we've ever had or ever will again. Totally resourceful, absolutely fearless. They could withstand tremendous levels of pain simply by blocking it out with their minds. Their logical perceptions were flawless, their situation analysis quotient incredible. Their absorption rate was seemingly endless. Chinook could speak five languages at the time he was restored. Their most valuable trait, of course, was their complete lack of . . . conscience, I suppose you would call it."

"By restored, you mean brought back to their original condition?"

Something stirred briefly in his eyes, a flare of something not unlike pain.

"According to Burchwalder, that was theoretically possible. But I saw some of his . . . misfits. *Retards* would be a complimentary word for them. But Burchwalder considered the restoration technique a success. Just like his original mind-expansion subjects. He considered them a howling success also. He simply closed his eyes to the fact that in giving them what he considered to be a priceless gift of mental superiority he had robbed them of all benevolence, turned them into emotional eunuchs."

"And yet you used them," I repeated sourly. "You provided funds for his research."

"It was my job," he said tonelessly, his face blank.

"That's what they said at Auschwitz and Buchenwald."

I crossed my legs and reached automatically for a cigarette, then let my hand drop. "Chinook," I said. "Mittleton didn't attempt to restore him. He blocked his memory instead. The entire episode. He thinks he was in a coma during those two years."

He nodded. "I'm not surprised. Mittleton was as much a fanatic as Burchwalder. It was a mistake trusting him. But that's hindsight. If he's dead, it really doesn't matter much. You'll never be able to unlock Chinook's hypnotic block."

"Nobody's trying," I said dryly. "I'm just trying to save his damn life."

He smiled thinly. "If Willow's after him, he'll get him eventually." The smile grew even thinner, hard. "Believe me, that would be a blessing."

"Maybe so," I said. "But he's got a sister. A nice lady who almost got in the way once. She loves him and that's good enough for me. And like you said, Colonel, that's my job."

"I hope it's not your last." He appeared honestly amused.

I took out my billfold and extracted three hundred-dollar bills. I laid them on the coffee table. "This should restore your tables. I'm sorry about that."

He nodded unconcernedly, but it was easy to see the relief. "It doesn't matter."

I stood up and crossed to the doorway. "Don't

bother, Colonel, I can find my way out." I cleared my throat. "Thanks for the drink, and you don't have to worry about your pension. Not from me. And I'm sorry about your tables."

"Don't mention it," he said. "We all do what we have to do."

/ 16 /

"Hi, Dan," she said, her face radiant. I stood up and went around the desk and she kissed me almost shyly. I hugged her briefly, awkwardly, and patted her shoulder.

"I'm sorry I haven't been by to see you sooner, but I've been pretty busy."

"Yes, Captain Sellers has been telling me about your trips to Indiana and California. I'll say you've been busy."

I went back to Homer's chair and she sat down in front of the desk.

"How have they been treating you?"

"Fine." She patted her stomach and smiled. "They let us order our meals from outside and I've been eating too much. Getting fat."

"Looks good on you."

She grimaced prettily. "I look like a cow."

I grinned. "You're fishing is what you're doing."

"I am not. I look terrible when I put on too much weight."

"You're luscious and you know it."

She blushed and looked down. She crossed her legs

and picked imaginary lint from the black pants. She raised her head and wet her lips. "Have you . . . found out anything?"

"A lot," I said soberly. "But not the one thing that's most crucial. I know who's after your brother, but it doesn't help much because I don't know where to look for him or really what he looks like if I found him." I shifted uneasily and fumbled with Homer's letter opener. "There's something you have to know, Anne. About your brother . . . there was no coma."

"What?" She stared at me incredulously. "What are you saying, Dan? Of course there was! He had some medical papers . . ."

"It doesn't matter. Warren wasn't in a coma. Take my word for it. During those two years he was—" I broke off, uncertain how to say it. "He was engaged in an experimental program with twenty-four other men. He was an agent for the Army Intelligence Corps."

"Agent!" She started to laugh, smothered it when she saw my face. "Agent? Warren? Dan, you can't be serious!"

"He was, Anne. One of their best—if not the best ever, according to his control officers."

"War? My God, I can't believe it! He's so . . . so . . ."

"I know. There's more to it. He wasn't like he is now when he was an agent. They did . . . something to him, Anne. They blocked his memory. They gave him hypnotic amnesia. He doesn't remember anything that happened during those two years. Not consciously. I think that's the reason for his nightmares. His subconscious mind trying to break out, restore his memory."

"My God, this sounds . . . fantastic, unbelievable!"

"I felt that way myself," I admitted. "But it's true,

Anne. There's too much evidence to support it. They gave Warren a superintellect and made a superagent out of him. Then they removed all traces from his mind. But there wasn't anything they could do about his brilliance without making him a vegetable. The doctor in control refused to consider that. He blocked him with hypnosis instead."

"But what about his . . . childishness, the way he acts sometimes?"

"I don't know. A by-product of what happened to him, I guess. Maybe a personality change due to . . . whatever. I don't know, Anne. I doubt if the doctors who did this would know themselves—if they were alive."

One hand fluttered to her cheek like a wounded bird and she shook her head savagely. "How can they do this? How can they get away with it?"

I shrugged. "Like everything else they do. They cover it up. But this time they screwed up. They didn't bury their shit deep enough and it's working to the surface."

She was crying quietly, tears welling up in her lovely eyes, brimming over and racing down her cheeks.

"I'm sorry, Anne," I said gently. "Warren and the man who I think is after him were both victims. With a little luck maybe we can find him and this nightmare will end."

"It won't ever end, Danny. Not with War the way he is." Her voice was filled with a quiet helplessness and despair that made my insides tighten painfully. I wanted desperately to say something meaningful, something that would ease the hurt; I lit a cigarette instead. Comforting crying women is not something I do well.

"You haven't told War any of this." It was more a statement than a question.

"No. I didn't think it would help matters. Do you?"

"No, not at all." She twisted her hands in her lap. "He's getting awfully restless, Danny."

"That's too bad. Tell the big lummox to read a book or something."

"He reads two or three a day now."

"Speed reader too, huh?"

She looked up quickly, her expression on the verge of a smile. "Are you being nasty?"

"I'm probably jealous, if the truth was known."

She rubbed the corners of her eyes. "What do we do now, Danny?"

"We wait. There's nothing we can do until Homer gets a line on Peter Strobow."

"Who?"

"His name is Peter Strobow. His code name is Willow. He was one of Warren's fellow agents."

"Fellow agents. That sounds so strange. But why would he want to harm War?"

"I don't know for sure. Something happened on their last mission." There was no point that I could see in burdening her with Chapman's version of what happened in Poland.

We talked for a while longer and then she left, her face wan, her dark eyes deep-sunken. She walked slump-shouldered, listlessly, an air of desolation so thick about her that I felt something tug gently at my heart.

I spent most of the next morning at the kitchen window watching the squirrels tease Rowdy in between headlong flights up the tree trunk with their jaws crammed full of acorns for the coming winter. Occasionally I would roam through the house, restlessness, boredom, and loneliness hovering over me like a swarm of flies on a screen door. I felt a vague indefinable sense of foreboding, as if I were forgetting something important and the lapse in memory would spell doom.

Finally I said to hell with it and built a Bloody Mary. I dropped into my recliner, pushed all the way back until I was lying almost horizontally. I closed my eyes and thought about Susie, admitted to myself how much I missed her now that she was gone. I went through a whole silent stream of self-criticism and self-abuse over the reasons for her divorcing me. I denounced myself bitterly, cursed savagely my many failings, my numerous faults. But the human id will abide only so much self-flagellation before it begins in sly and subtle ways to restore self-esteem. By the time my first drink was finished, and while I was making another, I began to feel the first faint creep of anger at her egregious display of perfidy. She was leaving me again, wasn't she? I wasn't leaving her! I drank half my new Bloody Mary, sat sullenly in my chair and tried to think of all the reasons why a man my age shouldn't marry a woman sixteen years younger. Only one came to mind and I discounted that as being improbable and an old wives' tale. Feeling self-righteous, smug, and vindicated, I pushed back in the chair again, downed the rest of the Bloody Mary, and forgave her.

She seemed to be floating there in the doorway; the diaphanous gown billowing slightly as she drifted forward, the incredibly rounded contours of her lovely body projecting somehow the promise of more than earthly pleasures. Her smile was gentle and knowing, as if she understood the fire in my veins, knew and approved the tumult inside me that stuck my tongue to the roof of my mouth and brought the thickening rush of fever to my loins. I reached for her; she swayed just beyond the touch of my fingers, the smile rich and inviting now, the gown disappearing as if by magic as she sank slowly to the thick white rug before the fireplace. Her lips moved and the words burned like white fire in my brain:

"Here, Danny, take me here!"

I lurched up out of the chair, and magically, I too was naked. She was warm honey and velvet softness under my hands and I writhed and shuddered in an orgy of touching and stroking and kissing, my body hot and tight and swollen with lust. Minutes passed, or hours, and I hovered over her, deliciously delaying the moment of intussusception, prolonging the agony and ecstasy of anticipation. She sighed softly, touched me with gentle possessiveness, urged me downward, into the hot liquid depths, the first touch of her secret flesh branding me with flame, the ringing of the telephone dim and meaningless in the mystical exultation of the moment . . .

The ringing telephone . . .

I snapped awake, stared stupidly at the beamed cathedral ceiling above me, my mouth thick and dry, still feeling the fluid caress of her . . . my intumescence rapidly dying in despairing indignation.

It rang again, an insistent raucous peal of derision.

Son of a bitch!

I staggered into the kitchen and jerked up the receiver. "Hello, dammit!"

A second of startled silence, then, "Getting a little touchy, cowboy?" The sly, unctuous voice touched a coiled spring somewhere inside me.

I cursed him steadily and evenly for a good two minutes, not once repeating myself, not hesitating or faltering, taking a vague pride in that somewhere beneath the thick white cloud of anger that fogged my brain. He waited patiently for me to finish, a second or two more to be sure, then he said:

"Yep. Getting touchy all right."

I sucked in a deep hissing breath. "Give it up, Willow! It's all over. I know who you are. I know about Titan, about Chinook and you, about Poland. I know your name is Peter Strobow and it's just a matter of time before we run you to ground. Give it up!"

He chuckled dryly. "Such an impassioned speech. One would think you have a personal interest in this matter beyond your three hundred a day."

"I'm going to stop you, Willow. You're not going to get to Chinook. Believe that."

"Oh, we'll get him, cowboy. Never fear. We have all the time in the world. You can't keep him locked up forever."

"Long enough. Long enough for me to find you first. I know all about you, Willow. I know you were a victim, too, the same as Chinook. I know about your superintellect. I know what Burchwalder and Mittleton did to you at Greenville. I'm sorry for that, but it won't stop me from killing you if it comes down to it."

"It must be the sister," he said musingly. "It certainly couldn't be affection for Stillwell."

"You got it, pal. My way, I'd put you and Chinook in a locked room and toss in a couple of live grenades."

"You're a bloodthirsty shit, cowboy. You're also becoming a nuisance. You must know we could have dropped you any time we wanted."

"If I remember correctly you tried, asshole."

"That was just for fun, cowboy. To give you something to think about. My man could have blown up your head just as well as that smoker."

"Why didn't he?"

"Despite what you seem to think, we're not bloodthirsty savages. All we ever wanted was Stillwell. You're the one doing all the bloodletting." He sounded genuinely annoyed.

"What about Mittleton?"

"Retribution." There was a shrug in his voice. "That should have been done six months ago, but he was our only link to Stillwell and we had to be sure first. You brought that on him, cowboy."

"Dammit, stop calling me cowboy!"

"Dammit, stop calling me Willow." Unlike his voice, his laugh was dry, rasping.

"You don't like that, huh, Willow? That have unpleasant memories for you? They screw up and leave you with a little conscience, or what? Maybe Chinook is the lucky one after all. At least he doesn't remember what he did."

"I don't follow."

"They buried his mind, Willow. They wiped his Chinook years off his slate. All he has left are nightmares. What kind of nightmares do you have, Willow?"

"I sleep like a baby."

"Chinook is a baby, Willow. He doesn't remember anything. He doesn't remember what he did in Poland, what he did to you, if anything. If you did manage to kill him, you'd be killing a stranger, a helpless bewildered stranger who would die without knowing why."

"Then we'll just have to tell him, won't we?" His voice had changed; flat and hard and toneless.

"You'll have to go through me."

"That's a shame, cowboy. I was beginning to like you."

"I like you too, shitbag."

I hung up in the middle of his dry rasping laugh.

"It looks like you're going to have to take to the friendly skies again, son." Homer cupped his big nose in a handerchief and blew out half his brains. "Only permanent address he ever had, the one listed when he went AWOL in 1973."

"AWOL?"

"What it says. Listed as a deserter."

I shook my head. "That's one way of doing it. The guy supposedly gets killed while on an intelligence mission for his country and they list him as a deserter. Must make his folks proud."

"Alice and Peter Strobow, Doolittle, Arizona. That's right outside Phoenix. Peter Junior joined the army there, in Phoenix, in 1946—"

"When?"

"I said 1946. Went in when he was seventeen looks like."

"That'd make him fifty-nine now, right?"

"Yeah, I guess. So what?"

"I don't know. I just assumed he was about the same age as Stillwell."

He shifted in his chair and wiped his nose. "Does it matter?"

"No, I don't suppose it does."

"Well, you gonna go out there, or do you want me to have the local law check around?"

"Check for what, Homer? No. I'll go. Maybe they have a picture of him, or something. I would think they've seen all they want to see of law over the years with him listed as a deserter."

He grunted. "Yeah. You might be chasing your tail though. If he's fifty-nine they gotta be at least in their late seventies. They could be dead by now."

"You got any better ideas?" I picked up Strobow's record, went over the dry, impersonal statistics again: Peter S. Strobow. Sergeant. Busted twice during a twelve-year stint in Germany; served a total of five years in 'Nam, two tours on the line. Five years in Japan, three years in Iran, then back to the States for two years before being sent to Greenville for medical observation for an unspecified reason. Listed as AWOL from the facility in 1973, reclassified to deserter after the regulation amount of time had passed.

"He gave them twenty-seven years and his soul," I said harshly, "and they give him desertion."

Homer gazed at me dispassionately. "You feeling sorry for that bastard?"

"Maybe he wasn't always a bastard."

"He is now."

I got up and went to the door, then stopped and looked at him, emotions I didn't understand and didn't want to feel making my voice harder than it should have been. "You been a damn cop too long, Homer."

We looked at each other for a moment in silence, then I went out and closed the door gently.

/17/

They had pictures; from the obligatory one naked on a bearskin rug laughing and waving dimpled arms, to the latest one, a snapshot in front of the Eiffel Tower with his arm around a smiling blond woman who had been his wife for seven years. He was tall and solid-looking, with a mass of dark hair worn longer than I remembered regulations permitting, a strong narrow face that somehow looked familiar, and a wide handsome smile with the faintest trace of cynicism.

"He was always a good boy," the old lady told me, tears welling her rheumy eyes and dripping unheeded onto the backs of her palsied hands.

"He never deserted either," the old man said belligerently, shaking his head with the fringe of white vehemently. "Something happened to him, that's all. That boy loved this country. Why, he gave them lots of years. Why would he do a fool thing like deserting?"

"When was the last time you heard from him?"

He gave me a vague glance out of still-bright blue eyes. "I believe in 1971 . . . Wasn't that it, Mother?"

"I thought it was 1972," she said, as if the year made a difference, brought him closer somehow.

"This is the latest picture you have of him?"

"Petey wasn't much of a hand to take pictures," she said fondly. "Not like his daddy."

"How old was he here?"

"That was made while he was serving in Germany. That was his wife with him. Must have been 1954 or 1955."

"You don't have any idea where she might be?"

He peered at his wife, then back at me. "No, Elsie left him when he come back to the United States."

"She didn't want to leave her mama," the old lady said, mustering as much contempt as she could manage. She rocked gently, her son's picture clutched in skeletal fingers.

"When did you see him last?"

They looked at each other as if using their collective memories. "It was 1965, wasn't it, Mother?" He touched a gnarled hand to his forehead.

"I think they killed him," she said.

"They?"

"When he went in that hospital. We heard from him regular for a while, then he stopped writing."

"That was in 1971?"

She nodded. "Somehow they killed him in that hospital. We told them that every time they came here acting like they was looking for him. But they didn't fool us, did they, Dad?"

"Not a bit," he said. He looked away, his eyes worried. After a moment, he looked back at me. "I forgot who you said you was."

I smiled. "My name's Dan Roman. I'm a private investigator."

"You're not one of them?"

"No," I said, "I'm not one of them."

He leaned back in his rocker, satisfied. "If Petey's not dead, he'll come walking in here one of these days."

I don't think they were even aware of my leaving. I boarded the airplane wondering about the simplicity of old age. They had welcomed me warmly, as friendly and eager to please as pound puppies, ushering me into their small neat frame house on its fifty-by-one-hundred patch of desert, answering my questions about their son with the trusting innocence of children. They were nice people and they probably deserved a lot more out of life than they had received up to now. But don't we all? I wondered how it would be to be eighty, withered in body and lean in shank, wondered if nature compensated for the loss of faculties, the loss of urges and ambitions that propelled us from the cradle onward. Or was the mind trapped in a worthless body, seething helplessly, remembering the touch of loving hands, the feel of a soft nubile body, the fire of sweet kisses . . . but that way lay madness. I blanked my mind and slept.

It was almost dark by the time I collected my car and departed the organized insanity of DFW Airport. I drove by the Midway City Police Department, but Homer was gone. I walked downstairs to the front desk and asked the lady sergeant if she would give Anne a message for me.

A funny look came over her face. "Anne Stillwell?"

"Yes."

"I'm sorry, Mr. Roman. You just missed them. They—"

"What the hell you mean, just missed them? Where did they go?" I felt an old familiar prickle on the back of my neck, and something bubbled in my stomach.

"Home, I guess, sir." Her face was red and her voice was distinctly annoyed.

"Who let them go?" I asked ominously, already moving toward the door.

"They had a lawyer with a release order, sir. It was signed and everything—" Her voice was cut off by the swinging doors behind me.

The taxi was driving away when I got there. Warren was putting his billfold in his hip pocket and Anne was standing behind him with a large paper sack clutched in her arms. They heard my car and stood watching me drive up, looking as guilty as two kids caught playing doctor in the bushes.

I slammed into the curb and jerked to a stop. I was out and had the back door open before the wagon stopped rocking.

"Get your asses in there," I said tightly.

Anne stepped obediently forward, but Warren stood his ground, his face the color of old copper, set rigidly into stubborn, defiant lines.

"I ain't going," he muttered. "I'm going to stay in my own house."

I didn't waste time arguing; I stepped back to the wagon, reached under the seat, and brought out the gun. I took one quick step and placed it against his cheek.

"Get in," I said evenly, "or this whole damn thing ends right here, right now."

He stared at me over the gun, and for a second I

thought he was calling me, and I wondered what I would do if he did. Then his eyes came back to the gun and he folded meekly.

"Okay, Dan," he said cheerfully.

Anne slid across the front seat, and I waited until he was seated in back before climbing in beside her. My hands were shaking a little and there was a sharp throbbing pain behind my eyes.

Anne leaned over and kissed my cheek as I started the car. "You wouldn't have shot him, would you?" she whispered.

I grinned at her weakly. "We'll never know."

I drove to the corner and turned around. "What the hell happened, Anne?"

She grimaced. "War called some lawyer yesterday. He came with a release paper a few minutes ago."

"Did you know about it?"

"Not until an hour ago. I tried to get in touch with Captain Sellers, but he was in Dallas, they said."

"As usual, he probably never told his people anything. He tries to do every damn thing himself."

She nodded. "The lady policeman at the desk said she had to let War go. I wasn't about to let him go alone."

"You're an idiot, Anne. Don't you know this is what they want, what they've been waiting for?"

"I couldn't stop him, Danny," she said miserably. "But he's my brother. I couldn't let him go alone."

I turned into my driveway and punched the button for the garage door. "It wouldn't help him," I said harshly, "for you to get killed too." I could feel her eyes as I drove inside. I waited until the door was down before I let them out. Then I remembered the latch on the kitchen door and raised the garage door again. I punched the down button and hustled them out under the descending door.

Inside, I breathed a sigh of relief and flipped the

lock on the dead bolt. "Well, we made it again," I said, then turned with a sinking heart as I heard the gasp from Anne and the oily voice:

"That you did, cowboy." He was standing in the door to the den, gun steady in his hand. A second later another man appeared in the main hallway, his broad flat face grim and hard. He had a gun in each hand. The .357 in my pocket might as well have been on Mars.

"Shuck your jacket, cowboy. Easy."

I slipped out of it and held it with one finger under the neckband. Anne and Warren were as still as twin statues, Anne's hand at her mouth, her face stricken. Warren quietly watched, his thick lips slightly parted, his bewildered expression just beginning to give way to alarm.

"Throw it through there." The short man motioned with his gun. I tossed the jacket into the living room and cleared my throat loudly as it landed.

"What's the matter, cowboy? Getting nervous?" He smiled, revealing small even teeth and a lot of gum. "Too late for that. I gave you your chance yesterday. Cecil, pat him down a little."

The tall man pocketed one of the guns and ran his hands over my waist and up and down my legs. "Take off them boots. Throw 'em in there with your coat," he snapped in my ear. I did as I was told. "He's clean," Cecil said.

The short man backed into the den. "Okay, friends, let's all come in here where it's cozy."

He watched warily as we filed into the room. "Okay, big man, you sit there in the recliner. Push it back as far as it will go, and don't move one lousy muscle or it'll be your last." He waited until Warren was stretched on the chair, then motioned to Anne. "Okay, sis, you get over there." He gestured toward the love seat. My heart hit bottom again. The gun in the cushions of the love seat had been my last hope.

"Okay, cowboy, you're next." He gave me his tight little grin and produced a thin nylon cord from his pocket. "Tie his feet, Cecil."

Cecil shoved the gun in my stomach. "Sit down in the corner." He pushed me backward against the wall, and I lowered myself to the floor and scooted into the corner.

He quickly knelt and tied my feet. He was wearing a baseball cap pulled low on his forehead. His eyes were pale green, cold and expressionless as he finished knotting the cord. He had a long face, concave cheeks, and a square chin with a Kirk Douglas cleft. He looked up and held out his hand and the short man tossed him a pair of handcuffs.

"Hold out your hands." His voice was as empty as his face. He ratcheted the metal bands tightly around my wrists and rose to his feet. He took out both his guns and moved to lean against the wall, his eyes swinging slowly back and forth between me and Warren. The short man relaxed for the first time. He let the gun fall to his side and fished in his shirt pocket for a cigarette.

"Okay," he said happily. He had black hair, thick and tightly curled, a tiny upturned nose, and a round fat face. I realized with a sickening thud that I had been wrong: he wasn't Willow. He was about six inches too short and lacked about an inch in nose. He went into the kitchen and picked up the receiver. He dialed and after a moment said something I couldn't make out. He came back smiling.

"What now, Willow?" I said.

"We wait," he said. He blew smoke at me and widened his grin.

"You're not Willow," I said.

"You finally figured that out. I knew you were smart, cowboy."

"Not too smart," I said amiably, "I let two scumbags like you two take me."

"Cecil!" The short man's voice cracked like a whip, but Cecil kept coming. He was wearing cowboy boots with pointed toes and he drove the right one into my thigh. He stepped back, grunted, and did it again.

I hardly felt the second blow through the pain of the first, blinding, searing pain like a charley horse gone wild. I drew my legs up, then straightened them hurriedly as the injured muscle began to cramp.

"Watch your mouth, boy, there's a lady present." There was a touch of amusement in his voice, but his expression didn't change. He went back to his place and resumed his careless slouch against the wall.

Anne sat huddled in one corner of the love seat. Her legs were drawn up beside her on the cushion and her head was bowed into one of her hands. I could see the sparkle of tears on her cheeks.

Warren was still stretched stiffly on the recliner, big hands knotted on the arms. His eyes were closed and his face was the color of old bleached sheets.

"I'd like to smoke," I said to no one in particular.

"Sure, cowboy," the short man said.

"Could I have an ashtray?"

He looked around, saw the heavy glass one on the stand by the chair and smiled.

"No ashtray. Spit on it."

I shrugged and fished my cigarettes and lighter out of my shirt pocket. I lit up and looked at him and opened my mouth to say something and he shook his head. "No more talking, cowboy. You'll just get in more trouble. It won't be long now."

I massaged my leg tenderly and smoked in silence.

I finished the cigarette and mashed it out against my boot heel. The cuffs were too tight and I moved them a fraction of an inch and rubbed the red, angry groove. I lit another cigarette and was halfway through it when the sound came at the front door.

"It's locked," I said, but the short man just smiled.

"He has a key," he said.

The brain is a marvelous intricate mechanism; it is a storehouse of facts, of bits of information, seemingly irrelevant scraps and shreds of data. The brain can absorb all these of its own volition, store them, assign the unconscious mind to worry over them, realign, juxtapose, correlate, and hold. Hold until required, until sufficient stimulation is received to galvanize the brain to action, to deliver to the conscious mind what the conscious mind probably knew all along and wouldn't recognize. All it takes is the right key. Key!

And that's what happened to me.

I knew who Willow was.

As impossible as it seemed.

The key turned in the lock; the door opened, and I heard the shuffling feet. And in that last second before he appeared in the doorway, I raised my head and called out:

"Hello, Mr. Whitecomb!"

He stood in the door looking down at me, his face arranged pleasantly, a slight smile, an approving gleam in his eyes.

"Very good, Mr. Roman. How long have you known?"

"About five seconds," I said ruefully. "I'm a slow learner."

"Ah," he said. "Then it wasn't anything I did."

"No, sir. You performed flawlessly. Right up to and including the day you took the impression of the key to my new lock."

"Ah," he said again. "I thought that was a rather nice touch—the glass of water."

"I should have known the night your two apes came. They went right through the door, lock and all. I just assumed at the time that Anne hadn't relocked the door. It wasn't until later it occurred to me that I had used the rear door that night. I kept forgetting to ask Anne about it. But reason should have told me she didn't unlock it. Like I said, Willow, I'm slow sometimes."

"Yes," he said absently, his eyes on Warren, still motionless on the chair. None of his features seemed to move, but something was happening to his face; something not very nice.

"Hello, Chinook," he said softly.

Warren didn't move, but there was a muffled sob from Anne.

Willow took a step forward and I noticed for the first time that he was using a cane. A thick wood cane with a rubber tip. He took another shuffling step forward, toward Warren.

"You were smart," I said quickly, and he stopped and turned back to me. "The first rule of warfare, eh, Willow? Invade the enemy camp, determine his fortifications, his strengths, his weaknesses. Know your enemy. That was it, wasn't it?" I watched the struggle going on in his face.

"Yes," he said, after a moment. "That and to provide a distraction—a diversion, as it were." He allowed himself a wintry smile. "It's to your credit that you took me on, Mr. Roman. A feeble old man, helpless, sick. You have a generous nature, sir, a kindness of the spirit."

"It's my one failing," I admitted modestly, my mind working, sending desperate messages to Anne . . . the gun . . . the gun . . . the gun . . .

He turned to look at Warren again, and I went on with a rush. "There really was a Mr. Whitecomb. Right? He died recently. There really was a Sherry Bascomb, too, wasn't there?"

He nodded. "I took a house in Sunset Gardens when we narrowed the search to this area. Bascomb was a neighbor. His father-in-law was Mr. Whitecomb. He died, and his daughter ran off with a man on a motorcylce. Just as I said."

"But it wasn't the same tag number, right?" *Anne . . . please . . . the gun . . .*

"No, I'm afraid not. I took that from a passing vehicle. I hope that didn't prove to be embarrassing for you." He shifted restlessly and I jumped in.

"One thing. How did you get Bascomb primed to react the way he did when I called him?"

He nodded. "I was afraid you might—eventually. We made a few calls . . . late at night, requesting to talk with his father-in-law. A few nights of that and he was making the right sort of response." He smiled slightly, a minute parting of his lips. "No more, Mr. Roman. I understand what you're doing, but the time is now for Chinook." There was a hissing in his voice when he spoke the name.

"What has he done to you?" It was Anne, her face wet, splotched with red, twisting helplessly in terror.

He turned toward her, his face as white as bleached bone, as hard as stone. "Ask him," he said softly.

"He doesn't know," she wailed. "He's just a child in his mind. Can't you see?" She sat upright, her hand across the split between the cushions.

The gun, Anne, remember the damn gun!

"Roman told me that yesterday," the short man said. "He told me they blocked his memory. I forgot to—"

"I know that," Willow said impatiently. "Mittleton

told me that. He also told me how to restore it." He swiveled his head to me. "Did he get around to that before my men got there?"

"No, he didn't. But he told me enough, Willow. I know your name, Peter Strobow. I've talked to your parents. We know all about you, Willow. Homer Sellers. You remember him? He sent you to me, remember? He knows everything I know. You can—"

"Please, Mr. Roman. It won't do you any good. I owe this man too much. His dying won't repay it, but it's as good as I can do." He shuffled across the floor and rapped Warren across the shins with the cane. "Sit up, Chinook!"

The big body jerked, and his hands came up to protect his face. He peered at Willow through the screen of his big arms. "Why do you call me that? What do you want with me?" He raised his head and I could see a sheen of tears. Willow saw it, too.

"Sit up, Chinook," Willow said more quietly. "Sit up please. I won't hurt you." There was almost tenderness in his voice.

Slowly, fearfully, the big man pulled himself into a sitting position. "I don't know you. Why do you want to hurt me, please?"

"I don't," Willow said. "Not the way you are. Look at me, Warren. Please. Look at me. I promise you I won't hurt Warren Stillwell."

Anne, please, Anne, the gun . . . remember the gun, Anne!

She covered her face with her cupped hands, her shoulders shaking.

Cecil watched without expression, the short man with morbid fascination.

"Warren. Listen to me, Warren. I promise I won't hurt Warren. It's a man named Chinook I'm angry with, not Warren Stillwell. Do you understand?" His voice was soft, almost crooning.

"Yes," Warren said eagerly. "I knew there was something wrong. I knew nobody could want to hurt me." He poked at his eyes with a big thumb, then looked at his sobbing sister in bewilderment. "See, Anne. It was all a mistake."

"Oh, God," she moaned, her body shaking, rocking back and forth.

Dammit, Anne! Remember! Remember! Remember the gun! The cushion, Anne! Under the damn cushion!

"Warren," Willow said soothingly, "listen to me now. I want you to listen closely to my voice . . . relax and listen closely . . . Warren, listen . . . *Mount Rushmore is erupting.*"

The big head fell forward on the wide, thick chest, eyes closed, face passive.

Willow's head swiveled in my direction as if for approval, but for just a second his face was slack and defenseless, and I saw something that made my heart leap—I saw pity. But just as quickly the resolve returned, and the pale face hardened.

"Think what you're doing, man," I said urgently. "He's not to blame for what was done to him—any more than you are."

"Shut up, Mr. Roman," he said harshly. "Stay out of this. I don't wish to harm you. But I've paid too much for what he did to me. This must be done."

"What? What did he do that was so terrible? What *could* he do that was worse than what you did in Poland?"

He turned all the way around to face me, skin stretched tautly across his cheekbones, his face a ghostly caricature in the artificial light.

"What did he tell you I did in Poland?" he almost whispered.

"He didn't tell me anything. A man named Charles Chapman told me."

He nodded stiffly. "And Chinook told him. What?"

I shifted uneasily. "I'm not sure . . ."

"Tell me, Mr. Roman."

"He said . . . he told me that Chinook said you killed a whole houseful of people. . . ."

His head moved jerkily, and his lips pulled back in a chilling smile. "Yes. Yes, he would do that." He drew in a deep breath. "Chinook did that, Mr. Roman. Exactly what he said I did. I followed his trail of blood that night, seven or eight people, I don't remember without counting them up. I caught him with the last one . . . a young girl . . . he was raping her . . . I tried to stop him. He shot me, left me for dead. But I wasn't dead, you see. I was left for them to vent their terrible rage on . . . for what Chinook had done." His voice rose slightly at the end and his body trembled. "They kept me for eight years," he whispered. "They did things to me . . . they broke my knees twelve times . . . I kept count, Mr. Roman. They cut me with knives."

"Willow," I pleaded desperately. "He's not worth it. Walk away from him. He's not worth dying for."

He whirled. "Look at me! Damn you! Look at me! I'm only fifty-nine years old . . . but I'm an old man . . . I'm an eighty-year-old man . . . worse! He did that to me." His eyes blazed, flakes of blue ice. Behind him the short man stirred restlessly, his eyes met mine briefly, then flicked away. The tall man leaned against the wall, his face impassive; a hired hand, the boss's problems no concern of his. Anne huddled moaning on the love seat, her face hidden in her hands—and Chinook slept.

Willow stood over him weaving, legs widespread and braced, the cane the third leg of the tripod.

"Chinook. Listen. Your memory has been taken away from you, but I am going to restore it. Do you understand me? I have the key that unlocks your memory. You will awaken when I speak the words and you will be Chinook. You will remember everything. Do you understand me?"

"Yes," Warren intoned.

Willow straightened slightly, removed his right hand from the cane, and held it out to the short man. The short man put a gun in it.

"When he awakens he will be extremely dangerous," Willow said without emotion. "But it is necessary that he knows." He took a step backward. "Chinook. When you awaken it will be without alarm. You will feel safe, secure. You will not feel threatened. Do you understand?"

"Yes."

Willow turned toward me. "Mittleton had one serious problem. It was necessary that he use key words that would be highly unlikely to occur in conversation by chance. Even without the initial phrase to put him under, accidental use of these words in the correct order in Chinook's presence could set up serious psychological disturbances." His voice was dry and curiously didactic, as if he were instructing an English class to be on guard against solecisms.

He licked his lips nervously, shifted his stance, changed his grip on the cane, and turned back to Chinook.

"Chinook, listen closely to me . . . *ambergris* . . ."

All eyes were on the face of the sleeping man. Even Anne had straightened, her fingers over her mouth, deep-sunken eyes riveted on her brother.

". . . *procrastination* . . ." Willow's voice rose slightly on the final syllable.

Cecil had moved away from the wall, guns dangling negligently at the ends of his arms. Only his eyes were alert. The short man was standing by the mantel, his left hand frozen halfway to his mouth with a cigarette. Anne hadn't moved.

". . . cannibal . . ."

For what seemed like minutes we were a living tableau, wax dummies incapable of sound, movement.

Then the big man opened his eyes. He looked up at Willow. "Hello, Willow," he said genially. "I thought you were dead."

There was a faint, sibilant susurrus of sound around the room as our collective breaths were expelled.

"Hello, Chinook," Willow said softly. "I trust you've been well."

"Very well, thank you . . . and yourself?" There was no trace of irony or sarcasm in his friendly voice—only indifference.

"Not too well, Chinook . . . you understand?"

The big man nodded. "I understand, Willow." He cocked his head and smiled. "You shouldn't have interfered, you know."

The white-haired old man smiled thinly. "Compassion . . . my one human trait. You wouldn't deny me that, would you, Chinook?" His tone was chiding, almost happy, a sick old man whose last good friend has come to call.

Chinook shrugged, his dark brooding eyes flashed around the room. I felt their power a moment before they came to rest on Anne.

"Hello, sis," he said. "I'm sorry about this." For a split second his face changed, softened, and he smiled. Then it was gone and he was facing Willow again, cold and hard and implacable.

"Get on with it."

"You understand fully, Chinook?"

He shrugged, lifted his hands in a gesture of acknowledgment. "I understand, Willow," he said indifferently. Then his hands came down on the arms of the chair and he was moving, hurtling through the air like the wind that was his namesake. His arms spread wide, engulfed the frail man before him, and I heard his rumbling bellow as they crashed to the floor, the huge hands already at the old man's neck.

Then Cecil and the short man were moving, standing over the thrashing bodies, their silenced guns cracking like tiny whips, and from the corner of my eye I saw Anne, out of her trance at last, her arms coming out in front of her, my .38 gripped tightly in white-knuckled hands.

"No! Anne, no! Not now . . . it's too late!"

But it was too late for her also, and the roar of the .38 filled the room. The short man winced, then jerked up his gun and snapped a shot at her. Her body buckled, bounced against the back of the love seat, but she rebounded and fired again.

The short man screamed, slammed against the mantel, his gun whipping out of his hand, sliding across the floor—away from me.

Cecil raised one gun, fired at Anne, and she jackknifed across the arm of the love seat, her body sliding limply to the floor in front of the kitchen doorway. Cecil stepped forward and put his gun against the back of Chinook's head—and I snapped out of my paralysis.

I hunched forward frantically, my clawing fingers catching the edge of the entry hall door. I jerked myself to my feet as the flat dull sound of Cecil's gun sounded. He was rising, turning toward me as I threw myself headlong into the hall. I slid on the tile, came even with the living room door, tucked my knees under my chin, and rolled. I heard the slap of his feet in the den, and I clawed at the jacket, my fingers catching in the cloth, ripping free, dipping into the pocket with the gun as Cecil appeared in the doorway.

No time—I swung the jacket toward him, found the trigger, and jerked it—and felt the double triphammer blows in my chest as he fired both guns at point-blank range.

Shock, unbelievable numbness—I watched him fall forward and squeezed the trigger again, saw with a vicious burst of satisfaction the hole appear as if by magic in his forehead, the bits and pieces fly from the back of his head.

There goes the damned carpet, I thought.

I pushed myself like a scuttling crab, over him and across the hall to the den door.

There was a scuffing, scratching sound, wheezing, labored breathing—and I saw him, the other one, the short man Anne had shot. He was crawling toward his gun by the fireplace hearth. He was leaving a wide swath of blood on my floor and in spite of the agony in my chest and the dark haze in my eyes, I managed to bring my handcuffed hands around in front of me. I propped my right hand with the left and looked down the barrel at the side of his head.

His hand touched the gun, then he flicked a glance in my direction and froze.

"Go on, shitbag, pick it up." My voice was thick, guttural, and I could feel something sticky and salty on my tongue.

His fingers tightened around the butt, then suddenly relaxed. He grinned. "No way, cowboy. You're dying, hero. Another minute and I can walk out of here."

"The hell you say," I said, and squeezed the trigger gently.

I had time to see him jerk, to see his head explode all over my fireplace; I had time to laugh—until the blood flowing into my mouth choked it off; and I had time for one last glimpse of Chinook and Willow, locked in loving embrace, one glimpse of Anne, dead in front of the kitchen door. All of them dead and I was dying.

I fumbled for a cigarette, but my hands wouldn't work and my eyes couldn't see, and I gave it up and laid my cheek against the cool tile of the hall and died with them.

And even when they resurrected me, I was still sure I had died and gone to heaven. There was this angel sitting beside me, hovering over my bed; a dark-haired brooding angel with haunted eyes and a haggard, beautiful face.

But then I groaned and moved, and the angel moved, smiled at me, a warm, loving smile, and I knew everything was all right. I was really alive after all and the angel was Susie brushing warm lips against my cheek and whispering in my ear: "Get your big ass well, old man, I need you."